"Do you love Elise? Max asked Sam.

"No," Sam answered his best friend. There was no hesitation, no hedging, just a flat statement.

"I see," said Max, caught off guard.

"I think she's beautiful, I admire her warmth and sweetness, and I want to make love to her," Sam admitted with characteristic directness. He paused to let that register, then added bluntly, "And I intend to have her."

"You may have a problem there, my friend. Somehow, I don't think Elise is the type for an affair."

"I'm going to marry her."

"What! You just said you didn't love her."

"I don't. But I want her."

"And you think that's enough to build a marriage on?"

Again Sam answered without hesitation. "Yes."

* * *

FOOLS RUSH IN
WHERE ANGELS FEAR TO TREAD....

There's double trouble when twin sisters sweet Elise and saucy Erin, first introduced in *Fools Rush In* (Special Edition #416), mix business and pleasure— and two volatile males—in this companion edition, *Where Angels Fear*.

Dear Reader,

If you're looking for an extra-special reading experience—something rich and memorable, something deeply emotional, something totally romantic—your search is over! For in your hands you hold one of Silhouette's extremely **Special Editions**.

Dedicated to the proposition that *not* all romances are created equal, Silhouette **Special Edition** aims to deliver the best and the brightest in women's fiction—six books each month by such stellar authors as Nora Roberts, Lynda Trent, Tracy Sinclair and Ginna Gray, along with some dazzling new writers destined to become tomorrow's romance stars.

Pick and choose among titles if you must—we hope you'll soon equate all Silhouette **Special Editions** with consistently gratifying romance reading.

And don't forget the two Silhouette *Classics* at your bookseller's each month—reissues of the most beloved Silhouette **Special Editions** and Silhouette *Intimate Moments* of yesteryear.

Today's bestsellers, tomorrow's *Classics*—that's Silhouette **Special Edition**. We hope you'll stay with us in the months to come, because month after month, we intend to become more special than ever.

From all the authors and editors of Silhouette **Special Edition**,
Warmest wishes,

Leslie Kazanjian
Senior Editor

GINNA GRAY
Where Angels Fear

Silhouette Special Edition

Published by Silhouette Books New York

America's Publisher of Contemporary Romance

To my niece, Ellen Conn, who scouted out a location and provided the crucial information I needed, complete with detailed descriptions and a hand-drawn map. Thank you, dear heart.

And to Ginny Smith, for the books and maps, and for being so gracious. One does meet the nicest people at writers' conferences.

Thank you both. Without your help, I would have had a great deal of difficulty writing *Fools Rush In*, and without that book, *Where Angels Fear* never would have been written.

SILHOUETTE BOOKS
300 East 42nd St., New York, N.Y. 10017

ISBN: 0-373-09468-X

First Silhouette Books printing July 1988

GINNA GRAY

A native Houstonian, Ginna Gray admits that, since childhood, she has been a compulsive reader as well as a head-in-the-clouds dreamer. Long accustomed to expressing her creativity in tangible ways—Ginna also enjoys painting and needlework—she finally decided to try putting her fantasies and wild imaginings down on paper. The result? The mother of two now spends eight hours a day as a full-time writer.

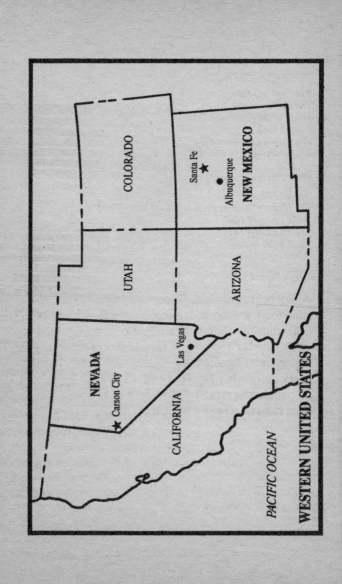

WESTERN UNITED STATES

Chapter One

Something was wrong. Even before she awoke fully, Elise Holman's instincts were clamoring out a warning not to move, not to open her eyes.

Her fogged brain registered several unpleasant things at once. Her throat was parched, her mouth held a terrible taste and her pounding head felt as though it were stuffed with cotton. She also had the uneasy feeling that her stomach would revolt at the least provocation.

Not wishing to test it, Elise lay perfectly still. Cautiously, she opened her eyes to mere slits, and her heart gave a little leap. Wherever she was, it wasn't her bedroom.

Through the fuzzy screen of her lashes, she examined the gray carpet that stretched away from the bed, the elegant Regency chairs covered in silver-and-maroon-striped satin, the marble bathroom visible through the open door.

From the impersonal decor, Elise guessed she was in a hotel room. And a ritzy one, at that. Certainly beyond the limits of her pocketbook. Judging by the slant of the sunlight filtering through the closed draperies, it was early morning. Other than that, she hadn't a clue about where she was or how she'd gotten there.

The beginnings of panic fluttered in her chest, but she shut her eyes again and willed herself to be calm. *Think. Think,* she ordered, trying to ignore the hammering pain behind her eyes. *What did you do last night?*

A tantalizing memory wavered just out of reach. Frowning, she shifted restlessly, then gasped as her foot came into contact with a hairy, muscular leg.

Good Lord! She was in bed with a man!

"So. You're awake." The mattress bounced as the man changed position beside her.

Elise cringed and squeezed her eyes shut tighter. It couldn't be. It just couldn't be. *Please, Lord, let me wake up and find this was all a bad dream*, she prayed.

But she was already awake. And she recognized that voice.

Only one man she knew spoke in that steel-edged monotone. The last man in the world with whom she'd ever expected to wind up in bed.

"Elise?"

She started at the gentle touch on her shoulder, her eyes flying open. Humiliation and fright seared her as she found herself staring straight into Sam Lawford's cold, silver-gray eyes.

There was no way she could avoid looking at him. Propped up on one elbow, he was leaning over her, his wide, bare shoulders blocking out the rest of the room. He was so close she could see each individual black eyelash, feel his warmth, the feathery touch of his breath.

Avoiding his penetrating stare, Elise lowered her gaze, but her misery increased when she encountered his naked chest. It was broad and dark and covered with a pelt of black hair that shone with the same blue highlights as that on his head. A silver medallion dangled from a chain around his neck, swinging lazily back and forth. Struggling for composure, she took a deep breath, and her senses swam as she drew in his scent. It was all around her, she realized, even on her skin, musky and male, tinged with soap. Heady. Intimate.

Shivering, Elise clutched the sheet closer, becoming aware at that moment that her sole item of apparel was a pair of bikini panties. Her gaze darted downward. The sheet draped just below Sam Lawford's lean waist, but she couldn't tell if he wore anything beneath it. If he did, it couldn't be much.

Oh, God. What had she done?

"Elise? Answer me."

Gathering her courage, Elise met Sam's eyes and felt her face grow hot. "I...that is..." She bit her lip and blinked. She wished he wouldn't look at her like that. She wished he would move away. She wished she were anywhere in the world but where she was. If only she could drop through a hole in the earth.

Battling panic, Elise swallowed hard and felt her stomach give a sickening lurch. "What ... how..?" She floundered under Sam's merciless gaze and, with a moaned "Oh, Lord," covered her face with both hands.

The mattress moved again as Sam leaned closer, and the effect on her stomach was disastrous. Against the top of her right breast Elise felt the weight of his silver medal, warm from his skin. She squeezed her eyes shut and shivered.

"How do you feel?" Hard fingertips brushed a tendril of hair from her face with a surprisingly gentle touch.

"I...I don't know," came her muffled reply. Making a strangled sound, she rolled away from him onto her side.

Elise knew at once that she'd made a mistake. Her stomach rebelled at the sudden movement; and moaning again, she lurched from the bed. As she stumbled for the bathroom she tried to pull the sheet with her and wrap it around her body, but it got stuck and she became tangled in the thing instead.

Before she could fall flat on her face, Sam was there beside her. He was wearing only a pair of skimpy white briefs, and even in her distress Elise experienced a flutter of panic as his arms came around her. She struggled against both his hold and the twisted sheet. "Let me go. I-I'm going to be sick!"

"I'd be surprised if you weren't," he said in that calm voice of his, and bent to scoop her up. "Just hang on."

"No, please, I—"

Ignoring her weak protest, he jerked the sheet aside and lifted her effortlessly.

Elise closed her eyes, partly in an attempt to control her roiling stomach and partly to shut out the sight of Sam's muscular chest just inches from her nose.

Her head swam with the jostling movement as he covered the distance to the bathroom in half a dozen strides. With each one her bare breasts rubbed against him, the sensitive tips burying themselves in the silky thatch of chest hair. Acute embarrassment added to Elise's discomfort as she felt the heat of him pressing against her from hip to shoulder.

"Here you are," Sam said, lowering her to her feet in the bathroom. He whipped a towel from the rack and draped it around her as she sank to her knees and hung her head over the white porcelain bowl. "Go ahead. Don't fight it. You'll feel better when you're done."

She felt him brush the hair back from her face, felt his broad palm gently cup her forehead. Lord! She didn't want him helping her while she was sick! Things were mortifying enough without that!

"No, please. I'll be okay. Just leave me alone," she begged, trying to wave him away.

But it was too late. Her nauseated body would not wait another moment, and once the retching started all she could do was give in to it.

Sam continued to hold her head and stroke her neck and shoulders. When she was done, he wet a cloth and washed her face. The cool wetness was blessedly refreshing, and Elise released a shuddering breath as he bathed her clammy skin.

The tenderness of his touch brought her eyes open, and she found he was kneeling beside her, his rugged face as emotionless as ever. His silver eyes met hers without a flicker.

"Feeling better?"

"Yes, thank you," she murmured with absurd politeness. His eyes impassively followed the movement of the washcloth, and Elise dropped her gaze, only to swiftly raise it again when she encountered his bare thighs and abdomen and the tiny white briefs that so boldly molded his manhood. Trembling, she clutched the towel around her and stared at the hollow in the base of his throat, wishing she could curl up and die on the spot. She had never been this close to Sam Lawford before, and it was her fervent hope that she never would be again.

"I gather you have a low tolerance for alcohol," he said as he stood and tossed the cloth into the sink. Bending, he cupped her elbows and helped her to her feet. "You didn't have that much champagne last night."

Champagne? Elise frowned. "No, I . . ."

Then reality hit her.

Of course! Erin and Max had gotten married last night! Which meant she was still in Las Vegas. Probably at the hotel where they had celebrated after the ceremony. Elise shuddered, recalling vaguely the toasts they'd drunk to the bride and groom. She must have been out of her mind to drink champagne.

She cast Sam a quick, sheepish glance. "That is . . . I . . . I only have a problem when it comes to champagne. It just doesn't . . ." She started to shake her head for emphasis, but the movement made her feel as though her skull were going to explode. She groaned, placing her palms flat against her temples. "It doesn't agree with me," she finished weakly.

"Then why did you drink it?"

"I don't know. I . . . I don't remember." Elise buried her face in her hands. "Could you please just leave me alone now?" she pleaded.

Not for one more minute could she continue to stand there, wearing only a pair of skimpy panties and a towel, talking to this man. Especially when he was also nearly naked. Sam Lawford scared her half to death even under the best of circumstances.

Sam neither spoke nor moved. It wasn't necessary for her to look at him to know he was studying her. She could feel his scrutiny like a physical touch. Elise gritted her teeth, her frayed nerves unraveling. In another minute she was going to either scream hysterically or break down and bawl.

"Very well," he said after an interminable time. "If you're sure you'll be okay."

"I'm fine," she lied. "But I'll . . . I'll feel better after I've had a shower."

"I'll get your bag for you."

Elise lowered her hands and, out of the corner of her eye, watched him stride back into the bedroom with unselfconscious grace. She was amazed that he could appear remote and formal even walking around in his underwear.

He returned with the small suitcase, set it down and left without a word, pulling the door shut behind him.

Bracing her palms against the counter, Elise closed her eyes and slumped, her head dropping forward until it almost touched her chest.

Well, you've done it now. To wake up in bed with a man—any man—and not remember how you got there was bad enough, but *Sam Lawford*? Not only was he her new brother-in-law's best friend, but he and Max were co-owners of Global Imports. Indirectly, that made him her employer—though technically she was Max's secretary.

Heaven above, you idiot! If you had to step out of character, why last night? And with this man, of all people?

Sam Lawford made her nervous, edgy. There was no real basis for her uneasiness, but her reaction wasn't something she could control. He had never been anything but the soul of politeness. He'd never done or said anything to make her dislike or fear him. Yet when he came within six feet of her, she felt threatened.

His coldness was what unnerved her, she had decided months ago. The remote aura he projected was almost menacing. It surrounded him like an invisible wall. Everything about him was controlled—his voice, his expression, the way he moved. He was always perfectly groomed, his attire impeccable, his manner flawless. But when he looked at her with those beautiful, pale, emotionless eyes, she felt something akin to panic.

And now, apparently, she had slept with him.

"Oh, God," she groaned, rubbing her aching eyes with her thumb and forefinger. How had it happened?

Elise raised her head, peered at her reflection and groaned again. She looked as bad as she felt. Her short, vivid red hair, now a riot of tangled curls around her face, accentuated her greenish pallor. Her brown eyes were bloodshot and bleary, and circles beneath them made her look as though she'd been in a fight . . . and lost.

For all you know, you could have, her conscience prodded.

Straightening, Elise cast a wary look at the closed door. What had happened? She remembered the wedding. She'd been almost as nervous as Erin, mainly because throughout the ceremony Sam had kept staring at her. Now that she thought about it, she realized he'd been doing a lot of that lately.

Elise took a bottle of shampoo from her suitcase, stepped into the shower and adjusted the water until it was as hot as she could bear it. Little by little, as she stood beneath the pounding spray with her eyes closed, massaging her throbbing temples, the events of the previous evening came creeping back.

After the ceremony the four of them had gone to one of the plush hotels along the strip for a celebration dinner. They had all been in high spirits. Even Sam had unbent far enough to smile a time or two. He'd even insisted on ordering champagne to toast the newlyweds. Elise remembered joining in, but at first she'd taken only a tiny sip of the bubbly wine.

As always, Sam had made her a bit uneasy, but everything had been going fine until he asked her to dance....

"I don't know about you, but I feel *de trop*," he'd said, casting a wry glance at the newlyweds, who were gazing into each other's eyes as though they were the only two people in the universe. "Why don't we dance and give them a few minutes alone?"

Unabashed, Max had pulled Erin closer and turned to his friend with a wicked grin. "Sounds like a good idea to me. That'll give me a chance to whisper lewd suggestions in my wife's ear."

Giggling, Erin aimed a playful poke at his ribs. "Pervert."

"Damn right," Max agreed cheerfully.

Without a word, Sam rose and extended his hand to Elise.

The last thing she wanted to do was dance with him, but she had no choice. She barely allowed her fingertips to touch his, breaking the contact the instant she was on her feet. Like a prisoner going to the gallows, she preceded him onto the dance floor, and when she turned to step into his arms a shiver rippled down her spine.

As they moved to the slow music she stared at the perfect knot in his silk tie, aware of his large hand pressing into the small of her back, the brush of his legs against hers, the combined scents of citrusy cologne and expensive wool worsted. As always, Sam's suit was superbly tailored to his tall, elegant body. It felt pleasantly scratchy beneath her hand, which rested on his shoulder. Against her other hand, his palm was dry and warm, his long fingers encircling hers in a firm grip.

Elise danced in silence and struggled against the tension that made her insides quiver like a plucked wire.

"Don't look so stricken. You'll get over it," Sam said, breaking into her agitated thoughts, but when she looked up the ghost of a smile that hovered around his thin lips did not touch his eyes. "You know the old saying. Time heals all wounds."

"What?" Elise blinked. "What are you talking about? What wounds?"

"I'm referring to your broken heart."

"My bro—" She gave a startled laugh and shook her head. "My heart's not broken. Why on earth should it be?"

"Come on, Elise. Surely you aren't going to pretend that you're not in love with Max."

"I don't have to pretend; I'm not."

It was the truth, but the taunting accusation had been close enough to the mark to make her blush. Not very long ago Elise had truly thought she was in love with Max, but seeing her sister and him together had proved to her that she was wrong. What she had felt had been nothing more than infatuation born of loneliness, which, next to the real thing, had seemed paltry indeed.

Moreover, though she admitted to being a dreamer, no one had ever accused her of being stupid. Once she had accepted the situation and sorted through her muddled feelings, she'd realized she had been indulging in a foolish, impossible dream. Max was handsome and dashing and utterly charming, the stuff fantasy lovers were made of, but he was not the man for her. She craved stability, the warm glow of hearth and home. Max was footloose and daring, always eager for the next adventure, the next challenge.... In Erin, he had found his soulmate.

Sam examined her rosy cheeks. "Ah, I see. Sorry. My mistake," he said with such patent insincerity that Elise ground her teeth and blushed more deeply. "Then I suppose it was the prospect of dancing with me that caused that unhappy look."

"No, of course not," she denied too quickly. Her gaze skittered away from his mocking stare. "I, uh...I was thinking about something else. That's all."

"You mean like imagining your sister in Max's arms? Wishing it could be you?"

"No!"

"Ah, poor brave Elise," he continued in that calm, even voice, as though she hadn't spoken. "Life isn't fair, is it? You wore your heart on your sleeve for six months, and Max never even noticed, but he took one look at your twin sister, who looks exactly like you, and fell head over heels."

Elise stiffened, but he pulled her closer and maneuvered them around another couple. Sam was so contained she had expected him to move mechanically, but he was a surprisingly good dancer, his rangy body gliding to the rhythm with fluid grace. The music flowed around them, slow, soft and sultry, but Sam's face was as warm and animated as stone.

Elise stared over his shoulder, humiliated, annoyed and thoroughly frustrated. She had thought she'd kept her feelings hidden, but apparently she hadn't. She wondered if anyone else at Global knew of her infatuation with Max. Did Margo and Peggy? Was she the subject of gossip and speculation among the other women on staff?

Probably, Elise realized, horrified. Even so, it was unkind of Sam to point it out. Lifting her chin a fraction, she shot him a sullen look. "There has never been anything personal between Max and me."

"I know. But you were hoping there would be, weren't you?"

"I . . . Oh, all right! Yes, I was. But that was just a . . . a crush. If you'll recall, I was the one responsible for getting Erin and Max together."

"Very noble and self-sacrificing of you," Sam mocked. "But since you were the cause of their being apart, it seems only fair. Your sister knew how you felt, and she'd sooner cut off her arm than hurt you."

"I know that," Elise replied, her expression softening.

But Sam was relentless. "In the end, though, you had no choice but to accept defeat." His level tone and steady gaze prodded her. "Any idiot could see that Max loved Erin, not you."

"Look, I told you—"

"I know, I know. You aren't in love with Max. You're delighted about this marriage. Happy for both of them." The music stopped, and the other couples started to drift back toward the tables, but Sam still held Elise close. He looked at her pityingly and smiled his chilly smile. "Just keep telling yourself that. Who knows? Someday it might even be true."

Unlike her twin, Elise had been blessed with a mild temper and an abundance of patience, but Sam's goading had pushed her to the limit, and beyond. She forgot her nervousness. She forgot that he was part-owner of the firm where she worked. She forgot where they were and who might be listening. Jerking out of his arms, she took a step backward.

"It's true now! And I'm sick and tired of trying to convince you." Her voice shook, though more from hurt than anger, and she felt a momentary spurt of amazement and fear that she had dared to speak to him so. "But even if it weren't, my feelings are none of your business. I don't have to take this from you or anyone."

Sam cocked one brow, a look of faint surprise on his face as his gaze swept over her. His mouth twitched in what might have been a smile. "Well, well, well," he murmured.

"You amaze me, Elise. I had no idea there was a temper beneath all that gentle sweetness."

Elise sucked in an affronted breath. Far from smoothing things over, his words ruffled her hurt feelings even more. All of their lives, when people compared her and Erin they'd called her the quiet one, the angelic one. It was meant as a compliment, but the older she got, the less it seemed so. It irritated her that people saw her as sweet and soft and placid, with no fire, no passion.

It wasn't strictly true. Yes, hers was a milder nature, less adventuresome, perhaps a bit softer, but Erin had always been such a daring, impetuous, impossible scamp that compared to her, anyone would have looked saintly.

Well, saints were boring. Men didn't fall in love with saints. And she was fed up with being considered one.

With a final affronted glare at Sam, Elise spun on her heel and stalked back toward the table, her stride long and determined. *I'll show Sam Lawford, and everyone else, that I'm no Goody Two-shoes*, she vowed. *I can be as spontaneous and free-spirited as Erin, any day. They'll see.*

Sam followed more slowly, his expression thoughtful as he pulled out Elise's chair. The instant she sat down she reached for her glass of champagne and held it high.

"I'd like to propose a toast," she said, shooting Sam a defiant glance when he took his seat beside her. "To Erin and Max. May you have a long, happy life together."

Glasses clinked, and Elise drained hers in one long swallow. Recklessly, she'd held her glass out for a refill, then raised it high again. "To love. May yours..."

The memory grew fuzzy around the edges, and for the life of her, Elise could not remember the rest of the toast. She moaned and rested her forehead against the cool tile of the shower wall, her eyes closed as the water sluiced over her. Several more toasts had followed—she remembered that much—but they, along with the rest of the evening, all ran together in a blur.

With a disgusted groan, she turned off the water and stepped from the shower. As she patted herself dry, she shook her head at her bedraggled reflection.

Pride. Done in by her own foolish pride. What an idiot. She had known better than to drink that second glass of champagne. Not to mention God only knew how many after that. One had been her limit since high school. She had learned the night of her senior prom that she had no tolerance for the stuff. Luckily, that night she had double-dated with Erin, and her twin had been there to protect her from her own folly *and* her date's amorous intentions.

Elise sighed as she dressed in the camel wool slacks and forest-green sweater she'd brought for the return trip to Santa Fe. Ever since she could remember, Erin had watched out for her, from their playpen days, during all the years of school and college, right up through that hair-raising episode last July, when they'd both been in danger.

But last night Erin had not been there to protect her. She and Max hadn't even stayed in this hotel. For some incomprehensible reason of their own, they had wanted to spend the first night of their honeymoon in some dive called the Red Rooster.

"And, bombed out of your mind, you ended up in Sam Lawford's bed," she snarled at her mirror image, slapping makeup onto her pallid cheeks.

Elise struggled to remember how it had happened, but all she could recall of the evening were disturbing, disjointed little snatches—waving goodbye to Erin and Max, giggling as Sam held her against his side, being carried and undressed by strong hands, flirting outrageously with Sam, trying to coax a smile from him. And she seemed to remember... Oh, no. Had she actually nibbled on his neck? Elise closed her eyes and shivered. Where had she gotten the nerve?

No matter how hard she strained, she couldn't remember much else. What had happened between her and Sam? They had slept in the same bed—that much was obvious—but had they...?

No. No, surely not. Sam wouldn't have taken advantage of a woman in her condition. At least...she didn't think so.

Chewing the inside of her cheek, she gazed at the closed door. She had to know. She wouldn't be able to stand it until she did. Which meant she was going to have to go out there and ask Sam, point-blank.

Fretting over the situation, she finished applying her makeup, then automatically tidied up the bathroom, scarcely even aware she was doing it. The last thing in the world she wanted to do was face him again, Elise admitted shakily as she dried off the counter and straightened the towels. But she didn't have much choice. He was right outside the door, and he wasn't going to go away. She closed the shower curtain and put the lid down on the commode. With a sigh, she snatched a tissue from the dispenser and wiped the water spots off the mirror. "So you might as well go out there and get it over with," she told her reflection.

Without giving herself a chance to reconsider, Elise tossed the damp tissue into the wastebasket, finger-combed her wet curls, squared her shoulders and reached for the doorknob.

Her courage almost deserted her when she saw Sam standing at the balcony doors, sipping a cup of coffee as he gazed out at the pool and the golf course.

He had pulled on the pants of the dark blue suit he'd worn the night before, and the same white shirt, though he hadn't bothered to tuck it in. He was barefoot, his hair was still tousled and the tail of the shirt hung about his hips in a wrinkled mess.

For a moment, Elise just stared. In the nine months she had worked for Global Imports, she'd never seen Sam any way but impeccably groomed, the picture of sartorial elegance.

As though sensing her presence, he turned, and she saw that his jaw and upper lip were shadowed with a dark stubble. It made him look dangerous and devastatingly male.

He strolled toward her, his bare feet silent on the plush carpet. "Feeling better?" he inquired.

Elise nodded.

"I ordered coffee." With a flick of his finger he indicated the tray on the table in the corner. "Would you like some?"

"Yes. Thank you." *How could he be so calm?*

On shaky legs, she crossed the room and poured the dark brew, adding her customary two teaspoons of sugar. The cup rattled in the saucer like castanets as she picked it up. She took a sip, scalding her tongue, but she was too grateful for the fortifying caffeine to care. Though quaking inside, she forced herself to look at him, and she felt her stomach lurch as she met his piercing silver-gray eyes.

"Uh, Mr. Lawford...about last night..."

"What about it?"

"What...that is...I can't seem to remember...." She paused hopefully, but he simply continued to watch her, his expression unreadable. She cleared her throat and tried again. "Uh...Mr. Lawford, I—"

"Sam."

Elise blinked. "What?"

"My name is Sam. After last night, don't you think it's a little ridiculous for you to keep calling me Mr. Lawford?"

The soft words caused her heart to give a little leap. Last night? Oh, dear. She closed her eyes and pressed her hand against her abdomen. She was trembling so, her coffee splashed over into the saucer, and she carefully placed it back on the tray before facing him again. "Mr. Lawf—uh, S-Sam, last night I was...that is..." She glanced at the rumpled bed and bit her lower lip. "Did we...I mean..."

Sam deposited his empty cup on top of the television set and braced himself against the dresser, his long legs stretched out in front of him and crossed at the ankles, arms folded over his chest. Beneath the gaping shirt the silver medal winked at her from its nest of dark chest hair, and his lean middle looked hard and brown, his navel disappearing into the horizontal fold created by his casual posture.

Sam tipped his head to one side and studied her flushed face. Then, to Elise's astonishment, he smiled—a small, devilish smile that made her stomach clench and doubled her apprehension. "I take it you're trying to tell me you don't remember last night."

"Not much, no," Elise admitted sheepishly.

"And you want to know what happened. Right?"

Lord, no, she thought. "Yes," she said.

"Well, for one thing, I learned that you're not as shy and retiring as I thought."

Elise felt her cheeks heat up, and his smile flickered again.

"In fact, when you loosen up a bit, you're quite an amorous lady. One might even say...frisky."

In a horrifying flash of memory, Elise saw herself nibbling Sam's neck, her body pressed against his, her fingers working open the buttons on his shirt....

"Mmm, Sam, you have the most delicious neck. Did you know that?"

"Elise, what are you doing?"

"I'm helping you undress. You can't sleep with all these clothes on. Mmm, you do taste good."

"Elise, behave yourself."

"And smell so good. So...masculine."

"Elise..."

"And I just love a man who has hair on his chest."

"Elise, cut it out. You don't know...what...you're doing. No, don't...stop.... Ah, sweetheart...."

With a groan, Elise covered her face with both hands, but Sam's unexpected reaction caused her to snatch them away again.

Shocked, she gaped at him, her embarrassment all but forgotten. Sam's head was thrown back, and deep, rumbling laughter rolled from his throat—warm, rich, masculine chuckles of pure delight that bounced off the walls. Never had she expected to hear such a happy sound come from this man, and she found herself wondering why he didn't laugh more often.

Sam's mirth finally subsided, and he gave her a teasing look, his pale eyes sparkling for once with life and good humor. "I didn't know there was a woman who could still blush like that. What's the matter? Are you afraid we made mad, passionate love? That I had my wicked way with you? That I took advantage of your inebriated state and ravished that lovely body?" Lowering his eyelids halfway, he gave her a slumberous look, and his voice dropped to a suggestive murmur. "Or are you more afraid that you may have ravished me?"

"Mr. Lawf—Sam. Please." She cast a desperate glance toward the bed and looked back at him pleadingly. "Just tell me what happened."

"Nothing."

"What?"

"Nothing happened." All trace of teasing vanished from Sam's face. Once again his beautiful eyes were cool, his expression austere and remote.

"But . . . I don't understand." Elise made a helpless gesture that encompassed the bed and the room. "If we didn't . . . that is . . . if nothing happened . . . then why . . . ?"

"Did we share this room?" Sam finished for her. "Simple. It was the only vacancy the hotel had." He straightened away from the dresser, took his garment bag from the closet and headed for the bathroom. "By the time we said goodbye to Erin and Max, you were in no condition to be left alone. Anyway, it was too late for me to go searching for accommodations elsewhere. I was afraid you were going to pass out on me." He stopped at the bathroom door and

looked back at her. "Which, by the way, you did, five minutes after we stepped into the room. So don't fret. We
shared a bed, and you spent most of the night in my arms,
but nothing happened."

Elise wanted to believe him, but his offhand manner
failed to convince her. Granted, her experience was limited,
since the only man she ever made love with had been her late
husband. But she knew enough about the male sex drive to
question if any man had that kind of self-control. Especially when he found himself in bed with an almost naked,
willing woman.

And, she had to admit, if those humiliating snatches of
memory were anything to go by, she *had* been willing. Even
eager.

"I see," she said quietly as Sam turned to enter the bathroom, but something in her voice must have revealed her
doubt, for he stopped and gave her a sharp look, his eyes
narrowing.

"You don't believe me, do you?"

"Well, I . . ."

"Never mind, it's not important." He gave a dismissive
shrug and said in that cool, disinterested voice, "Nothing
happened, but if you're worried about it, we can always get
married."

Chapter Two

With those few simple words, he managed to knock all the breath out of her. Elise gaped at him, the power of speech deserting her for a moment.

"Th-that isn't in the *least* funny," she sputtered.

"It wasn't meant to be." Sam gave her a long, steady look, then shrugged. "But since you're obviously not interested, forget it. It was just a suggestion." Before she could reply, he stepped into the bathroom and closed the door behind him.

She stood as though rooted to the spot and stared at the cream-painted panel, while her heart raced and her breath rushed in and out of her tight chest in painful little gasps. What did he mean, he wasn't joking? He had to be. Either that, or he had just wanted to shock her. He couldn't be serious about marrying her. An icy tingle feathered over Elise's skin at the thought.

Well, he'd shocked her all right—right down to her toes— but gradually that feeling gave way to anger. The longer she thought about the breezy, insulting offer, the more appalled and incensed she became. Was he so used to being intimate with women he scarcely knew that he could just pass off the whole thing so lightly? Even if, as he'd said, they had not made love, the situation wasn't something to joke about. It was embarrassing and humiliating and... and... extremely uncomfortable!

Releasing a long sigh, Elise raked a hand through her damp curls, fluffing them. But at least, if she could believe Sam, nothing had happened.

Doubt niggled at her, but she pushed it aside. Of course nothing had happened, she told herself.

By the time Sam emerged from the bathroom Elise had consumed two cups of sweet coffee, and though she felt miserable and self-conscious, her composure was once more in place. She sat in one of the chairs by the balcony doors, her hands folded primly in her lap, a third cup of steaming coffee beside her on the table.

"We're supposed to see Erin and Max off at the airport in an hour," Sam said, sparing her a glance as he repacked the suit he'd worn the day before and dropped his shaving kit into the garment bag.

A little dart of irritation pricked Elise when she noticed he was dressed in a beautiful navy blue blazer that fit his broad shoulders like a glove, and gray slacks with a knife-edge crease of which any marine drill instructor would be proud. He had teamed them with a crisp white shirt and a navy-gray-and-maroon-striped tie. Elise was neat and well-groomed, compulsively so, her sister had told her on numerous occasions, but next to Sam's perfection she felt positively dowdy.

In a morning that was shaping up to be one of the worst of her life, it was the final indignity. Gritting her teeth, she rose, picked up her overnight bag and said with as much icy dignity as she could muster, "I'm ready when you are."

* * *

She's still angry, Sam thought, two hours later.

As they waited for Erin and Max's flight, he watched her surreptitiously, paying scant attention to what his partner was saying. *Angry, and just a touch uncertain.* It showed in her stiff posture, that haughty little tilt of her chin. And in the unnatural tightness around that luscious mouth.

The drive to the airport had been made in absolute silence, and the moment they'd caught sight of Erin and Max she'd latched on to her twin and ignored him completely.

Of course, he'd known, even as he made the offhand comment about marrying her, that she would be angry. He wasn't even sure why he made it. Partly, Sam supposed, because he wanted to plant the idea in her mind. But also, he suspected he'd done it because her appalled reaction to spending the night with him had gotten under his skin. He had intentionally goaded her, hoping for precisely the response he'd gotten.

It was Elise's sweetness and serenity that drew him, but he had to admit, that tantalizing flash of temper he'd glimpsed for the first time the night before was intriguing.

Elise and Erin stood off to one side of the crowded boarding area, saying a last farewell before the newlyweds boarded their plane for South America. Sam wondered if Elise had told her twin that she'd spent the night with him. The two were very close, so it wouldn't surprise him if she had.

A hint of amusement entered his eyes. As fiercely protective as Erin was of her sister, he half expected her to come after him at any second with blood in her eye.

"They're an eye-catching pair, aren't they?"

The quiet pride in Max's voice was unmistakable. Glancing at him, Sam felt a peculiar sensation in his gut when he saw the adoration in his friend's face as he gazed at his wife.

Sam resumed his study of the two women. "Yes. Yes, they are."

They were, indeed, striking, he thought as he noticed the fascinated stares they were drawing from other people. Two identical tall, slender beauties with big brown eyes and flaming red hair. Oh, yes. They would stand out in any crowd.

To the casual observer, they looked as alike as the proverbial two peas in a pod, but there were differences—subtle, tiny ones you could detect if you were discerning enough, interested enough.

Sam doubted that he would ever confuse them again.

The differences weren't so much physical, though Erin's mouth was a bit wider than Elise's, her hair just a shade brighter. And the tilt of her eyes seemed more marked, giving her a bright, inquisitive look, where Elise's eyes were soft and dreamy. But their contrasting personalities and natures were what made them truly distinguishable. Erin was a feisty, intrepid soul, curious, energetic, adventuresome to the point of recklessness, in Sam's opinion. Elise was soft and gentle, an utterly feminine woman who projected a serenity he found irresistible.

Erin was a dancing flame, Elise a warm, steadily glowing coal.

"Did you have any problems after we left last night?" Max asked.

When Sam turned his head, he found that his friend was watching him, his expression amused. "What do you mean?"

"Only that Elise wasn't exactly herself. Erin told me she has no tolerance for alcohol. She wasn't comfortable leaving her. If it hadn't been our wedding night, she would've been hovering like a mother hen."

Sam shrugged. "We managed."

Their attention returned to the women, and after a moment Max said, "Erin thinks that you're in love with Elise, you know."

Surprise rippled through Sam, but he hid it, giving Max a dry look. "Erin has stars in her eyes," he said in a voice heavy with amused cynicism.

"True," Max agreed happily. "But that doesn't answer my question." He lifted one brow and fixed Sam with a probing gaze. "*Do* you love Elise?"

"No."

There was no hesitation, no hedging, just a flat statement. It seemed to catch Max off guard, for his expectant expression dissolved into a frown. "I see."

"I think she's beautiful, I admire her warmth and sweetness, and I want to make love to her," Sam admitted with characteristic directness. He paused to let that register, noting the look of faint surprise on Max's face, then added bluntly, "And I intend to have her."

"You may have a problem there, my friend. Somehow, I don't think Elise is the type for an affair."

"I'm going to marry her."

"What!" This time Max's surprise was anything but faint. "But you just said you didn't love her."

"I don't. But I want her."

"And you think that's enough to build a marriage on?" Max asked incredulously, pity shading his voice.

"Yes."

Concern and censure warred in Max's expression, but Sam met it without so much as a blink. Even if he wanted to explain, which he didn't, how could he make Max, a man who was besotted with his wife, understand that there was no place in his life for love?

Wanting was acceptable. Wants and desires—they could be satisfied easily and forgotten. But love...love wasn't that simple. It worked its way into your soul and into your heart, became a part of you. Love made you vulnerable. It weakened you and left you open to pain. He'd learned to block it out long ago, to live without it. He'd had to.

"Sam—"

"Drop it, Max." Sam met his friend's exasperated look with a cold stare that made it clear the subject was closed.

At that moment Elise glanced their way. Her eyes met Sam's for an instant, but she quickly looked away.

Oh, yes, Sam thought with a touch of amusement. *She's still angry. But what the hell!* Anger was a damn sight better than that frightened-fawn look she usually wore whenever he came near her.

Elise turned back from looking at Sam to find her sister studying her.

"All right. What's going on between you two?" Erin demanded.

Feigning innocence, Elise widened her eyes and gave an elaborate shrug. "Why, nothing. Nothing at all."

"Don't give me that. I saw that look. And I've been picking up some strange vibrations from you ever since you arrived. Now, I know you're angry and upset with Sam, so you might as well tell me about it."

Elise gritted her teeth. There were times, like now, when she regretted that uncanny ability she and Erin had to communicate their thoughts and emotions to each other. The telepathy, or whatever you wanted to call it, was a part of that special bond between them, and they enjoyed it, but it also made it almost impossible to keep a secret, which could be downright inconvenient at times.

"All right, yes, I am upset," Elise admitted grudgingly. "But it's really all your fault."

"*My* fault! What did I do?"

"You let me drink all that champagne, then ran out on me, that's what."

"As you've pointed out to me before, sister dear, you're a grown woman, capable of taking care of yourself."

Even as Elise had made the accusation she'd known it was unfair, even childish of her. She was upset and angry, with herself mostly, and looking for someone else to blame.

"You're right," she conceded with a sheepish grimace, but then couldn't resist adding, "But I still don't understand why you wanted to spend your wedding night in that dive."

"For sentimental reasons. Max and I stayed at the Red Rooster the first time we made lo—uh, that is . . . when we were searching for you, last summer," Erin replied, her lips twitching.

Elise shuddered. Last summer was a time she would just as soon forget. Even after almost three months, the mere mention of that harrowing experience made her stomach clench with fear.

It was impossible to forget, of course. If she lived to be ninety she would always remember how shocked—then terrified—she'd been that night when she'd stumbled onto Sam's secretary, Wilma Crenshaw, and her partners as they were uncrating a shipment of smuggled diamonds. Nor would she ever forget the horrifying five days that had followed, when she had fled for her life, moving from place to place, constantly looking over her shoulder, going without sleep or rest and sometimes food. It had taken every ounce of intelligence and cleverness she possessed just to stay one step ahead of her pursuers.

Typically Erin, with Max in tow, had been hot on her trail also, intent on protecting her. Instead, she'd almost gotten both of them killed.

Erin cocked her head to one side, her eyes narrowing. A wicked smile blossomed on her face, and Elise experienced a sinking feeling, knowing her twin was picking up on her discomfort.

"What I don't understand is why it bothers you so. Unless . . . Oh, my . . . don't tell me that Sam took advantage of you?"

When Elise's face flamed, Erin crowed with delight. "Why, Elise Marie Holman! You risqué thing, you. Do you mean you actually let him seduce you?"

"Yes. No! That is..." Elise glanced over to where the two men stood talking. Squirming, she looked back at Erin guiltily. "According to Sam, the hotel had only one vacancy, and...well...when I woke up this morning, I...I was in bed with him."

Erin's eyes widened. "According to Sam? You mean you don't remember?"

"Well...no," Elise admitted reluctantly, then rushed to add, "But Sam assured me that nothing happened. We just slept together."

"Oh, really," Erin drawled.

"Erin! Stop that! We didn't *sleep* together, we just—" flustered, Elise flapped her hands "—just shared a bed, that's... Oh, you know what I mean."

Her sister's lips twitched as she tried to stifle her amusement, but it was hopeless, and finally she threw her head back and let the peals of laughter pour from her. At last, spying Elise's affronted look, Erin made a valiant effort to regain control.

Taking one of Elise's hands, she squeezed it and said, "I'm sorry, love. I shouldn't tease you, I know. Forgive me."

Erin's laughter had drawn the men's attention, and Elise tensed as they began to head their way. At the same time Max and Erin's flight was announced.

Erin put her arm around Elise's shoulders, gave her a quick hug and said under her breath, "Don't look so tragic. Even if something did happen last night, it's not the end of the world. In fact, I think it's wonderful that you and Sam have finally gotten together."

"Wonderful!" Elise's jaw droppped. "How can you say—"

"I hate to break this up," Max said, taking his wife's arm, "but they're calling our flight. Come on, sweetheart, we've got to go."

"Oh, but—"

"Don't worry, sis. We'll be back in six or seven weeks," Erin assured Elise as she embraced her. "In time for Christmas, anyway." Stepping back, she took both of Elise's hands, her eyes suspiciously moist. "Now, remember, if you need me for any reason, we'll be at the International Hotel in Montevideo for the next week. After that we'll spend a week in the Bahamas, then fly to Europe so Max can iron out a few problems with his suppliers."

"I know," Elise assured her, wavering between amusement and tears. "I typed your itinerary, remember?"

"Yes, of course. Oh, but there's one other thing—"

"Come on, sweetheart." Max placed his hands on either side of Erin's waist and attempted to edge her away. "It's time to go."

"Just one second," she replied distractedly, clinging to her twin's hand. "Elise, when you talk to Mother and Dad, and David, too, tell them I'm sorry we had to rush the wedding, but otherwise, with our hectic schedules, we would've had to wait months. I was already committed to work as interpreter for this beauty pageant in South America, and Max can't postpone his trip. Oh, and—"

"For cryin' out loud, Erin, say goodbye." Max rolled his eyes, and Elise laughed at his beleaguered look.

"So long, sister-in-law," he said, giving her a hug and a kiss on the cheek. "Take care of yourself, and we'll see you at Christmas."

Erin darted in for one last embrace and whispered in her ear, "I expect to find you and Sam married, or at the very least, engaged by the time we return."

"Erin!" Elise gasped.

Her twin's brown eyes twinkled. "Don't look so shocked. You know our lives have always followed parallel paths. So it's only a matter of time now before you get married, too," she said smugly. Ignoring Elise's sputtered denials, she smiled and patted her hand, then allowed Max to tug her toward the boarding tunnel.

They had gone only a few steps when he stopped and turned back to her.

"Oh, by the way, Elise, I forgot to tell you. We decided that since Sam is without a secretary and I plan to spend a great deal of the next year or so out of the country, you'll work for him from now on."

The announcement, coming on top of Erin's teasing, made Elise's head reel. Appalled, her mouth slowly dropping open, she stared at Max as he hustled his bride down the tunnel.

Work for Sam? No. No, she couldn't. Even if last night had never happened, she couldn't cope with Sam. He made her too nervous. And now . . . now . . .

She shook her head. No. It was impossible. She couldn't.

But, short of quitting her job, she would have to. What excuse could she give for refusing? *I can't work for you, Mr. Lawford, because you're as cold and unemotional as granite, and you frighten me to death when you stare at me with those lifeless silver eyes.*

Elise shuddered. It was the truth, but she couldn't tell him that.

No matter what excuse she used, if she quit now people would think she was still nursing that foolish crush on Max and was heartbroken over losing him to her twin. That would be even worse.

She had to stay. Sam made her jittery and ill at ease, and working for him under any circumstances would be difficult, but after last night, it was going to be awkward and uncomfortable as well. Elise sighed and firmed her mouth. But, after all, she reminded herself, you're twenty-seven years old, almost twenty-eight. You've been married and widowed. By now you should be mature enough to weather a little embarrassment.

"Well, Elise, shall we go?" Sam asked, taking her arm. "Our flight will be boarding soon."

Elise started at his touch and looked up. For an instant she'd thought she heard mocking amusement in his voice, but the pale eyes regarding her steadily were as lifeless as ever. She stared at the lean, rugged face, so devoid of emotion, and nodded numbly. As he led her down the concourse toward the gate where they would board their flight for Santa Fe, a shudder rippled through her.

Oh, God, she thought desperately. Erin must have been joking. Surely her sister couldn't seriously think that there could ever be anything between her and this unfeeling man.

As it turned out, Elise was right to be concerned. Working for Sam proved every bit as difficult as she'd anticipated...though not in precisely the way she'd expected. Though Max was charming, he had not been an easy man to work for. Hard-driving, quick, energetic, he had been a demanding boss, and Sam was an equally hard taskmaster. The difference was, Max handled the overseas end of the business, which meant that he was frequently out of the country, but Sam was there most of the time. He oversaw the domestic side of Global Imports, and his infrequent business trips seldom lasted more than a day.

In five minutes, Sam could pile on more work than the average person could finish in a week. He never raised his voice, never flew off the handle, never showed the least sign of anger or impatience, but when he issued orders in that flat, clipped voice, it had the effect of a whip cracking, and Elise found herself scrambling to do his bidding. She was an excellent secretary, but it was a daily struggle just to keep her head above water.

Sam's remoteness continued to make Elise edgy, but he kept her so busy she didn't have time to dwell on it. Nor did she have time to fret over the night they had spent together. He, mercifully, made no reference to it at all. It was as though the whole thing had never happened. Except for his insistence that she call him by his first name, Sam Lawford was all business in the office.

By the end of the first week Elise was so exhausted she went home on Friday, fell into bed and slept until after ten the next morning.

By the end of the next week she was in slightly better shape, and each one that followed seemed to get a tad easier, until finally she began to think she would survive after all.

But despite the fatiguing demands of her job and Sam's blessed indifference, Elise was restless and uneasy, for niggling at the back of her mind constantly was her sister's parting comment.

"You know our lives have always followed parallel paths. So it's only a matter of time now before you get married, too."

It was true. The major events and turning points of their lives had always coincided—broken bones, triumphs and disappointments, beginnings, endings. What happened to one always, within a short time span, happened to the other, also. They had accepted it as inevitable long ago.

And in truth, Elise welcomed the thought of finding a new love and getting married again. What was scary was that the man might turn out to be Sam.

At first she denied the possibility vehemently, until it occurred to her that, because she hadn't dated at all since losing Tommy, she really didn't know any single men . . . other than Sam. Horrified, she realized it could happen by default.

The very idea unnerved Elise, so she tried to push it from her mind by indulging in a frenzy of activity. For weeks she went Christmas shopping almost every evening after work, even though most of the time she was so tired she trudged out of the office like a chicken dragging its tail feathers. When all her shopping was done, she resorted to cleaning out immaculate closets, washing clean curtains and waxing the kitchen floor. She even wallpapered her bedroom.

Nothing helped, and finally one evening the problem, and the feelings she'd been trying so hard to outrun, caught up with her.

Sam had left early to straighten out some difficulty at their Albuquerque store, so for once Elise was leaving on time. As her dragging steps carried her down the hallway the thought of a luxurious long hot soak, of reclining up to her chin in jasmine-scented water and bubbles, was uppermost in her mind.

"Night, Peggy," she called, giving the young receptionist a tired smile as she passed her desk.

At the entrance she paused to pull on her wool, leather-palmed driving gloves, stopping beside Margo North, who was studying the overcast sky through the glass door.

"It will snow before morning," Elise observed.

Her friend shot her a disgruntled look. "I know. And you don't have to sound so darned pleased about it, either."

"Oh, come on. It's not so bad."

"Not if you happen to be a penguin."

Elise chuckled. Margo, an attorney on staff, was a tough but dedicated career woman who used her acerbic tongue to hide a soft heart. She and the other women friends Elise had made at Global had difficulty understanding her fondness for snow and were constantly issuing dire warnings that she would soon be as sick of it as they were.

Elise knew that it was an inconvenience, especially since Global's office and warehouse were located several miles out of town in an isolated spot partway up a mountain. But, being from Crockett, Texas, where it seldom snowed, she still found the white stuff enough of a novelty to truly appreciate.

"Well, I don't know about you, but I have a fascinating man waiting for me at home, and I intend to be snuggled under the covers with him before it hits. See you tomorrow, kiddo." With a wave, Margo pushed open the glass doors, and Elise felt a blast of frigid air swirl around her legs.

She watched her friend hurry away. Then, in the act of tugging a green knit cap over her fiery curls, her gaze was caught by the cars pouring out of the parking lot. Elise's hands stilled, and as she stood motionless, watching the string of glowing taillights winding down the mountain road, an aching heaviness formed beneath her breastbone.

They're all hurrying home to loved ones and families, she thought, as an inexplicable rush of melancholia engulfed her. Suddenly the idea of going back to her empty apartment, of whipping up an omelet and eating it alone at the kitchen table, was depressing. Even the thought of a sybaritic soak had lost its appeal.

Oh, stop it! Annoyed, Elise rammed her hands into the pockets of her coat, shoved open the door with her shoulder and walked out into the gathering dusk, her head lowered against the icy wind.

It's fatigue. Or this gloomy weather, she told herself, fighting the sharp surge of self-pity that threatened to bring tears to her eyes. She climbed into her blue Chevy and started the engine, but then, as she waited for it to warm up, she sighed and slumped back against the seat.

Who was she kidding? Loneliness had caused this maudlin mood. She had been alone for the past two years and had thought herself reasonably content, but all that had changed since she returned from Las Vegas. Somehow, Erin and Max's marriage, their obvious delight in each other, had brought home just how empty her own life had become.

And yes, she admitted reluctantly, the incident with Sam was also to blame for her unsettled mood.

Pensive, Elise put the car in gear and drove out of the parking lot behind Margo's red BMW. As they joined the small convoy heading toward Santa Fe, her friend waved and honked, and Elise returned the farewell.

She followed the luxury car down the twisting road, negotiating the hairpin curves without conscious thought. Before that mad weekend in Las Vegas, it had been a long time since she'd lain in a man's arms and felt that warmth, that special closeness that only a man and woman can share. Too long.

Never mind that it had been the wrong man, the wrong time and for the wrong reason. The experience had awakened needs that had been dormant for more than two years. Needs that not even her infatuation with Max had stirred. That had been pure fantasy, a girlish, impossible daydream.

But she was not a girl. She was a woman. A woman who had known love.

The string of cars reached the foot of the mountain and turned onto the highway, heading toward Santa Fe. Elise followed Margo automatically, paying scant attention to where they were going. Yes, she thought, with a twinge of melancholy, she knew what it was like to love and be loved.

The night spent with Sam had stirred needs and desires, brought back memories and reawakened cherished dreams. Dreams of an abiding love, of a home, a family, contentment, the kind of happiness she'd tasted so briefly once before. And now her heart yearned to know that joy again. Her heart, her body and her soul.

If Max had not come along for Erin, her sister would have been perfectly content, living her life alone, a will-o'-the-wisp flitting happily about the globe with no ties. But not Elise. She knew herself well enough to know that she would never be truly happy alone. She needed commitment and roots. She needed a partner, someone to share life's ups and downs. She needed a mate.

"And if you don't want him to be Sam Lawford, then you'd better get busy and meet other men," she muttered.

Firming her mouth, she drew a deep breath and released it slowly. She would do it. She would do whatever was necessary to find a man she could love and—hopefully—marry. Even if it meant joining one of those computer dating services.

Chapter Three

The next evening Elise had dinner with four friends from the office. When she told them of her plan, they all stared at her as though unable to believe their ears.

Colleen recovered first.

"You're kidding, right?"

"No. Not at all."

"Gosh," Tracy said in an awed voice. "You mean you're just going to start... *husband hunting*? Just like that?"

"Yes." Elise smiled at the wide-eyed look of admiration in the younger woman's plump face. Marriage was Tracy's most cherished goal, but Elise could see that even as man-crazy as she was, she'd never considered launching an all-out campaign.

"Now wait a minute. Let me get this straight," Margo said, frowning. "You expect us to believe that you—sweet, soft-spoken, gentle Elise—are just going to intentionally and cold-bloodedly cut some poor unsuspecting male from the bachelor herd and wheedle a proposal out of him? Uh-huh.

Sure. Honey, the day you become a manipulating femme fatale I'll burn my ERA card.''

"I think you've overstated the case a bit, counselor," Elise said with a tolerant smile, placing chiding emphasis on the last word. "I have no intention of 'wheedling' a proposal out of anyone. If I meet the right man, I don't expect it will come to that."

For an instant she considered telling them about how her and Erin's lives had always taken identical turns, but quickly decided against it. They probably wouldn't believe it anyway.

"You're serious about this, aren't you?" Margo said in a softer tone.

"Yes, very. A career is all well and good. For some women, it's everything, but not for me. I want a husband and a family. It's what I've always wanted. And let's face it, I'm not getting any younger."

"Personally, tying yourself down to one man sounds perfectly dreadful to me," Colleen drawled.

"Oh, I don't know." Peggy Denton's pixie face took on a faraway expression as she sighed dreamily. "I think it sounds kinda romantic."

Colleen gave the younger woman a dry look. "I might have known you'd think so. You're so obsessed with that husband of yours, no doubt you'd think a walk in a swamp was romantic."

"Well, it would be, if Charlie were with me. But I don't expect you to understand, since you've never been in love." With that, Peggy loftily tilted her chin, gave an affronted little sniff and pursed her full lips into a pout.

Colleen shuddered. "Love, my sweet Pollyanna, is a four-letter word. Believe me, Elise will be better off if she stays single and plays the field."

Elise sent Peggy a consoling glance before turning to the older woman. Colleen Mahaffey was the assistant personnel director at Global. Cool and sophisticated, she seemed to value men for little more than the physical pleasure they could give her. At times, considering the differences between them, it still amazed Elise that they were friends.

"Actually, Colleen, I was hoping that the four of you would help me." She paused, her gaze sweeping the others. "Do you think you could?"

"Well, we're an odd assortment of matchmakers," Margo said with a grimace. "Peggy's married. Tracy wants to be. Colleen is single by choice, and I've been divorced twice. But I suppose, between us, we should be able to at least get you back into circulation."

"I think you're nuts," Colleen drawled. "But if you're determined to do this, I suppose I could round up a few candidates."

"Me, too," Peggy said. "That is, provided you don't mind going out with divorced men."

"If she does, I'll take them. I'm not choosy." Sitting forward, Tracy looked eagerly from one woman to the next, but the offer produced only looks of dry amusement.

"My cousin Norman is single."

"Forget it, Peg. I've seen your cousin."

"How about Earl Robbins, that new accountant?" Colleen suggested. "He's single. And he scored high on all the preemployment tests."

"No, he's too short." Margo dismissed him with a wave of her hand. "Besides, accountants are dull."

"I like dull men," Tracy inserted hopefully.

"Oh, I know! How about Jonathan Leeds?"

"That creep? Uh-unh. No way."

The waiter arrived with their order, and throughout the meal they continued the lively, sometimes hilarious discussion, ticking off the merits and shortcomings of every unattached male they knew, and the various methods of meeting more.

"Well, there's always church," Peggy said, as she polished off the last bite of quiche and pushed back her plate. "That's where I met Charlie."

"You know...that's not a half bad idea," Margo said thoughtfully. "And my church has a yummy new assistant pastor who's single. He'd be just perfect."

Colleen waggled her fork at Elise. "Unless you're an atheist, I suggest you haul your bustle down to that church Sunday morning."

"Okay. Okay," Elise promised, laughing. She had no intention of trying to ensnare the minister, but, who knew, she just might meet someone nice.

"Fine. You be there next Sunday," Colleen instructed. "And in the meantime, as a backup, I'll try to set you up with a blind date."

"Well, if you're all so determined to fix Elise up with a man," Tracy said huffily, "what's wrong with Sexy Sam?"

The other women exchanged glances. "Mmm. Wouldn't that be something?" Peggy said, sighing.

Puzzled, Elise looked from one to the other. *Sexy Sam?* "Who are you talking about?"

"Why, Sam, of course." When Elise's stare remained blank, Colleen rolled her eyes. "Sam Lawford. Your boss. Who did you think we meant?"

"Oh, God, that is one hunk of a man." Margo groaned, her eyes becoming heavy lidded and dreamy. "Of course, Max isn't bad, either. In fact, I've always thought we worked for the two sexiest men alive. But...I don't know...there's just something about Sam."

"I'll say," Tracy agreed in a breathy voice. She batted her lashes extravagantly. "It's those beautiful pale eyes—that voice—that get to you. Whenever he comes near me I swear I get the shivers."

So do I, Elise thought. But obviously not for the same reasons. Sexy Sam? She couldn't believe it! These women thought Sam Lawford—cold as ice, Sam Lawford—was *sexy*?

"I know what you mean," Colleen said. "There's something so appealing about brooding men. They're so mysterious, so . . . so . . . intriguing."

"Mmm." Peggy propped her chin in her hand. "He's the only man I know who might be able to tempt me away from my Charlie."

"Ha! Don't hold your breath," Margo said with a snort. "I've worked here nine years, and in all that time, he's never been seriously involved with any one woman."

"I'd settle for a roll in the hay," Colleen drawled in her sultry voice. "God! Can you imagine what that body looks like under those impeccable suits? What he must be like in bed?"

"Oh, Lord, yes." Margo gave a rapturous shudder. She closed her eyes for a second, then drew a deep breath and opened them, shaking her head as though coming out of a hypnotic trance. "He would be perfect, but I doubt that Elise stands any more of a chance than the rest of us. I heard he was engaged once, to someone named Sherry Phillips. They say he was crazy about her, but for some reason it didn't work out. Since then he's played the field. Sam is all man, but marriage? Uh-unh. He never lets anyone get close enough for that to even be a possibility."

"Thank the Lord."

A hush fell, and Elise found herself the target of four stupefied stares. Only then did she realize she had voiced aloud her heartfelt relief.

"You mean you don't find Sam attractive?" Peggy was incredulous.

"I . . ." Self-conscious, Elise glanced from one stunned face to the next. "Uh . . . he's . . . he's just not my type, that's all."

Colleen tapped a cigarette against her crimson thumb-nail and arched an elegant brow. "Honey, Sam is *every* woman's type."

"He's a hunk!" Tracy insisted. "A rugged, sexy, thor-oughly masculine hunk." She rolled her eyes at the others and made a disgusted sound. "I swear, there's simply no justice. Elise works for the most fascinating man in the company, and she's not even interested. Me, I'd kill to have that job and be around Sam every day, but I'm stuck in ac-counting. The most interesting man there is Percy Filway, and he's fat, fiftyish and going bald."

Tracy's expression drew a laugh from everyone, but after a moment Peggy looked at Elise and said thoughtfully, "She's right, you know. It is a shame. Regardless of what Margo says, you do have the inside track since you work for him."

Elise shook her head. "To tell you the truth, Sam fright-ens me."

"Me, too." Margo gave a slow, Cheshire-cat smile as she rubbed her forearms and shivered. "But, mmm, what deli-cious fear."

They argued back and forth for another half hour. The other women expressed doubts about both Elise's intelli-gence and taste, but in the end they agreed to disagree on the subject of Sam Lawford.

They parted outside the restaurant, and Elise drove home humming off-key, happily conscious of a buoyant feeling inside, a renewed eagerness and sense of expectancy she hadn't felt in a long time.

For more than two years after Tommy had died she'd been drifting in a kind of limbo. Most of that time she'd been too grief-stricken to think about the future. Then, though she'd known deep down that it was a foolish fan-tasy, she had wasted another six months mooning over Max.

But she had always been a person who needed purpose and direction to her life. Unlike Erin, whose restless spirit delighted in the new and the unexpected, she liked to plan and set goals, work toward them, no matter how long it took. Erin gladly consigned herself to fate and let the four winds blow her where they would, but something in Elise, something deep in the core of her being, needed the security of a carefully charted course.

A bemused smile tilted Elise's mouth. Husband hunting. It was a bold thing to do. More like something Erin would tackle than her. Her twin might believe in fate, but she wasn't above giving it a hand when she wanted something.

"Maybe it's time I started acting more like Erin," Elise mumbled to herself as she parked her car in the assigned space behind her apartment and climbed out.

Elise entered her apartment through the back door. Without thinking about it, she flipped the lock and put on the chain, closed the blind over the kitchen sink and tested the soil of the potted ivy on the window ledge. Finding it dry, she added a half cup of water.

Haven't you always admired Erin's adventuresome spirit? Her zest and daring? Her spontaneity? she asked herself as she drew the draperies across the large living-room window that looked out over the enclosed courtyard. *Haven't you often wished you were more like her?*

Lost in thought, Elise hung her coat in the closet, then glanced around. Finding nothing out of place, she turned off the light and walked down the hall to her bedroom, unbuttoning her blouse and pausing once along the way to straighten a picture.

If there was one thing she'd learned in the past few months it was that men preferred a woman with a little zip— a woman like Erin, who rushed out to meet life—not timid souls afraid to reach out for what they wanted.

And at least this way, she thought with a touch of aggression as she finished undressing and neatly hung her clothes, fate wouldn't have a chance to sneak up on her blind side. If she was destined to marry again, her spouse was darn well going to be someone of her own choosing.

On Sunday, Elise attended church with Margo and Paul Jennings, the man with whom she was currently involved, and during the fellowship hour that followed the service, they introduced her to Reverend Hawthorne.

He was all Margo had claimed and more. Not only handsome and single, he was warm and outgoing, and possessed the kindest blue eyes Elise had ever seen, eyes that made no attempt to hide his appreciation and interest whenever they lit on her.

In his early thirties, Keith Hawthorne was young enough to be in tune with children and teenagers, yet mature enough to inspire confidence in the older members of the congregation. He brought a vigor and zest to his calling, an enthusiasm that was genuine and unmistakable, especially when it came to his pet project. Scarcely three minutes after being introduced, he was telling Elise about his work with underprivileged children at the Pruitt Youth Center.

"It's one of the most rewarding things I've ever been involved with. Most of these kids have never known anything but poverty and neglect. Yet they have such potential, if only we can get them motivated and headed in the right direction." As he spoke, he gestured with his hands, his handsome face alight with eagerness, his kind eyes sparkling. "And that's what we try to do, not just provide them with a place to come for recreation, though, of course, we do that, too. We try to tap their creativity, spur an interest in a goal, act as role models. And most of all, we give them love and attention."

"It sounds wonderful," Elise said sincerely.

"Oh, it is. It is. The center was founded and endowed by Andrew Pruitt, a man who fought his way out of the slums by sheer determination and hard work, and went on to become a millionaire. It's run by a small staff of trained professionals, but they rely heavily on volunteers to keep the programs going." Pausing, he poured all his coaxing charm into the smile he directed at Elise. "Perhaps you might be interested in donating a few hours a week yourself?"

"Oh, I'm not sure . . . I mean . . . what could I do?"

"Any number of things—coach the girls' volleyball team, teach computer skills. Or just help out in the nursery. We've recently started a free Saturday morning play school, to give working mothers a few free hours to take care of necessary chores like grocery shopping and such. Believe me, we can always use another pair of hands around the place."

Elise laughed. Keith Hawthorne was a hard-sell idealist, and she was both touched and amused by his relentless dedication. "You've convinced me, Reverend. I think I could spare a few hours on Saturday mornings."

"Good, good. And please—call me Keith." He smiled, and his expression altered subtly. "I'll call you after the holidays and take you on a tour of the center, introduce you to the staff. Maybe afterward we can discuss your options over dinner."

The warm gleam in his eye produced a flutter of excitement in Elise's chest. "Thank you, Keith," she said, returning his smile. "I'd like that."

Elise left the church feeling optimistic. Keith was exactly the sort of man she'd hoped to meet: decent, kind, giving; a man whose values and aspirations meshed with her own.

However, it wasn't warm blue eyes or Reverend Hawthorne's dazzling smile that occupied her thoughts once she returned to her apartment. For the remainder of the day, as she had done all weekend, Elise kept recalling, over and over, the comments her friends had made about Sam.

That they found him so irresistible both bemused and disturbed her. What on earth was all the fuss about? The man was an iceberg—cold and, she was sure, just as dangerous. Margo and the others were entitled to their fantasies, of course, but Elise certainly didn't share them.

Whatever Sam's mysterious appeal, she, thankfully, was immune to it.

But the seed had been planted, and to Elise's chagrin, when she returned to work on Monday, she found herself aware of Sam in new ways.

For once she was at her desk before he arrived. When he entered the office she looked up, and her heart gave a strange little flutter at the sight of him.

He was dressed in a charcoal-gray suit, a crisp white shirt and dark red tie. As usual, his thick hair was brushed ruthlessly back from his face, framing his rugged features and gleaming beneath the fluorescent lights with the blue-black sheen of a raven's wing. As he drew near she could smell the faint scents of soap and after-shave.

"Good morning, Elise. Any calls?" He stopped beside her desk and picked up the stack of mail she had just sorted.

"No. None yet," Elise replied in a distracted voice as her gaze was drawn to his hands. Fascinated, she watched his long, blunt fingers riffle through the envelopes.

It struck her how beautiful his hands were. They were large and powerful, yet, at the same time, oddly graceful. Strange, Elise thought. She'd never noticed that before. As he shuffled the letters, she glimpsed calluses on his palms, and wondered what had put them there.

Sam extracted one envelope from the stack and studied it, turning it over, then back, finally tapping it against the others. Mesmerized, Elise studied the play of tendon and bone, her gaze gliding from his fingertips up to his broad, sturdy wrist. Against the strip of white shirt cuff that extended from his coat sleeve, his skin looked startlingly dark, and the dusting of silky black hair that grew across the backs of his hands enhanced their masculine beauty.

Elise stared, her mouth going dry as her mind formed a fleeting picture of that dark hand against a woman's milky-white breast.

Her heart began to pound and hectic color swept into her cheeks. She jerked her gaze away from Sam's hands, but when she looked up she found that he was watching her.

His eyes narrowed on her face as her flush deepened. "Is something wrong?"

"No! Everything's fine. I . . . I was just woolgathering. That's all." Flustered, she reached for the cup of coffee she had poured earlier, but in her haste she knocked it over.

"Oh!"

Elise jumped up as coffee flooded her desk. Snatching a wad of tissues from the box in the top drawer, she tried frantically to stem the tide before it reached the stack of files. Distressed sounds came from her as she fought a losing battle, but before the spreading brown liquid touched the folders Sam reached across the desk and calmly lifted them out of the way.

Elise felt like a fool for not having thought to do it herself.

He looked at her curiously, his head cocked to one side. "Are you sure nothing's bothering you? You seem a bit rattled."

"No, no. I'm okay."

The look he gave her expressed his doubt, but he didn't comment on it further. "Very well," he said, placing the stack of folders on top of the file cabinet. "When you've finished cleaning up this mess come into my office, please. There are several letters I want to dictate."

When he had gone Elise dropped the soggy tissues into the wastebasket and grimaced at her desk. The sugary coffee had streaked the polished surface and left it, and her fingers, disgustingly sticky.

What on earth had come over her—gawking at Sam that way? Just because a bunch of grown women had carried on over him like giddy, libidinous schoolgirls. *For heaven's sake, Elise! Get a grip on yourself*, she scolded as she stalked to the ladies' room to fetch wet paper towels.

She told herself it was merely the power of suggestion at work, and she returned to her desk determined not to succumb to it again.

But no matter how hard Elise tried to concentrate on business, over and over, her thoughts kept returning to Sam. Both her mind and her senses seemed strangely attuned to him, and she caught herself studying him at the oddest times throughout the day.

While she was taking dictation she became so mesmerized by the deep resonance of his voice that she forgot to listen to what he was saying. Twice, she had to ask him to backtrack, earning herself piercing looks that unnerved her even more.

She noticed for the first time the sinuous grace of his walk, the strength of character in that lean, rugged face, the way his thick hair curled over the tops of his ears.

Late in the afternoon he was leaning over her desk to sign some correspondence, when her gaze was helplessly ensnared by the startling beauty of his sooty lashes and the crystal clarity of his gray eyes. He was so close, his masculine scent surrounded her, making her head swim.

She sat perfectly still, unable to tear her eyes away from his face, enthralled by the strong bone structure beneath the tanned skin, the sculptured flare of his nostrils. Her fascinated gaze traced the intricate swirls in his ear, then dropped to the vulnerable spot just beneath it where she could see his pulse beating in his neck, sure and strong. Crazily, Elise experienced an almost irresistible urge to press her lips to that spot. She swallowed hard, panic and excitement flooding her.

At that precise moment, as though sensing her helpless scrutiny, Sam turned his head and looked straight into her eyes.

For a long, interminable time, like a small wild creature held immobile in a beam of headlights, she was caught by his fathomless silver gaze. Lord! Had she really thought his eyes were cold? At that moment they seemed to burn into her, their crystal depths glittering with sensual heat.

Elise knew she should move. At the very least, look away.

But she couldn't, and, as they held their unblinking gazes, something passed between them, something hot and hungry and intimate that shook her to the core of her being.

Time seemed to stand still. Her heart began to pound so hard she was certain he could hear it. The tightness in her chest was almost suffocating. Then his gaze lowered to her mouth, and for an instant her lungs stopped functioning.

The intent look on his face sent a quivering awareness streaking through Elise. Her blood slogged hotly through her veins. Her breasts swelled, and their aching tips strained against a lacy confinement. She watched his thin, sensuous lips part, and felt as if he had kissed her trembling mouth.

When at last his eyes met hers again, they held a look of sensual awareness that told her he knew exactly the effect he'd had on her.

His lips curved upward in the faintest of smiles, and Elise went rigid as he raised his hand to her face. "Hold still," he murmured. "You have an eyelash that's about to fall into your eye."

His callused palm curved around her cheek. His fingertips slipped into the hair at her temple. Elise's eyes drifted shut and her insides trembled as his thumb feathered over her lashes, then smoothed across the delicate skin beneath her eye. His touch was electrifying, sending an incredible heat radiating outward from each tiny point of contact.

His thumb stilled, and her eyelids fluttered open. Dazed, her insides quaking, she looked at that firm, sensuous mouth so close to her own, and thought her thudding heart would surely burst. She could feel his breath feathering across her cheek like a caress. It smelled faintly of mint and the strong black coffee he consumed in such quantity. He smelled of masculine soap and expensive worsted wool. And male.

His gaze shifted to her temple, where his fingertips were buried in her bright curls. Slowly, he removed his hand, and his smile broadened as he watched the silky red tresses twine about his fingers and cling as though loath to let go. When the last strand slipped through, he grasped a curl between his thumb and forefinger and tugged it out full length. "You have the most beautiful hair," he whispered as he let it go and watched, fascinated, as it sprang back into place.

The soft words scattered what little sense Elise had left, and she blinked at him, speechless. Briefly, his enigmatic gaze met hers.

Then, without a word, he straightened, walked back into his office and shut the door, leaving her so confused and shaken she couldn't move. She could barely breathe.

What had happened? Elise stared at the closed door, her eyes wide and frightened. She placed four fingers over her trembling lips. *Everything has changed.*

The moment the thought formed she rejected it. No! No, of course it hadn't! That was insane! Nothing happened. Nothing at all.

But deep down she knew that in those few tense moments her relationship with Sam had been irrevocably altered.

She began to gather up the letters Sam had signed, but her hands were shaking, and they slipped through her fingers, fluttering to the floor in every direction.

Closing her eyes, Elise clenched her fists and gave a distressed moan. This was crazy! How could she be attracted to Sam? She didn't even particularly like the man, and at times he frightened her witless. It made her feel prickly and on edge just to be near him. She thought about Tommy's laughing eyes, his blond, clean-cut looks, his openness and sunny disposition. Lord, Sam wasn't even her type!

You're letting yourself get worked up for no reason, she scolded as she dropped to her knees to retrieve the papers. *Nothing is going to happen if you don't let it.*

She was reaching under her desk for one of the letters when her sister's teasing comment came back to her, causing her hand to still, her heart to give a little lurch.

"I expect to find you and Sam married, or at the very least engaged by the time we return."

"Oh, no," Elise muttered in a shaky but emphatic voice. She scrabbled across the floor on her hands and knees to snatch up the last of the scattered letters. "Absolutely not."

"Elise? What on earth are you doing?"

At the sound of Colleen's voice, Elise jumped and spun around, falling back on her bottom with a jarring thud. Only the woman's head was visible around the edge of the door, and she was staring at Elise as though not certain it was wise to enter.

"Colleen! Come in." Elise made a wry face. "And don't mind me. I was just picking up some papers I dropped."

"Oh, good." Colleen looked relieved. "I came by to see if you'd be interested in going out on a blind date Friday night," she said as she stepped inside and closed the door behind her.

"Yes. Of course. When? With whom?" Elise scrambled to her feet and hastily straightened her clothing.

"Whoa. Wait a minute. Don't get so excited. The guy's just a friend of my brother's, not Robert Redford."

Elise didn't care. The important thing was, the man wasn't Sam.

Sam lounged back in his chair, his expression meditative as he tapped the eraser end of a pencil against the desk top. Interesting, he thought, as he reviewed the scene at Elise's desk.

He hadn't planned it. If he hadn't caught her looking at him that way he would not have provoked it. At least…not yet. Satisfaction glittered in his eyes at the memory. He doubted that she knew just how revealing her expression had been.

Sam tossed the pencil aside and swiveled around. With his elbows propped on the arms of the chair, he steepled his fingers beneath his chin and stared out the window. From the mountainside office the view was spectacular, with arid mountains and valleys, rugged arroyos and endless sky stretching away into infinity. Sam saw none of it.

Squinting his eyes against the glare of brilliant sunshine, he pursed his lips. It appeared that his patience was beginning to pay off. At least he knew now that she wasn't immune to him. That had not been fear he'd seen in Elise's face. Nor indifference. It had been stunned awareness, the pull of male to female. And in her lovely brown eyes there had been such sweet, unconscious hunger he had almost kissed her right there on the spot.

He was glad he had restrained himself, though. It was too soon. Instinct told him that it would be all too easy to spook her.

From the beginning he'd been drawn to Elise, to her beauty, her gentleness, that sweet serenity that was so much a part of her. But most of all, to her warmth.

He wanted that warmth for himself. He craved it—with an intensity that edged very close to outright need. That concerned him. But not enough to back off.

Because Sam knew in his gut that Elise could put the sunshine back into his life and give it meaning again. Her sweet loving nature would dim the memories that still clawed at his soul. In time, he might even forget that tiny cage, the filth, the darkness . . . the pain. And worst of all, that awful despair and aloneness that had made him shiver even in the oppressive heat of the jungle. Elise was the perfect woman for him—sweet, biddable, undemanding. She would make a restful mate who wouldn't disrupt his life.

Once she was his, this desperate desire would pass. He was sure of it. In the meantime, he knew all about patience and self-control.

At first, aware of Elise's feelings for Max, he had stayed clear of her. But when his friend had fallen in love with Erin, then Sam had begun biding his time, watching to see how it would all shake out.

Now that Max and Erin were married nothing stood in his way, and he was determined to have Elise. But he had to take care not to push too hard too soon. Despite what had happened earlier, he didn't think she was quite ready yet for what he had planned.

Sam laced his fingers behind his head and rocked back in his chair. His eyelids lowered until he was looking out through mere slits. Slowly, the crease lines that fanned out from the corners of his eyes deepened as a genuine smile curved his mouth. But with a little luck, he thought with relish, soon ... soon it would be time to make his move.

Chapter Four

By Friday afternoon Elise was a wreck.

She couldn't believe she had committed herself to spending an entire evening with a total stranger.

Oh, Lord. She propped her elbows on her desk and buried her face in her hands. What had she done? What if Craig Watson turned out to be a lech with eight hands? Or a bore? Or worse, what if he was wonderful and she did something really stupid... like spill wine in his lap, or unintentionally insult his mother or... or... get a piece of spinach stuck on her front teeth?

Elise knew she was acting crazy, but there wasn't a thing she could do about it. All week she'd vacillated between anticipation and dread. It had been more than seven years since she'd dated, and she felt as green as a schoolgirl.

It hadn't helped that she couldn't seem to forget that disturbing incident with Sam. It was always there in the back of her mind, taunting her. The memory of those few, intense moments, the sharp sensual awareness that had taken her by surprise, was so vivid that just thinking about it made her shiver.

Her preoccupation was embarrassing, especially since Sam had obviously forgotten the whole thing.

All week she had covered her discomfort by acting as though it had never happened. And she had taken care to keep her distance from Sam.

Whenever she even considered calling off the date with Craig Watson, she had only to remind herself of that little encounter, and her reaction, to change her mind.

It was a bit late for that anyway. Elise raised her head and glanced at the clock. Craig was supposed to pick her up in a little less than three hours. As it was, she was going to have to rush to be ready on time. With Christmas only three days away, shoppers would be out in force, snarling traffic. Getting home would take forever.

Elise had finished her own shopping weeks ago, but the evening before she had braved the crowds to buy a new dress for that night, even though she'd promised herself she wouldn't.

It was a beautiful, romantic dress, the kind she'd always preferred. With its softly draped neckline, fitted sleeves and flowing skirt, it made her feel deliciously feminine, and she could hardly wait to wear it. The luscious teal-blue wool garment was already laid out on her bed, along with fresh underwear and stockings.

A rueful smile tugged at Elise's mouth as she recalled how, before leaving for work that morning, she had dashed around setting out everything she would need—her shoes, the purse she would carry, jewelry, makeup, an evening wrap.

So much for spontaneity.

She could just imagine the pithy comments her sister would have made had she seen her frantic preparations. In her place, Erin would have simply breezed in at the last moment, taken a quick shower, slapped on a little makeup and dressed in whatever struck her fancy...and still managed to look ravishing.

With a sigh, Elise cleared her desk and slipped the plastic cover over the computer. Oh, well. A person could change just so much. At the same moment, Sam walked out of his office with a sheaf of papers in his hand.

"Elise, here are the figures for that government report we have to file. When you get it typed, bring it in."

"Now?" Elise caught her lower lip between her teeth.

"Yes. Since we'll be closed Monday for Christmas, I want to be sure this thing is complete and ready to go when we return." He turned to go back into his office but stopped when he caught sight of her stricken expression. Frowning, he walked back to her desk. "Do you have a problem with that?"

"No, it's just that...well...it's Friday. And it's already after five."

"So? You've stayed late many times."

"I know, but...that is...I was wondering...would it be all right if I came in tomorrow and typed it instead?"

"Is there some reason you can't work late tonight?" Sam persisted.

"Well...yes. There is." She hadn't planned on saying anything to Sam, but now she had no choice. She shifted under his piercing stare and needlessly straightened the items on her immaculate desk. "I, uh...I have a date tonight."

Absolute silence followed her announcement. For several seconds Sam simply looked at her. His expression did not alter one whit. He didn't move so much as a finger, or even blink.

Elise squirmed, uncomfortable with the strange undercurrents.

"I see," he said finally. "Well, in that case, by all means, go." His remote smile appeared briefly before he turned toward his office once again. At the door he paused and glanced back at her over his shoulder. "Oh, and Elise. Don't bother to come in tomorrow. The report can wait until Tuesday."

She opened her mouth to thank him, but Sam didn't wait around to hear. He stepped inside his office and closed the door behind him with a soft click.

Her expression thoughtful, Elise slipped into her coat, picked up her purse. After casting one last, troubled look at Sam's office, she walked out, feeling oddly uncomfortable, almost guilty somehow.

Which was absurd, she told herself as she hurried down the hallway. Sam hadn't appeared to be annoyed. But then, with Sam, who could tell?

Most of the staff had already left. Only a few dim lights still burned in the reception area, and when Elise stepped outside, except for a handful of cars, the parking lot was empty. Hunching down in her coat, she lowered her head against the biting wind and dashed to her little blue Chevy.

As usual in cold weather, the car was difficult to start. Shivering in the frosty interior, Elise pumped the gas pedal and turned the key several times before the engine sputtered to life. She knew from experience to let it warm up before attempting to drive, so she huddled down in her coat and tucked her hands under her crossed arms.

As she waited, her gaze was drawn to the lighted window at the end of the executive wing, and she felt her heart squeeze when she spotted the solitary figure standing there, staring out at the mountain sunset and the gathering darkness.

He looked so lonely. For the first time, Elise wondered what kind of life Sam had away from the office. Did he have any family nearby? Any friends, other than Max? He never talked about himself, so she had no idea. From comments Margo and the others had made, she gathered that he wasn't a monk, but apparently there was no special woman he cared about.

The thought saddened her, and she felt an ache in her chest as she studied the still figure at the window.

People shouldn't be alone. Especially not at that time of year. Elise didn't have a man in her life at the moment, but she had her family. Erin and Max would be back tomorrow, and the rest of them—her mother, father and brother, David—were flying in the day after that. They would have a good time, Elise mused with a soft smile. Laughing, joking, catching up on one another's lives, basking in that special joy of just being together, of being part of a family and knowing that you're loved. That you belonged.

She wondered if Sam had anyone with whom to share the holiday. Or if he would be alone . . . as he seemed to be so much of the time.

She put the car in gear, reversed out of the parking space and wondered why her heart felt so heavy at the thought.

Sam stood motionless with his hands in the pockets of his trousers and stared out the window, not at the vista of purple mountains silhouetted against a rose-streaked sky, but at the little blue Chevy.

His mouth set in a bitter line, he watched Elise dart across the windswept parking lot and climb inside the car. He'd miscalculated. While he'd been biding his time, she'd met another man.

A white cloud of exhaust billowed from the tailpipe of Elise's car. For a few moments the Chevy just sat there, rumbling, then eased backward out of the parking slot. Sam's jaw clenched as he watched it move off toward the gate. The hands inside his pockets curled with tension.

Only when the car had disappeared from sight did he return to his desk. Leaning back in his chair, with his elbows propped on the upholstered arms, he moved a pencil back and forth from one hand to the other, his eyes fixed on the middle distance.

It didn't matter, he told himself. He wanted her, but what the hell. He'd lost women before. He'd survive. After all, he'd survived worse. Holding the pencil at each end, Sam rolled it between his thumbs and fingers. Elise Holman was beautiful and sweet, but he didn't need her.

An instant later the pencil snapped in two.

"Damn!"

Sam flung the jagged pieces of wood against the far wall and lunged out of his chair. He snatched his overcoat from the closet and strode toward the door, ramming his arms into the sleeves as he went.

Whether she had been experiencing a bit of precognition or had jinxed the whole thing with her worrying, Elise wasn't sure, but in the end her fears were justified. The date with Craig Watson was a disaster.

The evening started out badly when he was half an hour late, and it went downhill from there. They had nothing in common, their personalities clashed, and there wasn't so much as a spark of physical attraction between them, at least not on Elise's part. She endured a boring evening listening to the man talk about himself while she glanced at her watch every five minutes. And then the jerk had the nerve to expect her to sleep with him just because he'd bought her dinner.

Thankfully, Craig Watson was eminently forgettable. Elise fumed for about fifteen minutes after he slammed out of her apartment in a huff, then she showered, went to bed and slept like a baby.

The next day Erin and Max returned, and the joyous reunion with her twin wiped the unpleasant incident from her mind completely.

Half expecting an inquisition, Elise was relieved when none occurred. With both their family and Max's due to arrive the next day on Christmas Eve, Erin was in a dither and concerned mainly with enlisting her help.

"Thank God you're here," Erin said as she led Elise through the multilevel house to the kitchen. "Except for Mother, you're the only one who can cook a roast the way Daddy likes it. Or make that wonderful pecan pie. Or—"

"Stop! Stop! I surrender!" Shaking her head, Elise chuckled and patted her sister's arm. "You don't have to butter me up. I'll do the cooking for you."

"You will? Oh, thanks, sis. You're a dear. I just knew I could count on you."

Elise gave her a reproving look, though her brown eyes were warm and filled with affection. "Our own know better, but you surely didn't think I'd endanger Max's parents by letting them eat *your* cooking, did you?"

For years, Erin's ineptitude in the kitchen had been a running joke in the Blaine family. Her culinary skills amounted to opening cans and packets and cooking frozen dinners, and even then the results were sometimes disastrous.

Erin wrinkled her nose at the gibe, then grinned. "I figured if your instinct for self-preservation didn't do the trick, your compassion for others would."

"Now, why do I get the feeling that I've just been neatly maneuvered?" Elise wondered aloud as they stepped into the kitchen.

Thanks to a jewel of a housekeeper who came in three times a week, the house was immaculate and the refrigerator and pantry were stocked with enough food to feed a battalion. While Elise spent the rest of that day and most of the next preparing a Christmas feast, Erin scurried around hanging garlands, mistletoe and wreaths, creating a centerpiece of pinecones and holly for the dining table, wrapping presents and trimming the gigantic tree that Max had set up in the living room.

Max's parents drove up from Phoenix on Christmas Eve, arriving at sunset to a house aglow with twinkling holiday lights and filled with the heavenly aromas of spicy apple pie, bayberry candles and fresh-cut greenery. A crackling blaze in the living-room fireplace added the pungent scent of burning cedar, and the soft strains of Christmas carols blended with the din of greetings.

Though she hadn't said so, Elise knew that Erin was nervous about meeting her new in-laws. As soon as the introductions were over she stood to one side and waited, ready to lend whatever support and help she could, but as she watched her vivacious sister charm Julia and Patrick Delany, she realized that everything was going to be fine. Swallowing around the lump in her throat, Elise smiled, her heart swelling with pride and pleasure, and just a touch of envy.

A half hour later, Elise and Erin's parents and brother arrived, and the hubbub started all over again.

Both sets of parents seemed pleased with their child's choice of mate and, much to everyone's relief, especially Max and Erin's, they took an instant liking to one another. Within minutes of meeting they were laughing and chatting as though they'd known one another for years.

After two days of frantic preparations all Elise wanted to do was relax and enjoy the holiday and the company, but any hope of doing that vanished an hour later when the doorbell rang.

"What is *he* doing here?"

Erin, bent over the tray of snacks she was arranging on the coffee table, looked up at her twin's frantic whisper. "Who?"

"Him," Elise hissed out of the side of her mouth, tipping her head toward the entrance hall, where Max was taking the coat of the latest arrival.

"Sam?" Erin's glance went back and forth between her sister and her husband's partner, a puzzled frown puckering her brow. "Why, he's here to spend Christmas with us, of course."

"I thought you had invited only family."

"Sam *is* family. He and Max grew up together. They're practically brothers." She returned her attention to the tray, realigning the plate of cookies. "Anyway, we wouldn't think of not inviting him. Max and his mother and dad are all the family Sam has left." Straightening, she brushed the crumbs from her fingertips. "Why? Does it bother you that he's here?"

"I just wish you'd told me he was coming, that's all." True, she'd hoped that Sam would have a family with whom he could share the holiday, but she hadn't meant *hers*. She saw more than enough of him at the office as it was.

"Uh-huh, sure. And if you think I buy that, think again."

Smiling, Erin slipped her arm through Elise's and urged her across the room to where Max was introducing Sam to their parents. "This is me you're talking to, remember. We'll discuss you and Sam later, I promise you, sister dear. But for right now, I suggest you paste a smile on your face. Mom has already been questioning me about your love life. If she so much as suspects you have something going with Sam, she won't give you a moment's peace." She slanted Elise a saucy look. "You know that, unlike me, she's not blessed with patience and tact."

Elise rolled her eyes at the blatant untruth and hissed, "Erin! I tell you, there is *nothing* going on between Sam and me!"

"Then smile, darling. We're almost there."

They approached the small group just as Sam withdrew his hand from Joe Blaine's and turned to greet their brother.

"Hello, Lawford," David said in that maddening, reserved way he had when he hadn't made up his mind about a person.

Sam dipped his chin in the faintest of nods. "David. Good to see you again. I'm glad you could make it back to Santa Fe under more pleasant conditions."

They shook hands with respectful wariness, two dominant males figuratively circling each other, each taking the measure of a potential enemy.

"Why, I hadn't realized that you'd met our son, Mr. Lawford," Dorothy Blaine exclaimed as cool gray eyes clashed with sharp brown ones in a silent duel that was destined from the start to be a standoff.

Releasing David's hand, Sam turned to her with a polite smile. "We met last summer, Mrs. Blaine, when David came here looking for his sisters."

"Sam went to Vail with me to track them down," David put in. "He and Max were the ones who actually subdued those two slimeballs who were going to kill Elise and Erin. Turns out, they're handy men to have around in a no-holds-barred slugout. I didn't get so much as a skinned knuckle."

"Oh, dear." Dorothy shuddered. "Whenever I think about—"

"Then don't think about it, love," Joe commanded. He put his arm about his wife's shoulder and drew her close against his side. "That whole nasty business is over and done with and best forgotten."

"Dad's right," Erin seconded. "This is Christmas, and I refuse to let anyone spoil it with talk of those scum. So let's just drop the subject. I suggest we all sit down and have a glass of eggnog."

Releasing Elise, she joined arms with her father. "Now, then, Dad. Aren't you at least going to give me a hint about what's in that long blue box that I saw you slip under the tree?" she coaxed shamelessly as she strolled with him toward the sofa that sat before the blazing hearth.

Joe laughed and shook his finger at her. "Erin Louise Delany, you've been peeking again." He gave Max a commiserating look. "I hope you've hidden her presents in a safe place, my boy. Curiosity is this child's biggest downfall."

Sam chose that moment to look at Elise for the first time. Direct and unnerving, his gaze held hers for an uncomfortable few seconds. "Good evening, Elise," he said softly.

"Hello, Sam." She twisted a curl around her finger and groped for something more to say, but the tension she always felt whenever he was near made small talk impossible.

He was dressed more casually than she was accustomed to seeing him, but his appearance was still flawless. His charcoal slacks were expertly tailored to his lean frame, and the loose, ruby-red pullover sweater was cashmere. Even his loafers were polished to a mirror sheen.

As usual, just looking at him made Elise feel unkempt. Unconsciously, she smoothed her long velvet skirt and ran a fingertip around the waistband to be sure her blouse was tucked in.

Clearing her throat, Elise summoned a weak smile. "Well. Shall we join the others?"

Without waiting for a reply, she walked to where the rest of the group sat before the fire, and perched on the arm of her mother's chair. Out of the corner of her eye, she saw Sam disappear into the entry hall. He returned a moment later with an armload of presents, which he arranged under the tree. When done, he walked to the sofa, carefully hitching up the legs of his perfectly creased trousers, and sat down beside Julia Delany.

"How's my favorite girl?"

To Elise's amazement, Max's mother reached up and kissed Sam's cheek, then took his hand between hers and patted it as she gazed fondly into his beautiful, remote eyes. "Oh, Sam, it's so good to see you. How have you been?"

Seated on her other side, Patrick leaned forward and entered the conversation, his voice and expression full of affection and warmth.

Watching them, Elise felt a little dart of surprise. The Delanys treated Sam as though he were another son.

Patrick Delany was a retired businessman with a commanding presence. Tall and slender, he had a full head of striking silver hair, chiseled features and laughing brown eyes exactly like his son's. His wife was a petite woman who wore her dark hair, which had grayed only at the temples, swept back over her ears, giving the effect of dramatic silver wings framing her lovely face. They were an extraordinarily handsome couple, which accounted for their son's good looks, and they were also, as Elise had discovered earlier, warm and friendly. And anything but fools.

Elise glanced at Sam and felt an uncomfortable niggle of doubt. People like the Delanys did not give love and loyalty where it wasn't deserved.

"Here you go, Elise."

"Oh, thank you." Accepting the cup of eggnog that Max handed her, she gave him a soft smile, but it faded when her eyes happened to meet Sam's.

He was watching her, his expressionless face somehow conveying censure. His pale eyes were as cold as ice. Whatever second thoughts Elise was beginning to have about him vanished.

When everyone had a glass of eggnog Max raised his. "Merry Christmas. May it be only the first of many we share."

As the others murmured their approval, Elise took a sip, savoring the rich creaminess mixed with the tang of rum, and the spicy aroma and subtle bite of nutmeg. She ignored Sam.

Settling back on the sofa, Patrick draped an arm about his wife's shoulders and looked back and forth between Erin and Elise. "I don't believe I've ever seen a prettier pair of young women in my life. But, I swear, son, I don't see how in the world you know which is which," he said with a bewildered shake of his head. "You'd better be careful. One of these days you might grab the wrong one."

"Don't worry, Dad, there's no chance of that. Anyway, there are differences. Once you've been around Erin and Elise a while, you'll be able to tell them apart."

"Besides, Patrick," Sam added quietly, "a man instinctively recognizes his own woman."

The words were innocent enough, but something in his tone and the way he watched Elise seemed to give them a double meaning.

She took another sip of eggnog, striving to keep her expression blank and look anywhere but at Sam as heat crept up her neck and flooded her cheeks.

"Now, that sounds like the voice of experience to me," Joe teased, his grin widening as he followed the direction of Sam's gaze.

Sam's unwavering stare remained fixed on Elise for several more seconds before he turned his head and looked at her father. "Could be."

While the others chuckled, Dorothy Blaine's gaze went back and forth between her daughter and Sam. Elise shifted on the arm of the chair, feeling her color deepen even more.

Standing beside the fireplace with an elbow braced on the mantel, David listened and watched, his eyes narrowed in a frown.

As though sensing her twin's discomfort, Erin jumped in and deftly steered the conversation in another direction. Within moments the talk had switched to reminiscences of earlier Christmases, and that led to a discussion of some of Erin's youthful high jinks, many of which she had led Elise into.

"I swear, we never knew what this little scamp would do next," Dorothy said, her fond gaze resting on her elder daughter. "And poor Elise was always so sweet and biddable, she went along with whatever Erin suggested without a qualm."

The description caused Elise's lips to firm into a thin line, but her mother was too occupied with her story to notice.

"Once, when they were five, we were frantic when they were both missing for several hours. We looked everywhere, and finally found them in the woods, treed by a wild boar."

"That porker was madder than sin," Joe added with a wry chuckle. "And there sat these two up in that tree, their eyes so big they looked like a couple of baby owls, holding on for dear life while that old razorback just kept ramming the trunk, trying his best to shake 'em out. Of course, they'd been expressly forbidden to go into those woods, but that didn't stop Erin."

Erin lifted her chin. "We were looking for the magic fairies. Johnnie Jenkins swore to me that they were in there. Besides, how did you know it was my idea?"

That brought a hoot of laughter from David and groans from her parents. Soon, egged on by Max, they were embroiled in a good-natured wrangle.

As the bantering words flowed around her, Elise rose and wandered around the living room, and finally out into the glass-enclosed solarium that flanked it.

Max's home was located a few miles above the Global warehouse and office, on the same road. The sprawling, multilevel house was built stair-step fashion up the side of the mountain, providing every room with a spectacular view, but from none was it so stunning as the solarium. Through the glass walls Elise could see patches of melting snow lying like tattered fleece over the mountainside. Bathed in moonlight, it glowed an eerie pale blue. The surrounding mountains were deep purple, crouched in the darkness like massive beasts. Thoughtfully, Elise sipped her eggnog and gazed at the twinkling lights of Santa Fe, below in the distance.

"You're quiet this evening. Something bothering you?"

She started at Sam's voice, and the eggnog sloshed over the crystal cup onto her fingers. Stiffening her spine, she drew a deep breath, then glanced over her shoulder at him and smiled politely. "No, of course not. I'm fine. I just wanted to look at the view. I'll return in a minute."

She expected Sam to take the hint and leave. Instead he came to stand beside her, so close she could smell his aftershave.

"It's impressive, isn't it?" he said, staring out at the panoramic scene. "Like looking down from an eagle's nest."

"Yes. It is."

Her nerves tightened at his nearness. With care she placed the cup of eggnog on a lacy iron table, hoping he wouldn't notice how her hand shook. Without giving it a thought, she licked the sticky drink from her fingertips, then flushed when she looked up and discovered that Sam was watching her, his silvery eyes glittering in the dim light, taking in each delicate flick of her tongue.

She jerked her hand down and curled it into a fist at her side. "Th-this house, all this soaring space and freedom, seems to suit Max."

For a moment she felt Sam's gaze boring into her. Then his attention returned to the mountain view.

The murmur of voices, punctuated by occasional bursts of laughter, drifted out to them. Elise looked up at the twinkling stars and groped for a polite excuse to rejoin the others.

A sharp rectangle of yellow light slanted through the open door from the living room, while overhead a three-quarter moon spilled its cool, luminescent glow through the slanted glass roof. The outside world was painted with shades of black, gray, blue and deep purple, stark with the coldness of winter, but in the solarium lush green plants of every kind flourished.

"It suits Erin, too." Sam reached up and fingered a waxy leaf of an ivy plant spilling from a suspended clay pot. The action drew Elise's gaze to his hand, to the long fingers and broad back with its dusting of crisp hairs. "They're a well-matched pair in every way."

"Yes, I know." Sam's hands fascinated her. They were so large and powerful. Yet, as she watched him stroke the heart-shaped petal, she recalled how gently those same hands had held her when she'd been sick, how they'd stroked her neck and forehead, how tenderly they'd bathed her face.

"So how was the date?"

The question caught her off guard, and she looked at him sharply. "Uh . . . fine. Just fine."

"Are things serious between you and this man?"

"It's, uh...too soon to tell. We haven't known each other that long."

"I see." He turned his head and looked at her. "Since you're dating, I take it you've gotten over Max. Or are you using this man for that purpose?"

Elise drew in a sharp breath. "There was nothing to get over. I told you that weeks ago."

"So you did. At the time I thought it was just face-saving, that you needed more time. It appears I was overcautious." He waited a beat, then added softly, "Foolishly so."

Her heart pounded in her throat. Confusion, suspicion, then denial flashed through Elise. It was absurd. Sam couldn't have meant anything by that remark. She was overreacting. "I . . . I'm sorry, but I don't care to discuss this," she said nervously, looking at anything but him. "If you'll excuse me, I think I'll rejoin the others."

She got only as far as the door.

"Running away, Elise?"

She stopped in the rectangle of bright light and turned to face him. "I don't know what you mean."

"Don't you?"

She shook her head and watched as he crossed to her with slow, purposeful steps, his shoes making a faint gritty sound against the solarium's stone floor.

An irrational urge to flee gripped Elise, which made her feel foolish. There was a roomful of people just a few feet away. Besides, logically, she knew she had nothing to fear from Sam. But her insides continued to flutter, her breathing becoming agitated. Just being near him produced the same fluttery thrill of fear and anticipation she'd experienced as a girl whenever she was about to ride a roller coaster.

He regarded her for several seconds. "You do have a tendency to run when things heat up, don't you?" he observed dispassionately. "If not literally, like you did last summer when those thugs were after you, then you hide behind a sweet smile and exquisite politeness and pretend a situation doesn't exist."

"Those men would have killed me!" she insisted, ignoring the last part of his statement. "What choice did I have but to run?"

"You could have come to me," he shot back. "I would have protected you."

Her eyes widened. He sounded almost resentful. But that was crazy. She had barely known Sam then. Had avoided him assiduously. For that matter, she didn't know him much better now. But the craziest thing was, she *had* almost turned to him.

Until that moment she had forgotten that. But, oddly, as she had fled from the Global warehouse that awful night last summer, her terrified mind frantically groping for a means of escape, someone to turn to, the first person she'd thought of had been Sam.

Sam, she realized now in amazement. Not Max.

"I . . . I couldn't. I had no way of knowing who was involved. Who I could trust. Not then."

Sam's eyes narrowed. "And now? If something like that were to happen today? Would you come to me?"

"I . . . I suppose so."

Her answer seemed to satisfy him. Though his expression didn't change, gradually the tautness around his eyes relaxed.

"Do you like to ride?"

Elise blinked several times, bewildered by the sudden change of subject. "Ride?"

"Horses."

"Oh. Well, I . . . don't know. I haven't been on a horse since I was a child."

"I could teach you."

Stunned, Elise stared at him. In all the months she'd worked for Global, Sam had never shown any personal interest in her. Even as she told herself she preferred it that way, in her mind she could picture riding with him, feel the hot wind, the sun, Sam's hands on her waist as he helped her dismount. . . .

Her heart began to thud. "Uh . . . no, thank you. I'm afraid I'm not the athletic type."

"You don't have to be. All you need is patience and a gentle touch. You have both."

"Maybe so." She twisted her hands together and glanced into the living room at the others. David, her mother and Erin were watching them. "But I'm afraid it would be a futile effort. As I recall, I could barely hang on to the saddle."

"You were a child." His gaze trailed over her. "You're a woman now."

"Yes." She cast another distraught look over her shoulder. "But I know how busy you are. I . . . I wouldn't feel right about taking up your time."

"I want to do it."

Her chest was so tight she could scarcely breathe. Sam was right; she didn't like confrontation, pressure. Her natural instinct was to turn away from it, but she could tell by his expression that he wasn't going to let her.

"Why? I don't understand—" When he reached up and brushed a curl from her cheek, the words simply melted away.

"Oh, I think you do."

"No." She shook her head, her eyes widening. "This is crazy."

"I know." He raised his other hand and cupped her face between his palms. His eyes weren't cold now. Longing swirled in their crystal depths, and she was unreasonably affected by the sight. "But I'm tired of waiting."

"Sam, no." She clamped her fingers around his wrists when he bent his head toward hers. "You can't!"

"The hell I can't."

He kissed her then, thoroughly, there in the brightly lit doorway, in full view of her family and what now passed for his.

It was stunning, electrifying. Elise's heart thundered. Her knees trembled.

She expected force. She got gentleness. His hands were powerful enough to crush, but he held her with great care, his fingers tunneling into her hair, thumbs stroking the soft underside of her jaw. That hard, unsmiling mouth should have been ruthless and forceful. Instead it rocked over hers with excruciating tenderness in a slow, soft savoring that stole her breath away.

With the tip of his tongue, Sam traced the line where her lips met, delicately urging them to part. Elise was powerless against the gentle persuasion, and when her quivering mouth opened, his tongue slipped inside to probe and stroke erotically. Elise moaned and shivered. Her fingers squeezed harder and harder around his wrists.

Sam was touching her with only his hands and lips. Elise could have pulled away with little effort. But she had neither the strength nor the presence of mind. She simply stood there, hopelessly ensnared by his ardor and the exquisite sensuality of the undemanding kiss.

Remotely, she was aware that the others had fallen silent. The only sounds were the soft strains of "Silent Night" drifting from the stereo. The sweet caress went on—it could have been minutes, or hours.

Several muffled coughs and a loud "ah-hem" sounded, and Sam slowly raised his head. Still holding her face between his hands, he studied her for several seconds.

When someone cleared a throat again Sam released her, slid his hands into his pockets and turned, unperturbed, to meet the speculative looks. "Sorry." With a shrug, he glanced up at the green sprig hanging from the door frame overhead. "Just taking advantage of the mistletoe."

Too shaken to move, Elise stood rooted to the spot, her cheeks flaming while everyone laughed and hooted.

"Well, I, for one am glad to see you getting into the Christmas spirit, Sam." Erin's eyes twinkled as she strolled over and looped her arm through Elise's. "But now I'm afraid you'll have to excuse us. Elise and I must check on dinner."

Sam watched them go, unaware, until he spoke, that David had joined him.

"I'll tell you the same thing I told Max." Sam turned his head and saw that David was also watching the twin sisters. When they had climbed the short flight of stairs to the kitchen level and disappeared from sight, David looked around, his eyes hard. "Hurt her, Lawford, and you'll answer to me."

Chapter Five

"Well? Are you going to tell me about it? Or am I going to have to drag it out of you a piece at a time?" Erin demanded the instant they entered the kitchen.

"What?"

"Don't play innocent with me. I'm talking about you and Sam. You've been so wound up ever since he walked in the door you've practically been having heart palpitations. What's going on?"

"That's just the trouble—I don't know." Elise crossed the kitchen and lifted an apron from the hook inside the pantry, shooting Erin a harried look as she tied it around her waist. "In the past week or so...I don't know...things have changed."

"How so?"

"Sam is... I keep feeling..." Elise made a face and flapped her hand. "Oh, it's impossible to explain."

As shock wore off, anger built. Elise took a deep breath, then another, and told herself to stay calm. She wasn't given to bursts of temper, and she certainly wasn't going to let Sam upset her.

She walked to the stove, lifted a lid from a pot and poked the carrots with a fork, then slammed it back down and whirled around. "Darn it! Why did he kiss me like that?"

Erin gave a startled little laugh. "That's easy. The man's crazy about you."

"Sam? You *must* be kidding! Sam doesn't have any feelings, period. The man's as cold as ice." Elise shook her head and began to pace, absently twisting a curl about her forefinger. "He's just playing some sort of cat-and-mouse game. He's probably getting some sort of sick delight out of tormenting me. That's all."

Surprise flickered across Erin's face. She leaned back against the table and crossed her arms, all trace of teasing gone as she watched her sister's agitated movements. "You can't really believe that."

Elise spared her a distracted glance as she walked past. "About Sam? Of course I can. You've been around him. You've seen what he's like." She came to the stove, swung around and headed back across the room. "He has all the warmth and emotions of a block of granite. It amazes me that he and Max ever became friends. Face it, Erin, the man is a cold fish."

"No," Erin disagreed in a quiet voice. "He's simply a man who's been badly hurt. And like any wounded animal, he's coping in the only way he knows how."

Elise frowned. "You're not making any sense."

There was a moment of silence as Erin studied her, her head cocked to one side. "You don't know, do you?"

"Know what?"

"Funny. I thought by now you would have heard. That maybe even Sam might have told you."

"Told me what? What are you talking about?"

"Elise...Sam was captured in Vietnam. He spent four years as a prisoner of war."

Elise halted and swung around. "What?" Her voice was little more than a whisper.

"Max doesn't know exactly what happened to him. No one does but Sam, and he doesn't talk about it. But it must have been horrible. He came back a changed man."

Conflicting emotions churned inside Elise, but she struggled to hang on to her fading anger. She didn't want to hear this. She didn't want to care. So, all right, she told herself. He'd had it rough. But he was just one of thousands. And he, at least, had come home alive and in one piece.

But in spite of her determination not to be, she was moved. "Changed? How do you mean?"

"According to Max, before the war Sam was friendly and outgoing, good-natured. He especially liked kids. In fact, he had plans to become a pediatrician. But whatever horrors he endured took their toll. He returned withdrawn and stoic, and he refused to even consider resuming his studies."

"But why?"

Erin shrugged and spread her hands. "He said medicine was yesterday's dream, and dreams were something he'd learned not to count on."

Something shifted and gave way within Elise—a crack in the defensive wall she'd built against Sam, and before she could shore it up, compassion flooded in and drowned the last remnant of anger.

With a sigh, she leaned back against the counter, rubbing her upper arms as though warding off a chill. The thought of him being held captive for all those years under God only knew what conditions, all he must have suffered, filled her with a trembling, achy feeling.

"Poor Sam."

"Yes," Erin agreed softly. "And on top of everything, he returned to find that both his parents had died without ever learning that he was alive. And that his fiancée had married another man shortly after he'd left for Vietnam."

"Oh, my God." Elise closed her eyes and pressed her lips together. Her tender heart hurt for him. How alone and abandoned he must have felt. No wonder he kept people at arm's length.

"So you see, I don't believe that Sam is really cold and unfeeling. I think he's just trapped behind all those defensive walls he built and doesn't quite know how to tear them down." She waited a beat, then added, "But you could help him."

Elise's eyes popped open. *"Me!"*

"He's in love with you."

"Don't be ridiculous!" She shuddered as a little thrill of fear rippled through her. "Look, I sympathize with him for all he suffered. I really do. And, to a point, I even understand why he's the way he is. But I still say that Sam's incapable of feeling any genuine warmth, much less love, for anyone. Whatever emotions he once had have atrophied."

"You're wrong," Erin insisted. "Once in a while Sam's guard slips. It happened last summer in Vail. Max was holding you in his arms, comforting you after that close call we'd had, and Sam was watching. I've never seen such longing and despair in a man's face before."

The revelation brought a sharp surge of emotion that made Elise's heart pound, but she quickly battled it down, resolutely refusing to analyze it. "I think being in love has turned you into a hopeless romantic," she scoffed. "But I assure you, you're dead wrong." She pushed away from the counter, marched to the stove and started banging pans. "Now, could we please drop the subject?"

"You're running away again, Elise," Erin accused her gently. "Just like you always do when you don't want to face something."

Elise's mouth firmed. She stirred the rice more vehemently, her hand clenching the spoon. It was the second time in less than an hour that she'd heard the charge, and she was sick of it ... even if a part of her did recognize that there was some truth to the accusation.

Turning, she met her sister's challenging gaze. "Why do you say that? Just because I refuse to consider a relationship, even one that exists only in your imagination, with a man I'm not attracted to?"

"No." Erin pushed away from the table and took a stack of plates from the cabinet. She walked to the door, turned to push it open with her backside, then paused to look at Elise once again. "Because you won't consider a relationship with a man you *are* attracted to."

Denial sprang to Elise's lips, only to die there the next instant when she found herself staring at the swinging door.

Attracted to Sam? Ridiculous. She wasn't even sure she liked him. She respected him. Sometimes admired him. And, after learning what she had tonight, she felt compassion, even pity, though she knew he would hate both. But attraction? No, Erin was wrong. Never in her wildest dreams had she even considered becoming involved with a man like Sam Lawford. He wasn't her type at all. He was much too tough, too stern, too ... too rawly male.

But throughout dinner and the rest of the evening Erin's statement nagged at Elise, and she found herself watching Sam, comparing him to Tommy, and even to Reverend Hawthorne.

Sam was once again distant and coolly polite. He spoke when spoken to, but most of the time he sat back, listened and observed, a bit apart from the others.

He acted as though he was isolated behind an invisible wall, Elise realized sadly ... a wall he couldn't or wouldn't pull down. Or maybe, as Erin had suggested, he simply didn't know how. Telling herself it was no concern of hers, Elise looked away. Nevertheless, a hard knot formed beneath her breastbone, and she had to blink rapidly to clear the sheen of moisture from her eyes.

A few times Sam glanced her way, but there wasn't so much as a spark of interest in his eyes. He acted as though that soft sizzling kiss beneath the mistletoe had not happened.

So much for Erin's theory, Elise thought, but deep down she wasn't sure if what she felt was relief or resentment.

In the Blaine household they had always opened presents on Christmas morning. *Early* Christmas morning. The tradition had begun when the twins were children because Erin, unable to curb her curiosity until a decent hour, had always routed everyone out of bed at the crack of dawn. It continued for the same reason.

"Wake up, wake up, sleepyhead!"

"Mmm."

A hand shook Elise's shoulder, and she burrowed her face deeper into the pillow. "Come on, Elise. It's Christmas!"

She lifted her head and peered at her sister through eyes that were mere slits. Her bleary gaze slid to the window, then the bedside clock. *"Erin,"* she moaned. "For heaven's sake, it's the middle of the night."

"Don't be silly. It'll be daylight soon. And there're loads of presents downstairs waiting to be opened."

Elise struggled to a sitting position, rubbing her eyes with the heels of her hands. She'd tossed and turned half the night, thinking about Sam, and all that Erin had told her. At the moment, the only present she wanted was another four hours of uninterrupted sleep. But with Erin wound up like a tight spring, she knew her chance of getting it was nonexistent. Resigned, Elise swung her feet to the floor and reached for her robe. "Lord help us. I was hoping that Max would put a stop to this early Christmas reveille routine."

"Max!" Erin whirled and scampered for the door. "He was sitting on the side of the bed with his eyes closed when I left. I'd better make sure he hasn't gone back to sleep. And hurry, Elise," she called over her shoulder. "Everyone else is already up."

Max and Erin's sprawling, multilevel home was a maze of interconnecting passageways and stairs. Half-asleep, Elise made a wrong turn and got lost, and by the time she finally stumbled into the living room everyone was there.

"Well it's about time," Erin scolded. "We've been waiting and waiting."

Max winked and gave her a sleepy-eyed grin. "Yeah, Elise," he drawled. "Can't you see we're all about to burst to get at those gifts?"

Elise glanced around and had to bite the insides of her cheeks to keep from laughing aloud. Patrick sat slouched on the sofa, his mouth stretched wide in a jaw-popping yawn, while beside him Julia was struggling to keep her eyes open and in focus.

Their parents, veterans of Erin's sunrise Christmas celebrations, sat in the fireside chairs, blinking sleepily and smiling with tolerant resignation.

With typical brotherly disdain, David lay stretched out on his back on the hearth rug, quietly snoring.

Other than Erin, only Sam appeared to be truly awake. He stood to one side in the wide solarium entrance, a shoulder braced against the door frame. He was wearing a deep maroon velour robe over blue-and-white-striped pajama bottoms, and leather house slippers on his bare feet.

The robe was belted at his narrow waist but the deep V formed by the crossed lapels revealed a naked chest covered by a cloud of black hair. Silver glinted in the dark thatch, and in a vivid flash of memory Elise could see Sam hovering over her in bed, feel that medal against her breast, heavy and warm from his body. A tingle feathered across her skin and her nipples grew taut and achy against the silk of her nightgown. Shocked, she tore her gaze away, but when her eyes lifted to Sam's face she saw that he was watching her.

Elise felt her entire body flush.

Then it hit her that she was standing there in her ratty old wool robe and fuzzy slippers, without so much as a speck of makeup on her face.

Ducking her head, Elise scooted across the room and sat down on the sofa beside Max's mother, and scrunched down into the cushions as far as she could. Trying casually to shield her face, she cupped a hand to her cheek, but then she felt the faint crease marks the pillow had made, and groaned. Lord, she hadn't even combed her hair. It probably looked like a mangled rat's nest.

It didn't bother her in the least for Max and his parents to see her looking a mess, with her face all scrubbed and shining and her eyes still puffy from sleep. They, after all, were family now. But Sam wasn't.

Erin was on her hands and knees in front of the tree, gleefully digging into the pile of gifts, calling out the names on the tags as she passed them to Max to distribute.

Accepting the bright red foil-wrapped box he handed her, Elise smiled vaguely. With care, she began to pry off the wide gold ribbon, and tried to ignore Sam's steady scrutiny.

That he'd seen her in worse condition that morning in Las Vegas was no consolation. At least then she'd had the excuse that she was ill. She didn't know why it mattered, but she hated for him to see her looking like a frump.

Of course, she looked no worse than anyone else, Elise told herself as she carefully peeled off the transparent tape. They were all still disheveled and rosy from sleep. Everyone, that is, except Sam, she thought sourly, peeking at him over the top of the box.

Dark stubble shadowed his jaw, but his eyes were crystal-clear and he'd obviously taken the time to brush his hair. As usual, it was swept ruthlessly back, the shining ebony creating a thick, luxuriant frame about his hard face, not a strand out of place.

Elise appreciated neatness, more so than most, she admitted, her mouth twisting in a self-mocking little smile as she removed the shiny foil and folded it into a precise square. All around her, the others were tearing into their presents with abandon, and the floor was already ankle-deep in torn wrapping paper, ribbon, tissue and empty boxes. But still, Sam's flawless grooming annoyed her. There wasn't so much as a crease in his pajamas, for heaven's sake!

Then it occurred to her that he probably hadn't slept in the pajamas at all, that he'd probably put them on this morning for the sake of appearance. In Las Vegas, she recalled, he'd slept in only his briefs, and she was beginning to suspect that even that had been a concession to her modesty. She had a strong hunch that Sam normally slept naked.

The intimate trend of her thoughts brought a fresh blush to Elise's cheeks, but she hoped if anyone noticed they'd blame it on the scandalous teddy she was lifting from the box in her lap. Made of ivory silk and ecru lace, it bore a French label. It was minuscule and semitransparent, the kind of garment a woman wore only so that a man could take it off. Trust Erin to give her something so provocative.

Everyone was pleased with their gifts, but the ones that surprised and impressed Elise the most were the ones from Sam.

He gave Erin a new piece of luggage with all sorts of intriguing compartments. To Max he gave three best-sellers that had been released while he and Erin were overseas. Julia, who had recently taken up painting, received a deluxe set of sable brushes in their own carrying case, and Patrick, a new golf bag. He gave Elise's mother a knitted wool cape from Ireland that delighted her so, she sat with it draped over her robe, her fingers stroking the soft garment. And for her father there was a software program on genealogy, which left Elise wondering how Sam had known of his quiet passion for tracing their family's history.

Certainly she hadn't told him. Nor had she done his shopping for him, as so many secretaries did for their bosses. Yet all his gifts had obviously been chosen with care, according to each person's likes and interests.

A strange warmth filled Elise as she took it all in. Thoughtfulness wasn't something she associated with Sam, and once again her opinion of him shifted subtly.

Elise meticulously worked her way through the stack of presents Max had handed her. By the time she reached the last one everyone else had finished with theirs, and as she opened it they all watched. It was a small narrow box, wrapped in silver and blue paper and tied with a silver lace ribbon. She held it in her hands, admiring it for a moment, then checked the tag.

Stunned, she flashed Sam a dismayed look. "Oh, Sam, you shouldn't have! You already gave me a gift."

Friday at work there had been an office party during the lunch break, and she'd given him a nice but impersonal pen and pencil set. Sam had given her, along with every other female employee, a small bottle of perfume.

"That was merely a token to a good secretary," he said, watching her impassively. "This is from me to you."

That made her feel even worse. She didn't want a "personal" gift from Sam. And she had nothing else for him. "But, Sam, I didn't—"

"Just open the gift, Elise."

A fine tremor shook her hand as she complied. The small narrow box was about the same size as the one she'd given him, but she had a sinking feeling it contained nothing so innocuous as a pen and pencil set. Even so, when she lifted the lid her mouth fell open. Nestled in the blue velvet jeweler's box was a delicate gold watch, its face encircled with diamonds.

Elise stared at it. "Oh, Sam," she said in an awed whisper. "I can't..." She looked up at him and shook her head, her soft brown eyes filled with regret and desperation. "I can't possibly accept this."

"Why not? Don't you like it?"

"Oh, no, it's not that!" she denied quickly, her voice stricken that he would even think that. "Of course I like it! It's beautiful! But it's . . . it's too expensive."

He shrugged. "If that's all that's bothering you, keep it. Expense is a relative thing. I can afford it."

"But that's not the point."

"I don't see why you shouldn't keep it," Erin put in, bending over Elise to examine the watch. "After all, Sam is practically family. And you told me you needed a new watch."

"Yeah, that's right," Max said. "So there's no problem."

Everyone else, with the exception of David, chimed in, agreeing.

"But—"

"Elise, for heaven's sake!" Her mother's aggravated voice cut off her protest. "Where are your manners, child?" Dorothy glanced at Sam and smiled, her expression radiating approval. "I think it would be extremely rude of you to refuse Sam's gift."

"Mother!"

Elise gaped at her, frustrated and dismayed. Dorothy Blaine was a sweet-tempered woman who had guided her children into adulthood with a gentle hand and a soft voice, which, on those rare occasions when she chose to employ it, made that commanding tone all the more effective. Her family knew it meant that opposition was futile. Elise knew it even more so than her siblings, since she had inherited her mother's nature.

"Don't worry, Mrs. Blaine, I'm not offended," Sam said in that infuriating matter-of-fact way. "Anyway, it would be pointless for Elise to refuse the gift because I can't return it. It's engraved."

Elise sucked in her breath, and with a sinking feeling in her stomach, she picked up the watch and turned it over. There, in flowing script were the words, "To Elise, Merry Christmas, Sam." Simple. Direct. And binding.

"Well, that settles it," Erin pronounced. "You keep the watch."

Elise sighed. "Yes."

She looked at Sam and smiled wanly. "Thank you, Sam."

When she entered the Global offices the next morning Elise was relieved to find that Peggy was not yet at her desk. Blessing her luck, she hurried through the reception room and down the hall.

The previous day she had called home and checked her answering machine. There had been several messages, all from her friends, wanting to know about her blind date. After the weekend she'd just had, she wasn't thrilled with the prospect of conducting a postmortem on her evening with Craig.

Her relief, however, turned to a groan a few minutes later when she stepped inside her own office to find, not only Peggy, but Margo, Colleen and Tracy, all waiting for her.

"Elise!" Margo cried, pouncing the minute she spotted her.

"It's about time you got here."

"Yeah. We've been waiting to hear about Friday night. So how was it?"

The women crowded around, all talking at once.

"Look, can we do this later?" Elise pleaded, trying to edge around them. "I don't have time right now. I have to—"

"Oh, no, you don't." Margo grasped her arm and tugged her across to the desk. With her hands on Elise's shoulders, she urged her down onto her chair, then placed herself squarely in front of her, hands propped on her hips. "Now then. Shoot."

"Yeah, tell us," Tracy echoed. "But hurry. I've got to be at my desk in three min— Saaay, will you look at that watch." Tracy grabbed Elise's arm for a closer look. "Did you get this for Christmas?"

"Uh . . . yes."

That drew a whistle from Colleen and oohs and aahs from the other women as they crowded closer to see.

"From your family, right?"

Peggy shot Colleen a puzzled frown. "Why do you say that?"

"Because if there was a man in her life giving her gifts like this, we wouldn't be bustin' our buns to find her one."

"Oh, right. I see your point."

They all laughed, and Elise didn't bother to correct the assumption. If they knew that Sam had given her the watch, they'd jump to all the wrong conclusions and she'd never hear the end of it.

"Enough about the watch," Margo insisted. "I came in here to find out about the date, and I'm not leaving until I do."

Elise sighed. "All right, all right. I'll tell you. It was a disaster. A complete and utter disaster."

"What!"

"Oh, no!"

"Ah, crud!"

"Shoot!"

They all spoke at once, looking so shocked and crestfallen that Elise almost felt guilty for spoiling their fun.

"What happened? Did he step out of line?" Colleen demanded. "If he did, my brother will flatten the jerk."

"No, no. It was nothing like that. Craig and I just didn't hit it off, that's all. He wasn't my type, and I wasn't his."

Colleen lit a cigarette and looked Elise up and down, her sharp gaze skimming over the bright red curls and the delicate features they framed, the slender curves beneath the lilac Victorian blouse and gray and lilac patterned skirt that hung in soft folds almost to her ankles. She blew a stream of blue smoke toward the ceiling and twisted her mouth sourly. "Choosy bastard."

Giving her a weak smile, Elise shrugged and looked away. Actually, Craig probably had no idea that she'd been less than impressed. He was so cocky and pleased with himself it would never occur to him that a woman didn't find him irresistible. As a salesman, Craig was no doubt very successful, but he was exactly the kind of man Elise abhorred.

"I told you blind dates were no good," Margo said, shooting Colleen an accusing look. "They always turn out rotten."

"Oh, I don't know," the other woman replied with a sultry half smile. "I've had a few that were fantastic."

"Yeah, but all you're interested in is how good they are in the sack. Elise is looking for husband material."

"I just hope this hasn't discouraged you," Peggy said, giving her a sympathetic look.

"Oh, no. Not at all. I don't give up that easily."

In truth, Elise did not give up at all—not when she had her sights set on something that was important to her. She didn't relish the thought of going out on any more blind dates, but she would do whatever was necessary.

Because of her nature, few people realized that Elise could be almost frighteningly tenacious. It was a fact to which any member of her family could attest, she thought with a wry little smile as she only half listened to the babble of advice from the women huddled around her.

At age eight, she had lost her heart to Tommy Holman, the boy next door, and made up her mind that she would someday marry him. Though he ignored her, and her family tried repeatedly over the years to dissuade her, she had refused to give up hope. It had taken thirteen years before Tommy finally looked at her as a desirable woman, instead of one of those bratty Blaine twins, but it *had* happened.

Patience and determination were traits Elise possessed in abundance, and she believed in them explicitly. They had never yet failed her, and she didn't expect them to now.

"I think we should try something different," Margo said. "Maybe give a party and invite all the single men we know."

"Hey, that sounds like a super idea!" Tracy exclaimed, her eyes lighting up.

"I thought you'd like it." Margo gave the younger woman a droll look and shooed everyone toward the door. "But for now, we'd all better get to work before Sam gets here. See you later, Elise."

Elise breathed a sigh and began to relax as the door shut behind them, but the next instant she nearly jumped out of her skin when a deep male voice cut across the silence.

"I wouldn't have believed it if I hadn't heard it myself."

Gasping, Elise whirled around and saw Sam standing in the doorway that connected his office with hers, his arms folded across his chest, one shoulder propped indolently against the jamb.

Chapter Six

S am! You startled me!"

Her face flamed as she realized that he had overheard everything. Taking refuge in indignation, she muttered, "You should have let us know you were here."

He ignored the comment and just looked at her, his brows arching skyward. "A blind date? You hotfooted it out of here Friday for a blind date?" Though pitched low, his voice was no longer devoid of emotion; it held scorn and disbelief.

Elise fidgeted, confused by his tone and the building tension. "I . . . I did offer to come in on Saturday and type the report."

"To hell with the bloody report," he fired back with that same quiet, unnerving forcefulness.

Sam pushed away from the door and stalked toward her with controlled steps, his rangy, elegant body taut. Elise watched him apprehensively, barely resisting the urge to push back her chair and flee.

He came to a halt beside her, and with one hand braced on the desk top, the other gripping the back of her chair, he bent over until his face was mere inches from hers.

Panic quickened Elise's breathing. He had her boxed in, trapped between his spread arms and the return section of her desk. She swallowed hard and pressed against the chair.

"Would you mind telling me why a woman as beautiful as you would resort to a blind date?" he demanded softly.

"I . . . I . . ."

"That's a pathetic device. Not only that, it's demeaning and potentially dangerous."

"It wasn't really dangerous. Colleen arranged it. Craig . . . Craig is her brother's friend."

"Colleen Mahaffey is a sharp woman, but I wouldn't call her discriminating when it comes to men. And you still haven't answered my question. Why are you letting your friends arrange your social life?"

"I . . . because I don't know anyone in Santa Fe."

Something flickered in his eyes, something cool and dangerous. "I see. So . . . now that Max is out of your reach, you've decided to find a replacement, is that it?"

Elise was watching his mouth form the words, so fascinated by the movement of those thin, sensuous lips that for a moment their meaning didn't register. When it did her eyes widened and she sucked in her breath, but he cut her off before she could speak.

"And as for not knowing anyone, that's not quite true," he insisted. "You know me."

That stopped her cold. His insulting comment and her denial were wiped out of her mind by those three, softly murmured words.

Elise's heart gave a little thump, then took off at a gallop. Her throat grew dry as she met his cool, unrevealing stare. "Y-you?"

"Yes, me. Does that surprise you?"

Her head bobbed up and down in a stunned nod.

"Why?"

Still holding her gaze, he picked up her hand and placed it against his cheek. The feel of his smooth shaven skin against her palm was incredible—intimate, arousing and, somehow, threatening all at the same time. Heat spread from the point of contact, zinging along her arm and shoulders and spreading all the way to her toes, raising gooseflesh in its wake and making her body tingle.

"You see? I'm flesh and blood and bone, the same as any other man," he murmured, his eyes narrowing as he watched her shivering reaction.

He straightened and sat down on the edge of her desk, then reached down and grasped her elbows, lifting her out of the chair and bringing her to stand between his spread thighs.

In her stupefied state the thought of resistance never entered Elise's mind. Docile as a rag doll, she obeyed the urging of his hands, her dazed brown eyes fixed on his hard face.

"I have the same basic requirements of life as Max, or Craig What's-his-name," he said, his soft voice growing steadily softer as he eased her close. "Peace. A degree of comfort. Moderate success. Physical satisfaction. Companionship." An almost imperceptible tug brought her closer still. "I sleep, I eat, I drink . . ." His gaze lowered to her mouth and lingered, and his voice dropped to just above a whisper. "I hunger."

The hard muscled thighs bracketing her hips tightened. One big hand left her elbow, slid up her arm, over her shoulder and curved around the side of her neck, the thumb beneath her chin tipping her head up and to the side at a waiting angle. He leaned forward until his parted lips hovered over hers. His warm moist breath feathered against her skin, and Elise waited . . . and waited . . . her heart booming, her starved lungs unable to function. Then his heavy eye-

lids lifted, and she met the silver fire of his gaze. "Especially when you look at me all doe-eyed like that."

"Mr. Lawford, I—"

"Sam," he murmured against her lips. "My name is
Sam."

After that, speech became impossible.

The shock of his mouth on hers sent a current straight to
Elise's feminine core. The kiss beneath the mistletoe had
been but a taste of Sam's sensual expertise. Never would she
have believed that he could kiss like that, that those thin,
hard lips could be so exquisitely tender and arousing. Or
that she would be so affected.

But her response was uncontrollable. Her heart pounded,
her knees went weak and the tight feeling in her chest was
almost painful. Her mouth opened of its own accord to the
probing of his tongue, and he swallowed her helpless moan
as he deepened the kiss.

Sam's arms enfolded her, pulling her against him. His
mouth rocked back and forth over hers, slowly, as though
savoring to the fullest the feel and the taste of the kiss, the
sensations it evoked. His tongue swirled in her mouth. His
big sensitive hands roamed her back, learning her shape,
pressing her tightly to him.

Elise's hands were trapped between them, and against her
palms she felt the fine silk of his shirt, the firm chest beneath it rise and fall, the heavy thudding of his heart.

Her own was banging away at her ribs. She felt engulfed,
overwhelmed, simultaneously hot and cold, excited and
panicky. The taste and feel and scent of Sam surrounded her
and set off a quaking deep inside that robbed her of the will
and the strength to resist.

Controlled excitement. It took her a minute to recognize
it, and when she did it surprised her. But it was revealed by
the tensile strength of the arms that bound her, by the insistence of his mouth, by the roughness and depth of each

slow breath he drew. She felt each one strike her cheek, an eddying current of warm, moist air that caressed her skin.

Elise was horribly aware that her nipples were pebble-hard against his chest. And standing as she was, wedged into the V of his thighs, the intimate alignment of their bodies made it impossible to ignore his arousal. With only thin layers of clothing separating them, he pressed hard and hot against her, and Elise felt that familiar quickening that brought a throbbing, hollow ache to the heart of her femininity.

She stirred, and made a desperate sound in her throat, and Sam's arms tightened.

The door to Elise's office opened, but she wasn't aware that anyone had entered until she heard Margo's voice.

"Elise, Sam left a note on my desk saying he wanted to talk to... me... about..."

As Margo's words trailed away, Elise struggled against Sam's hold, but he continued to kiss her leisurely. With her eyes open wide, she pushed against his chest as the other woman began to back away.

"Oh, Lord. I'm sorry. I should have knocked. I didn't realize... that is... I didn't know... uh... well..." Margo clutched the file folder she was carrying to her breasts and groped behind her for the door. "I'll, uh... I'll just come back later, when you're not busy... I mean... Oh, hell."

The incoherent babble came to an end as words failed her.

Just as Margo spun around to leave, Sam ended the kiss. He raised his head slowly, his lips clinging to Elise's as though breaking contact was difficult. Without taking his eyes from her flushed face, he said, "Don't leave, Margo. We need to discuss the import tax revision."

One roughened fingertip touched Elise's hot cheek and he smoothed an errant curl away from her temple, but for all the gentleness of his touch, his face was as inscrutable as ever, his beautiful silver eyes watchful, yet untouched by emotion.

After a moment, with his arms still around Elise, he looked over his shoulder, and said calmly, "I want to know how it's going to affect this quarter's profits before we close the books."

Watching them, Margo nodded, her shock already turning to avid curiosity.

With a sangfroid that left Elise speechless, Sam eased her back into her chair, stood up and gestured for the other woman to precede him into his office. "I have a twelve o'clock flight to Seattle, so we don't have much time."

Reluctantly, Margo complied, but not before sending Elise an indignant we're-going-to-talk-about-this-later glare over her shoulder.

Shaken, Elise sat immobile and watched the door to Sam's office close behind them.

Oh, Lord, she was in trouble. Closing her eyes, she pressed four fingers over her trembling lips. The kiss under the mistletoe she could dismiss as an impulse. Even her sister's claim that Sam cared for her could conceivably be chalked up to no more than vivid imagination, colored, perhaps, by wishful thinking and compassion.

But not this. There was no way she could brush aside what had just happened as casual or unimportant. She wasn't *that* much of a self-deluding fool. Sam had kissed her quite deliberately, with passion and a predatory hunger that stated, clearer than words could, his intent. He meant to have her.

It was an unnerving thought. Elise opened her eyes and struggled to bring her ragged breathing under control.

And she hadn't been unaffected, she admitted with grim honesty. It was a shock to discover that she was attracted to Sam physically, but there was no denying the mindless pleasure she had experienced in his arms. Worse though—much worse—she was very much afraid that she was beginning to respond to him on an emotional level.

Elise drew in a sharp, panicky breath and snatched up the telephone. No, she couldn't allow that to happen. Her hand shook as she punched out Colleen's extension. It rang once, and she drummed her fingers on the desk. Before it rang a second time it was picked up.

"Co—"

"Colleen, this is Elise...."

That evening after work, the minute Elise stepped inside Max and Erin's house, her sister pounced.

"Oh, good. You're here. I want to talk to you," Erin announced.

Elise had to stifle a groan. She'd sensed her twin's agitation even before she'd heard that aggressive tone, and she was beginning to rue her decision to stay here instead of returning to her own little apartment in town.

But it was too late to change her mind. Julia and Patrick Delany had returned to Phoenix that morning, but her parents and David were staying with Erin and Max until New Year's Day, and she'd promised that she would, also. Elise loved her family and wanted to be with them, but at that moment she would have given a lot for some privacy.

"Can't it wait?" she asked hopefully. "Right now, all I want is a long hot soak. I'm exhausted."

"No, it can't wait. Elise, Colleen Mahaffey just called. She missed you at the office. I told her you'd be here any moment, but she was in a rush so she said just to tell you that she's got a man lined up for you for Tuesday night."

Erin cocked her head to one side and looked at her expectantly, but Elise merely nodded.

"She also said to tell you that she and Margo are making up a list of candidates for a bachelor bash at her house a week from Saturday."

"I see. Well, thanks a lot, sis." Hoping she would let the matter drop, Elise gave her a bland smile and turned for the stairs, but Erin was right on her heels.

"Elise! What did she mean, she's got a man lined up for you?"

For an instant, Elise considered fibbing, but just as quickly gave up the idea as pointless. She and Erin were so attuned that keeping secrets was practically impossible. Affecting a casual air, she started up the short flight of stairs. "Oh, just that she's arranged a date for me. That's all."

"A date?"

"Uh-huh."

She barely made it to the landing.

"Wait a minute!" Erin grabbed her elbow and spun her around. "You mean a *blind* date?"

"Yes."

"Elise Marie Holman! Have you lost your mind?"

"No, I don't think so."

"I'm not so sure, if you don't have any better sense than to go out with strangers!"

Giving Erin a sweet smile, Elise gently disengaged her arm and started up the short flight of stairs that led to her wing.

As Elise entered the bedroom her sister stalked right along behind, nipping at her like a tenacious terrier. "And just what kind of party are Margo and Colleen planning? Or should I even ask?"

Elise unzipped her dress and stepped out of it. "It's simply one at which all the male guests are single and eligible."

"I think," Erin said in a stern voice, "that you'd better start explaining, sister dear. This is sounding worse by the minute." Holding her back ramrod straight, she crossed her arms and sat down on the edge of the bed, her whole attitude making it clear that she didn't intend to budge until she had some answers.

Elise sighed and accepted the inevitable. She had never been able to hide anything from Erin. She wasn't foolish enough to think she could start now.

Speaking in soft, gentle tones, she outlined her plan as she disrobed and ran her bathwater. By the time she had finished, her twin's expression had changed from disapproving to worried.

"Oh, Elise, honey," Erin said in a voice riddled with concern and dismay. "I don't think this is a good idea. The swinging singles scene isn't for you, believe me. You've led such a sheltered life, and you're such a naive innocent. It'd be like throwing a lamb into a pack of ravenous wolves." Erin shook her head. "No, I won't allow you to do this."

"Erin, I'm a grown woman," Elise reminded her in a gentle but firm tone. "I can take care of myself."

"Sweetheart, believe me—it's a jungle out there. You have no idea what—"

"Look, sis, I know that protecting me is more or less a habit with you. You, David, Mother and Dad—even Tommy—always have." Elise gave her a look of loving tolerance. "I know you do it out of love, and I appreciate that, but you can't hover over me forever."

"But, Elise—"

"It's no use, Erin. I'm going to do this my way."

"Oh, Lord." Erin groaned. "You've got that same sweetly stubborn look you wore when you were a kid and decided you were going to marry Tommy. We all argued and pleaded until we were blue in the face, but you were so damned immovable."

A slow, complacent smile curved Elise's mouth. "But I was right. I did marry Tommy."

"Yeah," Erin grumbled. "Thirteen years later."

"Well, don't worry. It won't take that long this time."

Erin continued to argue but Elise remained serenely implacable, and finally she threw her hands up in disgust and stalked out.

But Erin was no less stubborn, simply more volatile, so Elise wasn't surprised when David came storming into her room a half an hour later, just as she emerged from her bath.

"Just what is all this nonsense Erin's been telling me?" he demanded. "No sister of mine is going on the prowl for a husband at singles bars and swinging ski weekends. And that's final!''

"I should have known she'd sic you on me." With a sigh, she tightened the belt on her robe and sat down to wait out her brother's tirade.

David paced and glowered and lectured, then laid down the law. When that didn't work he tried reason, then pleading. Through it all, Elise smiled and stood firm.

"Dammit!" David bellowed, reverting once again to brotherly wrath. "You always were the most placidly stubborn, pigheaded, unreasonable female. But at least we never had to worry about you getting your butt in a crack like we did Erin. And now that we've finally got her married to a man who just might be able to handle her, *you* go off the deep end! If you want a husband, why the hell don't you just marry Sam and be done with it?''

Elise tensed. Her smile wavered a bit, but held. She gave a dramatic sigh. "First Erin, now you. Why does everyone keep trying to pair me off with Sam?" she asked with a feigned little laugh. "The man is my boss. Nothing more. Anyway... I thought you didn't like Sam."

"Lawford's okay," David muttered grudgingly. Scowling, he stuffed his hands in the pockets of his slacks and jingled his loose change. "He's an icy bastard and hard as nails, but he's reliable. He'd take good care of you."

"This may come as a shock to you, David, but I don't *want* anyone to take care of me. I want a husband, not a dragon slayer. Someone with whom I can share whatever life has to offer, both good and bad. Someone who will love and cherish me without trying to wrap me in cotton." She gazed at him, her brown eyes soft with entreaty. "Can't you understand? I'm tired of being protected and treated as though I were made of spun glass."

David cleared his throat and cast her an uncomfortable glance, his mouth twisting. "Well... it's hard not to," he grumbled defensively. "Even as a kid you always seemed... I don't know . . . fragile, I guess. Erin was a rowdy little devil with scabby knees, scruffy tennis shoes and grass stains on the seat of her pants. She was always getting into one scrape after another. But you . . . you were a sweet docile little angel in spotless pinafores and baby-doll shoes. Looking out for you has always seemed the natural thing to do.''

Elise winced at the familiar description, even though her heart was warmed by it. She stood up and went to him and laid her hand on his arm. "David, I'm not an angel. I'm a woman. I have the usual number of flaws and shortcomings. I'll admit that I may be a tad naive, but I am capable of running my own life." She rose up on her tiptoes and kissed his cheek, then linked her arm through his and led him to the door. "Now, you're just going to have to grit your teeth and accept that."

"Meaning you're not going to give up this crazy scheme, right?"

"Right." Smiling at his long-suffering look, she patted his cheek. "But one thing I can promise you," she said as she placed her palm flat on his chest and nudged him out into the hallway. "I'm definitely *not* going to marry Sam."

When he had gone she closed the door, rested her forehead against it and repeated in a shaky whisper, "I am not—absolutely not—going to marry Sam."

It would never work. It couldn't. She left the door and crossed to the window. Despite Erin and David's opinion, and even though her feelings about Sam had altered somewhat, she knew it was foolish to even entertain the idea. Whatever had happened to Sam during those four years of captivity, whatever unspeakable horror he had suffered, had stripped him of the ability to love anyone. Certainly the ability to show it. And if she knew nothing else about herself, it was that she was a woman who needed not only to love and be loved, but to hear the words. She needed to experience the tenderness, to see it in her beloved's eyes and hear it in his voice.

And face it, those are things you'd never get from a man like Sam, she told herself, turning away from the window.

Elise picked up a brush from the dresser and dragged it through her hair, watching the bright red curls twine about the bristles, crackling in the silent room. She felt wrung out. All she wanted was to crawl into bed and pull the covers over her head. Staring wistfully at her reflection, Elise wondered if Erin would let her get by with skipping dinner.

No, probably not. Knowing her sister, a request like that would only precipitate another confrontation. And God knew, she'd had enough of those today. First with Sam, then with Erin and David . . . not to mention Margo.

Sam and Margo had conferred together for more than two hours, two hours during which Elise had stewed and fretted over how she was going to face him, what she was going to say. When they'd emerged she'd cowardly latched on to her friend's suggestion to join her for a coffee break, even though she'd known it would mean enduring a third degree about her relationship with Sam.

Elise could still hear Margo's outraged, "Would you mind telling me why you're looking for a man when Sam's obviously got the hots for you?"

"Look, Margo," she'd argued urgently, "I know it looks bad, but—"

"Bad! Who're you trying to kid? It looked pretty damned good from where I was standing."

Elise had spent the entire coffee break explaining to Margo that Sam had kissed her on the spur of the moment in anger, and that there was nothing between them.

And she'd had about as much luck convincing her as she'd had in convincing herself.

Much to Elise's relief, Sam's business on the West Coast hit a snag, and he remained there the rest of the week. He called a few times to issue instructions or ask for information, but as always, he was terse and impersonal. If he'd even given a thought to those two breathless kisses they'd shared, it wasn't evident in his manner.

In the middle of the week Reverend Hawthorne called, and Elise gladly accepted his offer to show her around the Youth Center the following Saturday afternoon, though she had to decline his invitation to dinner afterward.

"I'm really sorry," she told him again on Saturday when she arrived at the center. "I'd like very much to have dinner with you, but David and my parents will be leaving on Monday and—"

"And until then you want to be with your family. I understand completely. No problem. We'll simply postpone our dinner until next week. Say...until Wednesday. If that's convenient?"

Elise smiled, relieved. She'd feared he would think she was trying to give him a polite brush-off. "Wednesday would be fine, Reverend."

Pleasure and a touch of masculine satisfaction shone in his kind eyes as he returned her smile. "Good. And now that we have that settled, shall we begin?" Lightly cupping her elbow, he led her down the hall. "And by the way," he added. "My name is Keith."

First he took her around and introduced her to the staff. The director of the center, Dr. Martha Connelly, a psychologist in her sixties, had taken the job after retiring from private practice. She was a calm, practical woman with a compassionate face and faded blue eyes that revealed hope tempered with realism and many years of experience. Her assistant, Dr. Bernard Rosenthal, was in his late twenties, and burned with the zeal and idealism of youth. Elise thought they probably made an excellent team.

In addition there were three social workers, an efficient but harried-looking older woman who ran the office, a program director and a general handyman. They were all pleasant and friendly, and seemed genuinely delighted when Keith told them she would be working as a volunteer.

After that, he showed her the classrooms and workshops where volunteers were teaching various hobbies and skills—on that morning, everything from cooking to carpentry. Then they toured the kitchen and dining hall, the indoor pool in the basement and the new wing that housed the play school for younger children.

"And here we have our gymnasium," Keith said proudly, pushing one of the wide double doors open just far enough for them to slip inside. "The boys' basketball team is practicing, but I don't think their coach will mind if we watch for a few minutes."

Standing on the sidelines by the door, the first thing Elise noticed was that this was no ordinary basketball team of young Goliaths. Two looked as though they might be edging close to the six-foot mark, but most of the sweaty youths running around the court were of medium height. A couple were even shorter than Elise. She felt a spurt of admiration for their coach as she realized that this was not a team whose only reason for being was to win. These boys were out there because someone wanted them to have the pleasure of playing the game.

Curious, her gaze sought the man on the other side of the court. He was standing with his back to her in the center of a cluster of boys, talking and gesturing, and they were hanging on every word. All she could make out was that he was tall—standing head and shoulders above his players—well built and had black hair.

Then the group broke apart and loped out onto the court as the man blew the whistle he wore around his neck. He swung around, clapping his hands. "All right, you guys, get the lead out! Get the lead out!"

Elise's jaw dropped and her eyes grew huge. There, standing directly across from her, wearing a baggy, sweat-stained gray knit warm-up suit and worn sneakers, his hair mussed and falling across his forehead in dark ringlets, was Sam.

And he was grinning.

She couldn't believe it! Sam? Sam was coaching a team of streetwise, underprivileged teenagers? Sam, who always held himself aloof from others, was giving freely of his time and himself?

And obviously loving it.

"Come on! Speed it up, speed it up! The other team's not gonna stop and give you goof-offs any free shots," Sam prodded from the sidelines.

Exuberant shouts bounced off the walls and the squeak and thump of sneakered feet pounding the wooden floor reverberated through the gym like rolling thunder. Racing up and down the court in a spread-out, elongated circle between the backstops, each player, after catching a gut-level, bullet pass from the boy stationed beneath the basket, attempted a one-handed lay-up shot as he went by.

"Rodrigues! Keep your eye on the basket when you throw!"

"Push up! Push up, Billings! Get some power on the ball!"

"Way to go, Hawk!" Sam shouted when a stout Indian boy made a basket. "Good follow-through!"

He kept up a hard, rhythmic clapping, urging the boys on as he shouted instructions. He taught constantly, couching his criticisms matter-of-factly, and praising whenever he could.

Elise could hardly believe what she was seeing and hearing. Gone was the stony-faced man she knew. This Sam was happy and relaxed, his eyes alive with pleasure and a ready smile on his lips as he made his team hustle. When a boy stepped out of the formation to make a teasing remark to him, she expected Sam to respond with a reprimand. Instead, he ruffled the boy's hair, then threw his head back and roared with laughter. Stunned, Elise leaned against the wall behind her and stared.

After a few minutes Keith asked if she was ready to go, but Elise shook her head, her gaze never leaving Sam.

He was wonderful with the boys, she realized with amazement. He handled them with just the right blend of firmness and affection. And though they tried to hide it behind a facade of toughness, it was obvious that they adored him.

It was several minutes before the occasional heckling jeer registered on Elise. Seeking its source, she noticed for the first time the small group of youths at the top of the bleachers behind Sam.

There were seven of them, and even as far away as they were, Elise could tell they were troublemakers by the insolent way they were sprawled over the bleachers, and by their cocky, slightly bored attitude.

At that moment one of the more gangly players missed his shot, then tripped over his own feet and fell flat on his backside. Instantly, jeering laughter and catcalls erupted from the top of the bleachers.

"Who are those boys up there?" Elise asked.

"A bunch of troubled misfits, I'm afraid." Keith frowned, his handsome face reflecting concern and frustration as he gazed across the gym. "Their leader is the stocky, black-haired kid with the beaded headband. Calls himself Stalking Wolf. Claims his father was an Apache." A sardonic half smile lifted Keith's mouth. "Actually, his name is Juan Aldondo. He's the illegitimate son of a woman named Lola Aldondo, a former cantina dancer turned cocktail waitress. And even she doesn't claim to know who his father is."

"And you let them just hang around here?"

Keith shrugged. "The center is open to anyone under the age of eighteen. I'll admit they're a nuisance sometimes, but they haven't caused any real trouble. They just sort of skirt around the edge of it. So far, that is. Anyway, I keep hoping that we'll be able to reach them eventually."

Beside them, the gym door opened a few inches and Dr. Rosenthal stuck his head inside. His eyes lit up when he spotted Keith. "Reverend, there's a telephone call for you. It's one of your parishioners, and she sounds upset."

"Thanks, Bernie. I'll be right there."

He turned to Elise with an apologetic look but before he could speak she told him to go ahead, that she would wait there for him. When he had gone, she eased farther into the shadows on the sideline and settled back to watch, her fascinated gaze homing in once more on Sam.

Fifteen minutes later, Keith had still not returned when Sam blew the whistle signaling the end of practice.

"All right, you guys, get over here."

The boys trotted off the court and gathered around him, winded and dripping sweat. With his feet braced wide, his fists on his hips, Sam looked at them sternly. "Tonight's game is a big one, so don't blow it. I want to see every one of you back here at seven sharp, bright-eyed and bushy-tailed and ready to beat the pants off those guys from Albuquerque. You got that?"

"Yeah, sure, Coach," one of the boys replied. Grinning, he elbowed the boy next to him. "But can we play 'um a game of basketball first?"

"Wiseacre," Sam growled affectionately. Cupping his hand around the back of the youth's neck, he gave him a little shake, and a shove toward the dressing-room exit. "All right, you goof-offs! Hit the showers!" he shouted with a grin in his voice as he ruffled a sweaty head and playfully cuffed another boy on the shoulder.

Bemused, Elise watched Sam and the boys head for the exit, keeping up a steady stream of good-natured banter and indulging in the rough-and-tumble affection typical of males.

Telling herself she should go find Keith to discuss her hours and duties, she turned reluctantly to go, but at that instant the door burst open and a small whirlwind raced across the gym.

"Sam! Sam! Wait for me!" Scrawny legs worked like pistons as a boy about four years old made a beeline for the dark man in the gray sweat suit.

The piping little voice stopped Sam in his tracks, and he swung around, his eyes lighting. "Paulo!"

The teenagers around him stopped also, grinning, and like Moses parting the Red Sea, they cleared a path between the man and the child. Bending from the waist, Sam spread his arms wide. The ragged little urchin hurtled into his chest at full speed and was scooped up in a great bear hug.

Infectious, high-pitched giggles blended with Sam's booming laugh and echoed through the rafters of the gym as he whirled the boy around. Then he tossed him high, and the giggles became a squeal of pure delight.

Catching him, Sam settled the child in the crook of his arm, poked his protruding belly with one long finger and grinned. "How ya doing, pal?"

In answer, the beaming child clamped his skinny arms around Sam's neck and planted a smacking kiss on his cheek.

Something altered in Sam's expression. Elise could see the change even from where she stood. The child was ragged and incredibly dirty, his face streaked with grime, his hair matted and dull, but Sam's big hand slid up the narrow little back to tenderly cradle the small head as he leaned forward and returned the salute.

The simple scene did strange things to Elise's heart. It was nothing more than ordinary affection, the kind that people exchange every day, yet seeing it demonstrated by this man made her chest tighten painfully and brought a sheen of moisture to her eyes.

As she watched, Sam hoisted the little ragamuffin onto his shoulder and carried him into the dressing room as though he were a victorious hero.

When they had disappeared through the doorway, Elise could barely swallow past the aching lump in her throat.

In a daze, she left the gym and wandered down the hallway toward the office, her emotions in turmoil. The scene she had witnessed had left her confused and shaken—vulnerable, somehow, and yet...deeply touched. She shut her eyes, picturing the way Sam's face had softened with tenderness, the gentle way he'd cupped the child's head, and felt a fresh rush of tears clog her throat.

Chapter Seven

Elise was so preoccupied she didn't realize that she was not alone until a young man stepped in front of her, blocking her path. She pulled up short, a spurt of apprehension making her catch her breath as she recognized the boy.

"Well, hel-lo, pretty lady."

He couldn't have been more than seventeen, but the black eyes that glinted beneath the beaded headband were cold and far from innocent. Insolent and calculating, they swept over her, and Elise gritted her teeth as his mouth curved in a suggestive leer.

She lifted her chin a fraction. "Excuse me, please." Pasting a polite but distant smile on her face, she started around him, but another boy appeared to stand shoulder to shoulder with the one who called himself Stalking Wolf.

Barely avoiding a collision, Elise jerked to a halt and took a step backward, only to bump into yet another youth. Her head snapped around, and her heart gave a little lurch as more boys moved in, surrounding her.

"Hey, man, this one's prime," one of the newcomers drawled.

"Yeah, Wolf, looks like you found a real fox." The remark came from a blond, pimply-faced teenager of about sixteen, who snickered and elbowed the boy beside him as though he'd made a hilarious joke.

"Whadda you doin' hangin' around here? You the preacher's ol' lady or somethin'?"

"I'm a new volunteer," Elise replied in a frosty tone. "Now if you don't mind, I'd like to pass. Reverend Hawthorne is waiting for me."

"Well, now." Wolf edged closer, and Elise started when he reached out and tugged a bright curl at her temple. "Things are lookin' up around this dump. Whatcha gonna teach? Maybe I'll even sign up for it."

This close, she could smell his fetid breath and the unpleasant sourness of unwashed flesh. His clothes were every bit as dirty as the little urchin's who had ridden away on Sam's shoulder, but Elise suspected that disregard of hygiene was part of the savage look Wolf affected. Jaw-length, straight black hair, held in place by the beaded headband, completed the image, the blunt style adding emphasis to his harsh features.

Elise grew more uneasy as the boys casually edged in closer. She glanced down the hallway toward Keith's office. A yell would bring someone running. She drew several shallow breaths and swallowed hard. But no. No, she wouldn't do that. Hadn't she told David she didn't need anyone to take care of her? She could handle this. They were just kids, after all. They simply needed a firm set-down.

"That's a very good idea," she said agreeably, hoping they wouldn't notice the slight quiver in her voice. "And you could certainly benefit from it." She looked him straight in the eye and smiled. "I plan to teach a course in manners."

Wolf's insolent leer vanished and his face hardened, but before he could reply the doors to the gymnasium were shoved open from the inside. After the barest moment of silence, Sam's voice boomed down the hallway.

"What are you boys up to?"

"Geez, Wolf," one of them hissed. "Let's get the hell out of here. It's the man."

Wolf's narrowed gaze flicked to Sam as he stared toward them. Grinning cockily, the boy held his hands up, palms out, and began to back away. "Hey, nothin', man," he said with feigned innocence. "Just talkin' to the lady, that's all."

The others followed him, flowing away from Elise as though they were steel shavings pulled by a magnet.

"Elise? Is that you?"

As the gang of youths slipped away she turned and watched Sam stride toward her.

"Elise!" Disbelief, amazement, then anger flashed across his rugged features so quickly she wasn't sure she'd actually seen them. By the time he came to a halt in front of her his expressionless mask had slipped back into place, and his face revealed only bland curiosity.

She hadn't seen Sam since the morning he'd kissed her in the office, and his sudden nearness was an assault on her senses. Attired as he usually was in impeccably tailored suits or classic casual wear, there was an air of restrained toughness about him, an elegantly cloaked but unmistakable virility that no woman, herself included, could fail to notice, though admittedly she had tried. But standing there with that damp, baggy athletic suit clinging to his leanly muscled body, his hair mussed, his skin flushed and glistening, he radiated a blatant sensuality that took her breath away. Heat emanated from him, and the earthy scents of perspiration and maleness made her head swim and sent a tingling sensation feathering over her skin.

"What are you doing here, Elise?"

"I could ask you the same thing," she replied with commendable calm, considering the way her heart was pounding. "I thought you were in Seattle."

"I flew in this morning." Sam shrugged and nodded toward the gym. "I coach the basketball team here. After the game tonight, I'm flying back." He looked in the direction the gang of boys had gone. "Were Wolf and his bunch bothering you?"

"No, not really." Bemused by the casual explanation, Elise shook her head. How many men, she wondered, would fly back and forth over the weekend just to coach a team of street-tough kids?

He grunted and sent her a skeptical look, but let the matter drop. "You still haven't answered my question. What are you doing here?"

She opened her mouth to tell him just as Keith came out of his office. "Sorry I took so long," he called out, hurrying toward them. "Oh, hi there, Sam. I see you've already met our newest volunteer."

"Volunteer?" Sam shot her a sharp look, his eyebrows pulling downward. "You don't mean you're actually planning to work here?"

"I . . . uh . . . well, yes," Elise stammered, taken aback by his obvious displeasure. "Why? Is there some reason I shouldn't?"

"I don't think it's a good idea."

"Why not? You do."

"Have you discussed this with your family? No, of course you haven't," he said, answering his own question and ignoring hers. "In case you haven't noticed, Elise, this isn't exactly the best neighborhood in town. I'm sure that Erin and David would have a fit if they even knew you were here."

It was the wrong thing to say. For the past four days Elise had endured her brother and sister's constant nagging and pleading lectures. She was sick of being protected.

"You're probably right," she replied, her soft voice icily polite. "But they could have ten fits, and it wouldn't affect my decision. I have no intention of living my life according to someone else's wishes."

"Somehow, I get the feeling you two know each other," Keith inserted dryly, looking back and forth between them.

Sam barely spared him a glance. "Elise is my secretary."

"Which gives you the right to order me around during office hours," she flared. "But what I do on my own time is my business."

Elise turned to Keith. "Thank you for showing me around, Reverend, but I must be going now." Ignoring Sam, she murmured a quick goodbye and headed for the front exit, her head held high.

Sam watched her march away, fighting back a smile. He'd forgotten the way her temper could shoot up so unexpectedly.

"Personally, I've always thought a little spirit in a woman was a good thing," Keith mused, drawing Sam's gaze.

He frowned when he saw that the other man was also watching Elise, his expression intent, interested. Sam's silvery eyes sharpened and narrowed as he looked back at her, noting the delicate grace with which she moved, the way the soft skirt flared and fluttered around her shapely legs with each unconsciously provocative sway of her hips.

Man of the cloth or not, he didn't like the way Keith was looking at Elise, as though he were imagining her, not only in his bed, but sitting in that first pew in church for the next fifty years or so. The undeniable fact that she would make an excellent minister's wife did nothing to alleviate the slow curl of anger that began to twist in Sam's stomach.

"I agree. A touch of spice keeps a sweet nature from being too bland. Of course, it doesn't hurt that she's a pretty woman." Sam made the probing comment casually, watching the other man, his body taut as he waited for his response.

It wasn't long in coming.

"Pretty?" Keith gave a derisive snort. "Man, are you blind? She's downright gorgeous. Both inside and out. The man who wins that lady is going to be one lucky son of a gun."

Sam didn't need Keith to tell him that. He'd been aware of Elise's warmth and soft femininity from the moment they'd met. He found the combination of flamboyant beauty and gentleness of spirit both soothing and strangely erotic.

He'd spent hours fantasizing about making love to her. The thought of that beautiful, serene face flushed with passion, her lips swollen from his kisses and begging for more was almost unbearably exciting.

In his saner moments, Sam realized that he was probably being unrealistic. Elise had not been unaffected by his kisses, but neither had she been rendered mindless with desire. Given her nature and the sheltered life she'd led, he wasn't even sure there *was* a more primitive, passionate side to her. It didn't matter though, since it was her warmth and serenity he wanted most.

But if there was passion there, he intended to be the one to awaken it. He might not deserve her, but he was determined that if any man ever saw those soft brown eyes dark and desperate with desire, felt that slender body writhing beneath him in hectic need, it would be him. As much as he liked and admired Keith Hawthorne, he'd be damned if he let him have Elise.

"I'm aware of her finer points," Sam said evenly, but his hard tone carried a warning that wasn't lost on the other man.

Keith looked at him sharply, his eyes widening. "Ah, so that's the way the wind blows."

Sam shrugged. "She's my secretary. And my best friend's sister-in-law."

"C'mon, Sam. My sister works as the church secretary, but I don't stand guard over her. Why don't you just admit it? You care for Elise."

"No." The denial came out with more force than Sam had intended, earning him a raised-brow look. Mentally kicking himself, he added in a quieter voice, "Not in the way you mean, anyway."

"Oh, well then. I'm relieved to hear that." Keith's eyes twinkled. "Because I've got a date with her Wednesday night, and I'd hate to cut in on one of my best friends." Looking pleased with himself, he put his hands in his pockets and strolled back toward his office, whistling softly. A few feet away he stopped and grinned back over his shoulder at Sam. "Not that I wouldn't, mind you, since the lady in question isn't wearing your ring. But I'd hate doing it."

Staring after him, Sam stood in the middle of the hallway, motionless except for the hands hanging at his sides, slowly opening and closing.

On New Year's Day Elise, along with Erin and Max, drove her parents and brother to the airport in Albuquerque. In the midst of the farewells, David drew her aside. Elise knew from his tight expression that he intended to take one last shot at getting her to give up her search for a husband, but she cut him off before he even started.

"David, please. I know what you're going to say. We've been over it all a dozen times in the past week." She smiled gently and put her hand on his arm. "Why don't you just kiss me goodbye and stop worrying? I'm a big girl now."

David started to say something, but when he met her soft, steady gaze he snapped his mouth shut and looked away, the muscles in his jaw working. Elise had the feeling he was silently counting to ten. When he looked back, his mouth was compressed in a tight line.

"You're going to go ahead with this crazy scheme, aren't you?" When she nodded he swore under his breath and shook his head in disgust. "I should have known it was useless to try and talk some sense into that sweet, hard head. It's never done any good in the past. You always just smile and forge right ahead in that blasted gently determined way of yours."

"I love you, too," Elise teased as she slipped her arms around her brother's lean middle and hugged him.

David's deep sigh signaled his defeat, and he laid his cheek against the top of her head as he returned the embrace. "Just be careful, okay?" he said gruffly.

Elise smiled against his chest and whispered, "I will. I promise."

Although her evening with Arnold Seavers wasn't exactly fabulous, it was a vast improvement over the first blind date. Arnold, a widower with three young children, turned out to be a very nice man. He was an attorney specializing in corporate law, and apparently very successful. In his late thirties, he was pleasant looking, a tad heavyset, had a receding hairline, a bald spot and what appeared to be a perpetual harried expression.

They had dinner at an elegant restaurant downtown. Afterward they returned to Elise's apartment for dessert and coffee, and talked for another hour or so, mainly about the problems Arnold faced as a single parent. All in all it was a pleasant, relaxing evening. However, she suspected that his main concern was not so much finding a wife, but a woman to mother his children. Which would have been fine with Elise, except that Arnold didn't have the least effect on her pulse rate.

On Wednesday, Keith took her to a play, then afterward, over a bottle of Chianti and a spaghetti dinner at a modest Italian restaurant, they exchanged life stories.

She was surprised to learn that he had been a premed student in college, but that after completing his internship he had decided against medicine as a career.

"I wasn't sure what I wanted to do with my life, just that being a doctor wasn't it. So, to have something useful to do while I made up my mind, I joined the Peace Corps."

"Really? I've never known anyone who belonged to the Peace Corps. What was it like?"

"Long hours, low pay, substandard living conditions, headaches like you wouldn't believe. But—" Keith smiled wryly and reached for a breadstick "—it turned out to be the smartest move I ever made. I learned that what I really wanted to do was help people. I suppose that was why I was drawn to medicine in the first place. But...I don't know...I wanted to do more than just patch them up when they were sick or injured, then send them home. I wanted to treat the whole person, help on a more personal level. I wanted to become involved in people's daily lives and be there for them when they needed me, for whatever reason.

"In Africa I helped treat malnourished children with open sores and adults with everything from tapeworms to goiters, taught the basics of hygiene and diet to women who'd never heard the words before, and modern agricultural techniques to men whose only farming tool up until that point had been a sharp stick. I set bones, settled squabbles, answered questions and gave guidance and advice where I could. And in the process, discovered that there's something very satisfying about helping on a person-to-person basis."

"So when you came home, you began to study for the ministry."

"Much to my grandmother's disappointment," Keith claimed, grinning at Elise's shocked look. "She said at eighty-seven, she didn't have any need for a preacher in the family, that if she hadn't already earned her ticket to heaven by then she was never going to, but that she sure as heck could have used some free doctoring."

Elise laughed and told him she didn't believe a word of it. She couldn't imagine anyone who wouldn't be proud of having a fine man like Keith Hawthorne for a grandson.

Over a sinfully rich dessert, Elise told him about growing up in Crockett, Texas, about her family and how she'd spent most of her life waiting for the boy next door to realize that he loved her, only to lose him to leukemia three short years after they married.

They discovered that they had a lot in common. They both liked sappy old movies, realistic art, guitar music and antiques. Elise didn't care much for football but, being from Texas, she was delighted to learn that Keith was a staunch Dallas Cowboys fan. They both enjoyed reading. Keith was mainly interested in nonfiction but seemed to understand her passion for western novels, though he was horrified when she confessed that she always skimmed the last scene of a book first.

When he took her home, Keith refused her invitation to come in for more coffee. They stood in silence before her front door in the courtyard of the Spanish-style apartment complex, looking at each other, their breaths forming puffy little clouds in the frosty air. Melting snow dripped from the roofs, and behind Keith the huge cottonwood tree swayed in the wind, its skeletal branches casting an eerie shadow on the moonlit flagstone.

Keith took her hand and, holding it between his, rubbed his thumb back and forth over the delicate skin on the back. "Would you like to go to a movie on Friday?" he asked with a touching diffidence that warmed her.

"I'd love to," she said softly.

He smiled. "Great. I'll pick you up about seven."

The silence returned. He made no move to kiss her, though she could tell from the warm look in his eyes that he wanted to, and somehow his restraint made her like him all the more. Finally, gazing at her tenderly, he touched her cheek with his fingertips and murmured a soft "Good night."

As he crossed the courtyard, skirting the drained fountain in the middle, Elise stepped inside her apartment, a thoughtful half smile on her face.

Keith had turned out to be every bit as nice as she had thought he would be. He was witty and warm, and an intelligent, interesting, attentive companion. Exactly the sort of man she was looking for.

Elise locked the door and made her customary check of the apartment. Then, feeling pleased and hopeful, she headed for her bedroom, humming her own hopelessly off-key version of the newest pop tune.

She hummed a lot over the next two days. With Sam still out of town her work load was light, her nerves were calm, and she had both the date with Keith and the party at Margo's to look forward to.

On Friday, with less than a half hour to go until quitting time, she was standing at the cabinet behind her desk, happily rendering an unrecognizable ditty as she caught up on her filing, when Sam marched in.

"Elise, I want to see you in my office." He glanced in her direction but didn't even slow down as his long stride quickly carried him through her office and into his own.

She stopped what she was doing and turned to stare at his retreating back, her lighthearted mood giving way to a heart-pounding excitement she recognized as part fear and part anticipation. Except for that brief, confusing encounter at the Youth Center, she had not seen Sam since the day after Christmas, when he'd kissed her senseless right there at her desk.

At the center, she'd been too surprised at the things she learned about Sam, then too annoyed with him for meddling in her life, to be embarrassed or apprehensive. But her anger hadn't lasted long. It never did. In any case, she was used to having her family fuss over her. Now, however, she'd had almost two weeks to dwell on that kiss and its implications.

"Elise," Sam called in his hard, toneless voice, and she jumped.

Grabbing up her steno pad, she squared her shoulders and hurried into his office.

Sam stood at the window, looking out at the mountains and sky, but when she slipped into the seat before his desk he turned around. Keeping her eyes downcast, she crossed her long legs, tugged her skirt down over her knees and sat waiting, her pencil poised over the steno pad. A pulse point at the base of her throat throbbed with a tom-tom beat, and she prayed he wouldn't notice. After a moment, when he didn't speak, she looked up and found he was studying her. Her heart gave a little leap and took off, and she flushed wildly.

Sam came around to the front of the desk and leaned back against it. His outstretched legs were so close to Elise's that she had to fight the urge to scoot her chair to the side. Crossing his arms over his chest, he tilted his head and regarded her, his pale eyes lazily intent beneath half-closed lids.

"So, tell me . . . how was your date with Keith?"

Elise's mouth dropped open. It wasn't at all what she had expected him to say. And how had he known? "I . . . uh . . . fine. Just fine. He's . . . he's a nice man."

"Yes," Sam agreed. "Though 'nice' is not a description many men like to have applied to them. However, I doubt that Keith would mind. And in his case, it's accurate."

Not knowing how to respond, she simply gazed at him. Was he angry? Amused? Just curious? What? It was impossible to tell. As usual, Sam's voice had not the slightest inflection, and his face could have been made of granite, for all the emotion it contained. Sadly, it occurred to Elise that he bore not the slightest resemblance to the laughing man she had seen at the Youth Center the previous weekend.

Several seconds ticked by, and finally Sam said, "And your blind date on Tuesday? How was that?"

"How did you—?"

"Erin told me. I assumed you were still staying with her, and I called there to tell you when I'd be back. When your sister answered the phone she told me you had a date. She seemed a bit upset that you were out with a man you'd never met." He raised one brow. "Another one of Colleen's friends?"

"No." Lifting her chin, she gave him a look of offended dignity. "As a matter of fact, he's a friend of Peggy's husband."

"I see." Sam studied her for a moment. "Then can I take it that this sudden flurry of dating means you're serious about resuming a social life?"

Elise blinked. "Well, I . . . uh . . . yes. I suppose you could say that."

"Good. Then after we've dealt with a few urgent items of business that I brought back with me, you and I can have dinner."

Elise was so flabbergasted she just sat there with her mouth open and stared as Sam rose and walked around his desk.

He glanced at his watch and reached for the telephone. "I'll make reservations at Henri's for eight. That should give us plenty of time to finish up here." Holding the receiver against his chest, he checked the small private directory on his desk and began punching out numbers.

The action snapped Elise out of her trance. "No! Wait! Sam, I can't have dinner with you!"

"Of course you can. When you were Max's secretary and the two of you worked late, he always took you out to dinner afterward. You didn't object then, so there's no reason to now."

"But you don't understand. It's not that." He punched the last two digits, and her voice rose in desperation. "Sam, I have a date tonight!"

His head snapped up. The beautiful, pale eyes impaled her, and she swallowed hard, returning the sharp look helplessly. "With . . . with Keith," she added lamely.

"I see." Sam replaced the receiver. Keeping his hand on it, he remained motionless, his intent gaze still holding her captive. "And tomorrow night?"

The softly voiced question made her heart skip a beat. Until that moment she hadn't been certain whether he was asking her out on a date, or merely suggesting a thank-you dinner for working late, as Max had been wont to do. Now there wasn't the least doubt.

"Well, uh . . . you see, there's this party at Margo's. . . ."

"I get the picture."

Sam sat down, snapped open his briefcase and withdrew some papers. "Very well then, let's get to work so you can get out of here. There are the letters that I want to go out today. I drafted them on the plane to save time, but I think they're legible. When you've finished them, you may go. The rest can wait until Monday."

It was a dismissal, and without a word Elise rose and took the papers. Back in her own office she sank down into her chair, shaken to the core.

A confusing turmoil of emotions gripped her, creating an aching tightness in her chest. She had been right to refuse him. Instinct, logic and common sense told her it was the only sensible thing to do. Unlike her twin, she wasn't the type to go rushing into dangerous situations or relationships, no matter how tempting they might be.

But she had been tempted by Sam's invitation, and that unsettled her. It was insane, she told herself. She wasn't interested in Sam.

All right. All right. She had to concede that Margo and the others were right; he *was* sexy. And attractive in a hard, forbidding way. She wasn't sure if it was animal magnetism or just woman's basic weakness for the mysterious, brooding male. Or both. Whatever, she had to admit, she wasn't immune to it.

But still, Sam made her nervous. When she was around him, she felt vulnerable. Threatened. Besides, he wasn't even her type. He was too controlled. Too cold and remote.

But is he? Really? her conscience prodded. *Or is the real Sam Lawford the man you saw last Saturday?*

The instant the thought formed, Elise pushed it away. The idea that behind Sam's cold mask lived a compassionate, caring man wasn't at all comforting. If anything, the possibility made her even more uneasy. An emotionless, unfeeling Sam she could ignore. But a kind, sensitive man— particularly one who'd been hurt . . .

Darn it! I don't need that kind of complication in my life, she told herself angrily as she accessed the word processing program on the computer. Her fingers flew over the keyboard while her mind silently railed against fate and wayward emotions.

Keith was perfect for her, just exactly as he was. And if that didn't work out, there was always the possibility that she would meet someone at Margo's party. Or on the skiing weekend they had planned.

Sam spelled trouble and heartache. She could feel it in her bones. A woman could spend a lifetime trying to get past those defenses, and still not succeed. To even try, she would have to be very brave or very foolish. *Or love him very much.*

The tightness in Elise's chest increased and her hands began to tremble. Well, she assured herself shakily as she corrected an error on the screen, none of those applied to her.

Chapter Eight

Over the next few weeks, the more Elise told herself that Sam meant nothing to her, the more preoccupied with him she became.

He was an enigma. Existing side by side in her mind were two disparate images of him that disturbed and intrigued her constantly. Which was the real man?

She watched him for a clue, but Sam was just as brisk and businesslike, and just as remote, as ever.

Still, Elise couldn't dismiss the memory of silver eyes crinkling merrily and teeth flashing white in a face alight with enthusiasm, a face transformed into handsomeness by warm, rich, unrestrained laughter.

Every time Sam spoke to her or dictated a letter in that steel-edged monotone, she could not help but recall the teasing and affection that had colored his voice as he had chided the boys at basketball practice.

And it took only the sight of him doing some small insignificant thing, like dialing the telephone, or straightening his

tie, to trigger images so clear and poignant she had to blink
back tears—those big hands sliding up a narrow little back,
lovingly cradling a child's head, ruffling a teenager's hair.
With no effort at all, she could recall the way they'd cupped
her brow while she'd been sick, their tender massage of her
shoulders, the touch of his callused palm against her cheek,
the gossamer brush of his thumb across her lashes.

They were not the actions of a cold man. Elise tried to
pretend otherwise, but deep down she knew better. The
more she began to suspect that Erin and Max might be right
about Sam, the more uneasy she became.

Her evening with Keith and the party arranged by her
friends was followed the next weekend by a ski trip to Vail
with Tracy, Colleen and Margo. After that came a flurry of
dating that left her exhausted and feeling vaguely depressed, though she wouldn't admit it.

The first party had been a disappointment, but she
doggedly attended several more, tagging along with either
Margo or Colleen, sometimes both. It was not at all the sort
of thing that Elise enjoyed, but nevertheless, with her usual
gentle tenacity, she gritted her teeth and made a determined
effort to fit in. She circulated, smiled, laughed at tired jokes,
fended off passes and danced until she could barely stand.
In the beginning she approached each party with a sort of
gritty eagerness, but after attending six in four weeks, both
her determination and optimism had begun to fade.

What am I doing here? Elise wondered when she found
herself cornered by yet another tiresome would-be Don
Juan. She smiled vaguely, took a sip of ginger ale and pretended to listen to his smarmy flattery, but as her mind began to wander, her gaze drifted over his shoulder.

Her senses were assaulted by the shifting montage of
sights and sounds and scents around her. Over the blare of
rock music, countless voices blended together in a dull roar,
punctuated by occasional bursts of laughter. Glasses
clinked, people shouted. The spacious contemporary house

SILHOUETTE GIVES YOU SIX REASONS TO CELEBRATE!

MAIL THE BALLOON TODAY!

INCLUDING:

1.
4 FREE BOOKS

2.
AN ELEGANT PEN AND WATCH SET

3.
A SURPRISE BONUS

AND MORE!

TAKE A LOOK...

Yes, become a Silhouette subscriber and the celebration goes on forever.

To begin with we'll send you:

4 new Silhouette Special Edition novels—FREE

an elegant matching pen and watch set—FREE

an exciting mystery bonus—FREE

And that's not all! Special extras— Three more reasons to celebrate.

4. Free Home Delivery. That's right! When you subscribe to Silhouette Special Edition, the excitement, romance and faraway adventures of these novels can be yours for previewing in the convenience of your own home. Here's how it works. Every month, we'll deliver six new books right to your door. If you decide to keep them, they'll be yours for only $2.49 each! That's 26¢ less per book than what you pay in stores. And there's **no charge for shipping and handling.**

5. Free Monthly Newsletter. It's the indispensable insiders' look at our most popular writers and their upcoming novels. Now you can have a behind-the-scenes look at the fascinating world of Silhouette! It's an added bonus you'll look forward to every month!

6. More Surprise Gifts. Because our home subscribers are our most valued readers, we'll be sending you additional free gifts from time to time—as a token of our appreciation.

You'll love your new LCD quartz digital watch with its genuine leather strap. And the slim matching pen is perfect for writing to that special person. They're yours free in this amazing Silhouette celebration!

SILHOUETTE SPECIAL EDITION®
FREE OFFER CARD

4 FREE BOOKS

ELEGANT PEN AND WATCH SET—FREE

FREE MYSTERY BONUS

PLACE YOUR BALLOON STICKER HERE!

FREE HOME DELIVERY

FREE FACT-FILLED NEWSLETTER

MORE SURPRISE GIFTS THROUGHOUT THE YEAR—FREE

Yes! Please send me four Silhouette Special Edition novels **FREE**, along with my pen and watch set and my free mystery gift as explained on the opposite page.   235 CIS R1XC

NAME
_____
(PLEASE PRINT)

ADDRESS _____ APT _____

CITY _____ STATE _____

ZIP _____

Terms and prices subject to change.
Your enrollment is subject to acceptance
by Silhouette Books.

SILHOUETTE "NO RISK GUARANTEE"
- There's no obligation to buy—the free books and gifts remain yours to keep.
- You receive books before they're available in stores.
- You may end your subscription anytime—just let us know.

PRINTED IN U.S.A.

Remember! To receive your four free books, pen and watch set and a surprise mystery bonus, return the postpaid card below. But don't delay.

DETACH AND MAIL CARD TODAY
If offer card has been removed, write to: Silhouette Books
901 Fuhrmann Blvd, P.O. Box 1867, Buffalo, N.Y. 14269-1867

FILL OUT THIS POSTPAID CARD AND MAIL TODAY!

Postage will be paid by addressee

BUSINESS REPLY CARD
FIRST CLASS   PERMIT NO. 717   BUFFALO, N.Y.

SILHOUETTE BOOKS®
901 Fuhrmann Blvd.,
P.O. Box 1867
Buffalo, N.Y. 14240-9952

NO POSTAGE
NECESSARY
IF MAILED
IN THE
UNITED STATES

was a moving mass of people and color—women showed great expanses of skin, draped in satins and silks of every imaginable hue, while men in their dark evening wear provided a dramatic foil for the bright plumage. The air was heavy with the mingled scents of tobacco, whiskey and a dozen different perfumes. Overhead, a miasmic blue cloud of cigarette smoke clung to the ceiling. One end of the living room had been cleared of furniture, and the floor was packed with people gyrating to the sounds pouring from the stereo speakers. Even the wall against which Elise was leaning vibrated with the pounding beat.

The parties were beginning to seem the same, she realized with a dispirited sigh as she surveyed the restless scene. All of them blurred together in her mind—noisy, frenetic affairs crowded with people working hard at convincing themselves and everyone else that they were having a good time. The music was loud, the food uninspired, the atmosphere artificial and, more often than not, the conversation ranged from vapid to subtly vicious.

It all seemed pointless, especially since most of the men she'd met at these things were either wimps, outrageous flirts or phonies. And at each one, she kept seeing the same faces over and over. One of them was Sam's.

Her gaze went to where he was standing on the other side of the room, talking with two other men. The first time he had shown up had been at Margo's party, and Elise remembered sheepishly how shaken and upset she'd been.

When he had walked in, she'd clutched her friend's arm in a death grip and wailed, "Oh, my Lord, Margo! I can't believe you invited Sam."

"Don't blame me. You're the one who told him about the party. When I went to the office this morning to go over some contracts with him, he mentioned it. What else could I do but invite him?" Margo shrugged her shoulders. "Besides, he *is* an eligible bachelor."

Elise had been a bit mollified by the explanation, but Sam's presence had ruined the party for her. At least, she'd thought so at the time, but she realized now that had been more her fault than his. Several times she'd caught him watching her, and he'd been one of the last to leave, but aside from a brief hello, he had stayed away from her.

It was the same at the other parties where he'd shown up. Privately, Margo teased her that he was watching to see if she left with anyone, but Elise didn't think so. Sam had not asked her out again or acted in any way interested since the day he returned from Seattle.

It had surprised her when he turned up at the other parties, until Margo explained that most of the people she and Colleen knew socially they had met through the company. It was logical that Sam would move in the same circles, though she hadn't thought he was the type to enjoy gatherings of this sort.

She certainly didn't.

And if I don't escape this one soon I'm going to go stark raving mad, Elise thought when Mark What's-his-name ran his finger over her bare shoulder and leaned forward to whisper in her ear. The music was so loud she didn't catch everything, but it was something about a water bed and a vibrator that sounded downright obscene.

He straightened and fixed her with a practiced, droopy-eyed look that she assumed was meant to be sexy. With a sweet smile, Elise removed his hand from her shoulder and dropped it as though it were something foul. Then, in dulcet tones, she said, "No, thank you. I'd rather be infected with a bad case of mange."

While he was still staring at her, thunderstruck, she ducked under his arm and strolled away.

Working her way through the crowd, Elise craned her neck for some sign of Colleen or Margo, while from all sides came snatches of conversation.

"Did you *see* that ghastly dress? My dear, it was—"

"—well, according to Babs, he's—"

"—a face-lift. Simply dreadful job—"

"Poor thing. Doesn't she know pink isn't her color?"

"—real hot little number. Frank says she—"

"—bad Karma—"

"—an affair with Roxanne. His wife hasn't a clue—"

Elise was weaving her way past a group discussing the latest fad diet when, through the inane babble, she heard someone call her name.

"Elise! Just the person I was looking for." A short blond man grabbed her arm and tugged her into the clutch of people surrounding him. "Tell me, love, would you like to join a witches' coven? Sensitive redheads are supposed to possess very strong supernatural powers, according to my spiritual leader."

"Uh . . . no. No, I don't think so." Elise disengaged her arm and backed away, striving to keep her wooden smile in place. *Crazies*, she thought, shaking her head as she made good her escape. *I'm surrounded by crazies and jerks.*

If only things had worked out with Keith, she bemoaned for what must have been the thousandth time. She'd had such high hopes. Even after their second date, she'd still been confident, telling herself that the reason his kisses hadn't stirred her was that she'd been upset over the encounter with Sam. That was all. But when they'd gone out again the result had been the same; Keith's kiss was pleasant, but it wasn't shattering. Nor did it make her heart pound and her blood race through her body until she thought she'd surely melt from the pleasure of it. Not the way Sam's did.

She'd tried. She'd tried desperately to respond, winding her arms around his neck and kissing him back with fierce urgency. But that had only made things worse. She would never forget Keith's face when he had broken off their last embrace and drawn back to look at her, his blue eyes full of regret. "It's just not there, is it?" he'd said sadly. "At least, not for you."

"Keith, I'm so—"

"No, don't apologize. It's no one's fault." He squeezed her hands, and his mouth twisted in a lopsided smile that held regret and resignation. "Chemistry is a strange, unpredictable thing. It's either there or it's not, and there's nothing any of us can do about it."

It was the truth, but she found it no more comforting now than she had then. It wasn't fair, she thought as she spotted Colleen's blond head. Why should the earth move when Sam kissed her, when Keith, who was absolutely perfect for her in every way, aroused nothing more than a pleasant warmth?

"Ah, there you are," Colleen greeted her. She and Margo murmured a quick excuse to the man they'd been talking with and took Elise aside. "So how's it going?"

"It isn't. There aren't any new faces, and frankly, there isn't a man here I'd have."

"Not even Sam?" Margo questioned slyly.

Elise's reply was a quelling look.

"She's right," Colleen agreed, gazing around. "This is a waste of time. I think we've exhausted the party circuit."

"So what do we do now? We've introduced her to every halfway acceptable male we know. On the skiing weekend all we got were propositions. She didn't click with the minister. What's left?"

Colleen glanced at her watch. "Well, it's early yet. Why don't we leave here and hit a singles' bar or two?"

"A singles' bar! Oh, I don't know," Margo protested. "I don't think Elise is quite ready for that scene."

"Well, we've exhausted all our other possibilities. Unless you can come up with something better, this is it. We're scraping the bottom of the barrel here."

"You can say that again," Margo muttered.

"C'mon, singles' bars aren't that bad. There are a lot of eligible men out there. You just have to know where to look and how to size them up." Colleen blew a stream of smoke at the ceiling and raised an eyebrow at Elise. "Well? How about it? Are you game?"

Far from it. Elise found the idea revolting. It was one thing to have your friends introduce you to men they knew. It was quite another to perch yourself on a bar stool and let some stranger, who only wanted a quick roll in the hay, look you over. It smacked too much of the auction block for Elise's taste.

Still, her friends had rallied around her and done everything in their power to help her achieve her goal. She wasn't going to be an ingrate and refuse Colleen's suggestion because of puritanical scruples. Taking a bracing breath, Elise nodded. "Sure. Why not?"

Scraping the bottom of the barrel was not an exaggeration. If anything, Elise decided, scanning the patrons in the dimly lit bar, the description was a bit generous.

The Old Bailey was packed with the usual Saturday night crowd. Elise supposed, as singles' bars went, it wasn't all that bad. At least the decor wasn't sleazy. The massive dark beams that spanned the room were reflected in the gilt-framed mirror behind the gleaming mahogany bar, both of which were at least forty feet in length. Watered-silk wallpaper, polished wainscoting, plush leather chairs and restrained prints of the English countryside gave the place a look of understated British elegance that lent an air of respectability. Clearly, it was a meeting ground for sophisticated, upwardly mobile types.

But for all that, the music was just as insistent, the talk just as superficial, the air of gaiety just as false as Elise had expected.

Within five minutes Colleen had made eye contact with a man at the other end of the bar and they were now sharing a table. Seated on the stool next to Elise, Margo was talking to the man on her other side. Elise glanced at her watch and wondered how soon she could politely make an excuse to leave. They had come together in Margo's car, but if she had to she could always take a taxi home.

A man stepped up to the bar beside Elise and ordered a drink. When he reached to pick it up, his chest brushed her arm, and Elise leaned aside.

"Hello," he said, pausing to look her over. His gaze lit with interest as it ran over her slender curves in the figure-hugging emerald-green dress. "Well, well," he commented aloud as he took in her face, feature by feature, and the glowing red hair that surrounded it. Elise squirmed and looked at him with cool disdain, but the effect was spoiled when her creamy complexion betrayed her embarrassment. "Very nice, indeed," the man added, as he noted the becoming rosy tint in her cheeks.

It annoyed Elise that he was looking her over as though she were a piece of merchandise he was thinking of buying, but she couldn't really blame him. She was there, after all. Plus, she'd seen the look of quiet desperation and hope on the faces of the other women seated along the bar and knew that for the price of a drink and a show of interest he could have his pick of any of them. Probably for the night.

"How about I buy you a drink?" he said with lazy confidence.

"No, thanks. I already have one."

He glanced at the full glass of ginger ale in front of her. "Fine. Why don't you bring it with you and we'll go sit at that table in the corner? We can get acquainted. By the way, I'm a doctor," he said, tossing out the information as though he was sure that once she heard it she'd fall all over herself to join him.

"No, thank you. I'm, uh . . . I'm waiting for someone."

He looked surprised for a second, then indifferent. "Too bad." Shrugging, he turned away and wove his way through the crowd.

In the mirror behind the bar, Elise watched him pause at a table where three young women sat alone. His measuring glance was met and returned boldly as all three looked him over with blatant interest. He said something that made their faces light up, and Elise looked away, her stomach twisting with disgust. It looked as though the good doctor would have his choice of companions tonight.

Trying her best to block out the din of music and voices, Elise took a sip of ginger ale, then fiddled with the soggy paper coaster beneath the glass. She peeked at her watch again and groaned when she saw that only ten minutes had passed. At the other end of the bar a trill of feminine laughter rose above the muted roar, and the sound grated on her exacerbated nerves like fingernails scraping down a chalkboard. *To heck with this. I'm getting out of here.*

She turned to Margo, but before she could tap her friend on the shoulder a hand encircled her arm. Startled, Elise looked around and found herself staring into a smoothly handsome face, just inches from her own.

"Hello, gorgeous. My name is Jim. What's yours?" Crowding in between her and the woman on the next bar stool, he stood with an elbow braced against the bar, leaning over her, a cocky, seductive smile curving his mouth as he took inventory of her assets.

He was so close his breath struck her face, creating a cloud of whiskey fumes that nearly choked her. Elise reared back until her shoulder almost touched Margo's. Warily she took in the styled blond hair, the suave smile, perfectly even teeth and blue eyes that glittered with cool calculation. A little shudder of revulsion rippled through her.

"I'm sorry. I was just about to leave." Draping her coat over her arm, she clutched her purse and slid off the stool.

The hand around her forearm tightened. "What's your rush? Stick around, sweetheart. I promise you won't be disappointed."

"No, I—"

A sharp jerk on her forearm brought her stumbling against the stool she had just vacated. They stared at each other, Elise's eyes wide and stunned, his narrowed now in a feral glare, all trace of charm gone from his face. "I've been watching you, lady. You're nothing but a little tease. But don't think you can fluff me off like you did that other poor slob. You came in here all hot to trot, looking for some action. Well, now you've found it."

"Look, I told you, I'm leaving."

"What's the matter? You think you're too good for me? Is that it?"

"Let go of me!" Elise tried to wrench her arm free, then cried out in pain when he twisted it viciously.

"What's going on here?" Margo demanded from behind her.

"Butt out, lady," the blond man snarled. "This is none of your business." His gaze sliced back to Elise, and he stepped away from the bar, giving her arm another brutal jerk. "C'mon. You want to leave? Fine. My place is just a few blocks from here."

"No! Stop it!" Elise clawed at the hand that circled her arm like a manacle. "Stop it!"

"Now, wait just a minute, you jerk." Margo slid off the bar stool as he started dragging Elise away, but before she could enter the fray another man stepped in front of him, blocking his path.

"Let her go."

"Sam." His name came out a breathy whisper of mingled surprise and relief as Elise stared at him, her eyes wide.

The blond man bristled. "Get outta the way."

"You've got two seconds to release her," Sam said in the same quiet voice.

"And if I don't?"

"Then I break both your arms."

Elise gasped. Before she had been angry and embarrassed, but not really frightened. Her tormentor would have had to drag her out kicking and screaming, and she knew her friends would never have allowed that to happen. But the matter-of-factness of Sam's threat chilled her to the bone. He meant it. She could hear it in his tone, see it in his icy gaze.

The other man could, too.

He appraised Sam through narrowed eyes. They were approximately the same height and build, both tall and muscular, but the lethal menace in Sam's tone and expression was unmistakable, and gradually the blond man's belligerent scowl dissolved.

He dropped Elise's arm, and instantly Sam reached out and drew her to his side. Holding his hands up, palms out, the man backed away. "All right. All right. You want her that bad, take her. Makes no difference to me. There's plenty more broads to choose from," he said with a touch of bravado as he turned and disappeared into the crowd.

"Thanks, Sam," Margo said. "Boy, was it ever a lucky thing for us you stopped in here when you did."

"I'm taking Elise home," he announced, ignoring her comment. "You and Colleen can do as you please, but in the future, don't let me hear of you taking her to any more places like this."

"Yes, boss," Margo said meekly.

"Sam!"

Ignoring Elise's scandalized exclamation and the sputtered protests that followed, Sam bundled her out into the crisp February night and all but stuffed her into his car.

Confused and shaken, she huddled in the plush leather seat of the Cadillac and stared straight ahead as Sam went around to the driver's side and got in.

He slammed the door so hard she jumped. "Buckle your seat belt," he ordered without even glancing at her, making her jump again. As she complied, he rammed the key into the ignition, gave it a vicious twist and sent the big car roaring out of the parking lot at a speed that made her heart leap right up into her throat.

Elise peeked at him and her breath caught. Sam was furious. Cold, unemotional, remote Sam was about to explode with rage. Elise jerked her gaze to the front and swallowed hard as her pounding heart took off.

It didn't seem possible. Unable to resist, she turned her head slightly and looked at him again out of the corner of her eye, and knew she hadn't been mistaken. Sam's hands were gripping the steering wheel so tightly his knuckles were white. His jaw was clenched, and a muscle jumped in his cheek. In the dim glow from the dashboard his face looked as though it were carved of stone.

"You followed us, didn't you?" she finally dared.

For a moment she thought he wasn't going to answer but then breathed a sigh when, in a voice much closer to his normal controlled tone, he said, "Not intentionally. I left the party right after you three and was heading home. I happened to be passing that joint just as you were walking in." He shot her a hard glance. "I couldn't believe my eyes."

"It's not a joint. It's a perfectly respectable place." Even though she had hated it and agreed with him wholly, she felt compelled to defend her actions.

"It's a flesh market," he contradicted bluntly. "Anyway, I didn't like the idea of you being in there, so I wheeled around and came back."

"I can take care of myself."

"Yeah, it looked like it."

Elise rolled her eyes and made an aggravated sound. "Not you, too! *Why* does everyone insist on treating me as though I were a glass figurine?"

"Let's drop it, okay? At least until we get to your apartment. Then I've got some questions of my own I want answered."

Elise shot him a wary look. She didn't like the sound of that. They were silent for the remainder of the ride.

With a hand planted firmly in the small of her back, Sam led her through the courtyard of her apartment complex straight to her door, and it hit her that he'd driven there without once asking for directions. She hadn't realized he even knew where she lived. That he'd obviously taken the trouble to find out puzzled her and brought a queer sensation to the pit of her stomach. She meant to ask him about it, but the moment they stepped into her apartment Sam went on the attack.

"Would you mind telling me what the devil you think you're doing, going to a place like that?"

Elise dropped her coat and purse into a chair and faced him. This time there was a hard edge to the carefully controlled tone that betrayed his agitation. A part of her was glad to see a crack in that icy reserve of his, but another part of her, the cautious part, was leery of the change. "You're acting like I committed a crime. It's not a dive, you know. And besides, I went with two other women."

"Why go at all?"

"For the same reason other people go—to meet someone."

"Why?" he probed relentlessly, watching her. "You can't be that desperate or lonely. Practically every night for the past month you've rushed home from the office to get ready for a date."

"Sam, I don't think—"

"Why, Elise?"

Rattled, and feeling as though she were being backed into a corner, she lashed back. "Because I want to remarry, darn it! Can't you understand that? I want a husband! A home, and a family. And I'm not getting any younger."

The instant the last word left her Elise realized what she'd blurted out and clamped her hand over her mouth, closing her eyes with a little distressed moan, humiliated beyond bearing. At that moment she could have gladly cut out her tongue. Sam was the last person she had wanted to know of her quest.

"A husband?" She opened her eyes and saw that he was staring at her. With an ironic lift of his brows he shook his head. "Didn't it occur to you that a singles' bar isn't the best place to meet potential marriage material?"

"Of course it did," she admitted dejectedly. Grimacing, she folded her arms over her rib cage and studied the floor. "But none of the other men I've met recently were right, that's all. And I'd run out of places to look." Hectic color burned in her cheeks, but she was beyond caring.

In the silence that followed, all Elise could hear was the distant measured plop-plop of the dripping kitchen faucet and her own slow, painful breathing. Sam remained perfectly still, and she could feel his eyes on her.

"I see. So, that's what this has all been about these past couple of months," he said in a low, thoughtful voice. "All those dates. The round of parties. Your little foray tonight into the sleazy side of single life. It was all to find a husband."

"Yes," she mumbled in a dispirited little voice.

"Well, if finding a husband is your problem, you didn't have to go to that much trouble. There's an easy solution."

Elise looked up at that. "What?"

"Simple. You can marry me."

Chapter Nine

Elise stared at him. "You . . . you can't be serious."

"Why not?"

"But . . . you don't want to get married."

"What do you know about what I want?" Sam asked in that soft, unnerving voice, his steady silver gaze impaling her.

"I . . ." Elise drew in several deep breaths in an attempt to slow her thudding heart. The first time Sam had offered to marry her she had thought that it was a flippant joke, that he'd been making fun of her. Now she had the uneasy feeling she had been mistaken. "But . . . why? Why me?"

Sam shrugged. "Because, with one exception, I want the same things you want: a home, someone with whom I can share my life, a stable relationship."

"But there are any number of women who can give you that. Several who work for Global, in fact."

"Ah, but you have something they don't." He stepped close and touched her cheek with his fingertips, and Elise shivered as a tingle rippled over her skin. He studied her dispassionately, his pale eyes revealing not a flicker of feeling. "You have this incredible warmth and sweetness about you, Elise. A gentleness that makes you special." His fingers trailed down her jaw. His thumb brushed the corner of her mouth. "I want that."

His touch, the heat and intensity in his voice, so at odds with his impassive expression, caused her stomach muscles to tighten. Mesmerized, Elise could only gaze at him while her breathing grew shallow and her heart fluttered against her ribs like a captured bird.

"But...but...what about love?"

"What about it?"

"Do you...that is..." Floundering, Elise made a helpless gesture with her hand. She hated asking, but she had to know. "Can you give me...love?"

"I can give you kindness and care. Respect." He stroked a silky curl at her temple and watched it twine about his finger. "And passion," he added in the softest of whispers.

She searched his face, her eyes touched with sadness. "But...don't you want to love and be loved?" she asked in a small, bewildered voice.

"No."

A flat statement. No explanation, no attempt to soften his reply, and Elise knew from his expression that the subject was not open for discussion.

Strangely, the knowledge that he didn't expect or want her love hurt, much more than she could have imagined possible. She stared at him, confused, not knowing what to say.

"Before you decide, though, there is one other thing I think I should make clear." Sam hesitated and frowned, as though unsure how she would take what he was about to say. His hand dropped from her face and he turned away and walked to the window. With his back to her, he twitched aside the draperies and stared out at the dimly lit courtyard. "I can give you what you say you want, except for one thing. If you marry me there will be no children."

Several seconds ticked by as Elise absorbed the statement. "You can't have children?" she whispered, her surprise evident.

"I can have them. I just don't want them."

He said it softly, with deliberate blandness, but Elise couldn't have been more shocked had he snarled the words.

It didn't make any sense. Sam loved children. And they loved him. She had known since the day she'd first seen him with the kids at the Youth Center that he'd make a wonderful father. Over the past month, while working in the nursery there on Saturday mornings, she'd been unable to resist peeking into the gym during basketball practice, and she'd seen the camaraderie and affection between Sam and the boys. Several other times, when he hadn't known she was around, she'd observed him playing with the younger children, even the babies, and the rapport between them had been beautiful to watch. Something like that couldn't be faked.

Stunned, confused, Elise studied Sam's rigid back, the stiff, unyielding set of his shoulders...and suddenly she knew.

Sam was *afraid* to love.

He could give his affection to other people's children with impunity, but a child of his own would steal a piece of his heart, make him vulnerable to pain and possible loss.

As Elise looked at this stoic, remote man, her heart seemed to crack. An overwhelming rush of tenderness welled up inside her, filling her chest and making it ache. Her chin wobbled and her throat worked with emotion as she struggled against tears. *Oh, Sam. Sam.*

He had, however, given her a way out. Not that she needed an excuse, she told herself. She had a perfect right to refuse his insulting, businesslike proposal. But still, Sam's deliberate exclusion of love from his life, especially the joy that children could bring, saddened her deeply.

Intellectually, logically, she understood. She didn't think he was right, but she understood. A human could take just so much, and Sam had already endured devastating losses, suffered unimaginable pain. He was merely trying to protect himself against more of the same.

But whatever his reason for denying himself, Elise wanted children desperately. Even more, she wanted love.

You're an idiot, Lawford, Sam raged silently. *A damned fool. Why in hell did you have to tell her that?*

She's going to say no. Sam glanced at Elise over his shoulder, saw the play of emotions across her face, and felt as though he'd received a kick in the gut with a lead boot. *Well, what else did you expect? You offer the woman a loveless marriage, and then, to really sweeten the pot, you tell her she can forget about having a family.*

You ass. A woman like Elise is made for motherhood.

He stared out the window at the bare cottonwood tree, the drained fountain filled with dead leaves and winter debris, the piles of dirty slush that were all that remained of the last snowfall, and felt in tune with the desolate scene. *Why the devil didn't you just keep your mouth shut? Then you might have had a chance.*

But he couldn't do that to Elise. He might not be able to give her the love she deserved, but he could give her honesty. She had a right to know what she'd be getting into. What to expect and not expect.

God, he wanted her. He couldn't ever remember wanting a woman this badly. Sam clenched his jaw so hard the bones hurt. At times he wished to hell that Max had never hired Elise. Then he wouldn't be battling this unremitting hunger. It was worse torture than he'd endured in Nam. Hell, every time she looked at him with those soft doelike eyes he felt another turn of the rack.

Dammit, he'd been satisfied with his life before Elise came into it. If it had been a bit lonely, it had also been orderly, peaceful, and he'd felt in control.

If you had any sense at all, Lawford, you'd tell her to forget the whole thing. She deserves more, and you don't need this complication in your life. Sam sighed and flexed his tight jaw. Good advice. But what the hell. He knew he wasn't going to follow it.

"Sam—"

Dropping the drapery, Sam turned. They looked at each other in silence, Sam questioning, Elise immeasurably sad and doubtful. No, by damn, he wanted her! And as long as there was a chance, he was going to do everything in his power to have her. He crossed the room to stand before her once again.

Elise sighed. "Sam, I can't—"

"Don't give me an answer now," he insisted. "Think it over for a few days. And please . . . don't be hasty. Remember, Elise, I can give you almost everything you want."

Except children. And love. Though unspoken, the thought hung in the air between them, and they both knew it.

She started to speak, but he put two fingers over her mouth, stopping her. "No. Don't say anything. Just promise me that you'll think about it. That's all I ask."

Elise hesitated, her soft brown eyes wide and filled with misgiving, and Sam held his breath. Finally, after what seemed the longest moment of his life, she gave a reluctant sigh and nodded.

It was not a difficult promise to keep. Over the next week Elise couldn't think about anything else. The idea was a metronome in her mind, ticking away, insistently demanding her attention.

It was madness to even consider the proposal, she told herself. She couldn't marry a man who neither wanted nor needed love.

But he does need it, an inner voice whispered. *He's afraid of it, but Sam, probably more than anyone, needs love.*

Okay. Maybe that's true, she conceded. But I'm not the one to give it to him. I'm not in love with Sam.

Aren't you?

No. Of course not.

So why does his slightest touch affect you? Why do his kisses, his unexpected tenderness, make you weak in the knees?

That's physical attraction. Nothing more.

And this heaviness of heart? How do you explain that?

Compassion. I feel sorry for him, that's all. It's normal, under the circumstances—although I'm sure Sam doesn't want my pity any more than he wants my love.

So, what are you waiting for? If that's all you feel for the man, why don't you tell him no and get it over with?

But somehow, Elise just couldn't bring herself to do that. Neither could she condemn herself to a sterile life devoid of emotion, so her internal battle waged on and on for days.

She thought about it in the shower, driving her car, shopping for groceries. No matter how hard she tried to concentrate on other things, her mind kept wandering back to Sam.

On Friday, almost a week after Sam's bizarre proposal, Elise was sitting at her desk attempting to proofread a contract she had just typed when once again her thoughts drifted back to the situation.

She knew with a heartfelt surety that if she agreed to marry Sam, he would be good to her. He had demonstrated his capacity for tenderness many times, though she doubted he had meant to. Elise looked down, and with a strange little smile touched the dainty, diamond-encrusted watch on her arm. Sam was a generous man, and a thoughtful one, too, she admitted, remembering the care he'd given to the selection of each Christmas gift. He would be protective of her, and cherish her in his own way. And she would never want for anything.

Whenever she thought of the physical side of marriage, of sleeping in Sam's arms, making love with him, a little thrill shot through her, but she wasn't sure if it was excitement or fear. Sam still made her nervous. Understanding hadn't changed that.

Elise longed to seek the advice of another woman, especially her twin, but Erin and Max were in China and weren't due to return for three more weeks. She didn't dare confide in any of her friends. To start with, she knew what their advice would be, since they all thought Sam was the sexiest, most desirable male walking. Mainly, though, she was afraid of the story getting out. Margo and Colleen could probably be trusted, maybe even Tracy, but Peggy was such an incurable romantic she would burst if she couldn't tell someone.

It surprised Elise that Sam hadn't pushed her for an answer. After a sleepless night, she'd spent all day Sunday prowling her apartment in a tizzy of indecision, half expecting him to call or ring her doorbell at any moment, but he'd made no attempt to contact her.

On Monday, she'd returned to work, apprehensive and nervous as a cat, not knowing what to expect, but Sam was as crisply businesslike as ever. Not once had he mentioned, or even hinted at what had passed between them. From his actions no one would suspect that he had proposed marriage to her at all, and Elise found his attitude disconcerting. Even irritating.

She was beginning to wonder if he regretted having asked her to marry him. Depending on her mood of the moment, the thought produced either vast relief, or incensed her so she barely restrained herself from marching into his office and demanding to know if he'd changed his mind.

With a moan, Elise propped her elbows on the desk and cradled her head in her hands. This whole thing was driving her crazy. And heaven help her, she was no closer to a decision now than she had been five minutes after Sam had proposed.

The door to her office opened, and Elise jerked to attention, self-consciously fluffing her hair as she smiled at the woman who entered. She was a stunning creature, somewhere in her late thirties, tall and willowy, with long blond hair and the most vivid blue eyes Elise had ever seen.

"May I help you?"

The question had barely left her mouth when the telephone rang, and Elise smiled apologetically as she reached for it. "Elise Holman."

"Elise, this is Peggy. Some woman just walked in and asked to see Sam. She didn't have an appointment, and when I told her I'd check with you she said 'Never mind' and just walked right by me. I tried to stop her, but—"

Elise glanced up at the woman. She was standing in front of her desk, staring at her in a challenging, self-assured way that immediately put Elise's hackles up. "That's okay, Peggy." She returned the woman's look with one of calm authority. "I'll take care of it.

"May I help you?" she asked again in a decidedly cooler tone as she replaced the receiver.

"Yes. I want to see Sam Lawford."

"I'm afraid Mr. Lawford doesn't see anyone without an appointment."

"Oh, I think he'll make an exception in my case. Why don't you just check? The name is Sherry Phillips."

The woman's tone made Elise grind her teeth. "I'm sorry. Mr. Lawford is very busy at the moment."

"Not too busy to see me, I assure you." She shrugged elegantly. "If you don't call him, I'll simply wait here until he comes out."

It took Elise only a few seconds to decide. The woman annoyed her right to the marrow of her bones. She'd rather risk Sam's ire than have that haughty creature camping out in her office for what could be hours.

Sam answered the buzz of the intercom with a brusque, "Yes, what is it, Elise?"

"Sam, there's a Ms. Phillips here to see you. I explained that you were busy, but she's very insistent."

"Tell her I'm not— Wait a minute. Sherry Phillips?"

"Yes, that's right."

A taut silence followed. Then, very quietly, Sam said, "Send her in."

Standing beside the desk, Sherry Phillips had heard every word, and she gave Elise a smug smile when she released the intercom button.

"You may go in now," Elise said tightly. An uncharacteristic rage boiled within her as she watched the woman saunter past.

Elise stared at the closed door for a long time after the woman had disappeared behind it. Sherry Phillips. Where had she heard that name before?

The question nagged at her for the next hour, but no matter how hard she groped for the answer, it remained just out of reach, tantalizing her.

Elise tried to remain busy, but curiosity about the woman made it impossible for her to concentrate. Every few minutes, as though drawn by a magnet, her gaze went to her watch, then to the closed door. What was taking so long? Elise had a strong hunch that whatever business Sherry Phillips had with Sam was personal. The idea did nothing to ease her mind or put out the slow fire of anger that was burning hotter inside her with every passing minute.

When the door finally opened, Sam escorted Ms. Phillips out, bringing her to stand in front of Elise's desk. Elise ground her teeth at the self-satisfied expression on the blonde's face. Evidently she had gotten whatever it was she came for.

"Elise, I want you to take Sherry down to personnel and tell Colleen I said to find a position for her."

"Did you have anything specific in mind?" Elise asked, careful to mask her dismay.

"Whatever suits her skills. I'll leave it up to Colleen." He turned a questioning look on the woman. "Does that suit you, Sherry?"

"Whatever you say, Sam," she said softly, giving him a submissive look that reeked of adoration. "I really can't thank you enough."

Elise clenched her fists so hard her fingernails dug into her palms, but Sherry's flattering thanks didn't seem to have the least effect on Sam. He shrugged, told her to think nothing of it and returned to his office.

"Sam is such a wonderful man," Sherry gushed as Elise led her down the hall toward Colleen's office. "So...caring. Don't you agree?" She smiled and looked at Elise slyly.

"Yes. He is."

"We haven't seen each other in years, but I knew I could count on him to help me. You see, I'm newly divorced. My husband was very successful so I never had to work, but my lack of experience has made finding a job very difficult. At least, one that pays adequately."

"I can imagine." It was all Elise could do to be civil, but she couldn't quite keep the note of sarcasm out of her voice.

"Do you have any idea of what positions are open?"

"Colleen will probably put you in accounting. I believe one of the clerks is about to leave to have a baby."

"Oh. I was hoping for something in the executive wing." She cast a speculative, sidelong look at Elise. "I don't suppose you're going to be giving up your job anytime soon, are you?"

"I'm afraid not."

"Hmm. I didn't think so. Oh, well, it doesn't matter," she mused aloud, as though to herself, but Elise had the distinct impression she meant the words for her. "I'm here. And just knowing that I'm close by is bound to bring back memories for Sam. Eventually I'll get what I want."

Elise almost stumbled. Suddenly she felt as though an icy fist were squeezing her heart. Sherry Phillips! Of course! She'd heard that name weeks ago from her gossiping friends. This woman was Sam's former fiancée, the one who had dumped him for someone else all those years ago. And now, if she read the situation correctly, Ms. Phillips wanted him back.

It was a struggle, but Elise managed to keep her expression impassive long enough to carry out Sam's instructions. As she hurried back to her own office, however, she gave her raging emotions free rein.

The nerve of that woman! Did she think she could come waltzing in here and have Sam back, just like that? After what she'd done to him?

Not if Elise could help it! She wasn't about to let that woman sink her claws into Sam again. He had suffered enough!

Without stopping, Elise sailed through her own office and into Sam's, slowing just enough to give his door a tap before thrusting it open.

Sam looked up at her entrance, a flicker of surprise in his eyes as he watched her militant march across the room.

"Sam, do you still want to marry me?" she demanded when she came to a halt in front of his desk.

With slow deliberation, Sam laid his pen down and folded his hands together on top of the desk. "Yes."

"Very well, then." Elise drew a deep breath. "My answer is yes."

Sam didn't turn a hair. He just sat there, pinning her with his crystalline gaze while a nerve-racking ten seconds ticked by in silence. Elise grew uneasy and had to fight the urge to squirm, but she returned the look.

"Are you very sure?" he asked quietly, at last.

"Yes."

Her reply galvanized Sam into action. He came out of his chair with the suddenness of a released spring and rounded the desk in three long strides. He bent, pressed a swift, hard kiss on Elise's mouth, then, ignoring her startled expression, slipped an arm around her waist and urged her toward the door. "Come on, let's go."

"What? Sam!" Startled, Elise instinctively tried to hold back, but her feet seemed to work independently of her brain, because she found herself tripping along beside him.

Before she could gather her scattered senses they were in her office, where Sam paused only long enough to retrieve her purse and their coats.

"Wait a minute! I—"

"Here." He shoved the leather bag into her hand. "Okay, now put this on," he ordered, and bundled her into her heather plaid cape as he hustled her out and down the hallway.

"But . . . but Sam, where are we going?" Elise managed to stammer as she was swept along.

"To get married."

"*What?* Sam, we can't—"

"Sure we can."

At that moment they burst into the reception area at something just under a trot, and Peggy looked up, her face comically startled. Sam didn't even slow down.

"Elise and I are leaving, Peggy," he said over his shoulder, heading for the exit. "Cancel my afternoon appointments and reschedule them for Monday. If anyone asks, tell them I'm out of town."

"But . . . but . . . where can you be reached in case of an emergency?" the flustered girl called after them.

"At the MGM Grand in Las Vegas, but if anyone calls me there it damned well better be a life-or-death situation."

"Sa-aamm!" Elise wailed as he hurried her outside. "We can't rush off to Las Vegas and get married, just like that!"

They could, and they did.

By nine that evening Elise found herself staring with disbelief at a shiny new gold band encircling the third finger of her left hand. She stood in the middle of an impossibly luxurious bathroom, similar to the one she'd found herself in a few months before, and like then, Sam was waiting for her in the next room.

Only this time, he was her husband.

Elise closed her eyes and pressed her balled fist against her middle. Oh, Lord! What had she done?

The worst of her anger with Sherry Phillips had worn off hours ago, and now she was amazed that she could have reacted so rashly. Erin was the impulsive one, not her. She had always planned her life carefully, plotted a course and held to it, and at no time had marriage to Sam been a part of that plan.

Slowly, her gaze lifted to her reflection in the bathroom mirror, and her jittery nerves received another jolt that made her heart thud. With an unsteady hand, she touched the shiny bodice of the ivory satin nightgown.

Sam had chosen it himself. It had surprised her that he'd come into the exclusive little dress shop with her at all, but she'd been amazed, and burning with embarrassment, when, while she was selecting a dress for the wedding, he had calmly flipped through the rack of scandalously expensive, sexy nightwear.

She would have preferred something more modest but she'd been so relieved that he hadn't picked a wispy, transparent gown that she had accepted it without a word. Now she could see she'd made a mistake.

Though the garment was opaque it was shockingly revealing, clinging to every curve and dip of her body like a lover's caress. Her nipples thrust against the soft fabric, creating two button-hard nubs in the glossy surface, and a tiny crater marked the indentation of her navel. The rounded upper curves of her breasts swelled above the plunging neckline like ripe fruit, and against the ivory satin, her pale skin glowed with a delicate peach tint.

Elise stared at her reflection and wondered how she could possibly walk out there and face Sam wearing the slinky garment. Not that she had ever really had any other choice. Today she had discovered that when Sam's mind was set on something he was like a steamroller. He'd met all her protests head-on, crushing them without even slowing down.

Her frantic cry that they couldn't just fly off to Las Vegas and get married had been met with a blunt, "Why not? Max and Erin did."

"But…we were there with them," she'd exclaimed as he assisted her into the car. She had watched him walk around to the driver's side, her eyes wide with something near panic. The instant he climbed in behind the wheel she'd taken up her plea again. "Sam, I-I want Erin to be at my wedding, too. And I would think you'd want Max to be your best man."

"If they were here, yes. But I'm not waiting three weeks to a month for them to get back."

As Sam headed the big car down the mountain road Elise had tried every argument, but by the time they reached the bottom she had accepted defeat. Even so, she had expected him to take her home so that she could pack a bag. When he had turned toward Albuquerque and the airport, she had been stunned, and had insisted that she couldn't fly to Las Vegas without even a change of clothes.

The afternoon shopping spree had been the result. Elise shivered as she recalled how, for a long, heart-stopping moment he had stared at her with a feverish intensity that had plainly told her he didn't expect either of them would have any need for clothes. Then he had informed her that they would purchase whatever they needed in Las Vegas.

A sound from the other side of the door made her jump. Elise stared at it, her mouth so dry her tongue cleaved to the roof of her mouth. She knew she was behaving foolishly. She hadn't been this nervous when she'd married Tommy, and she'd been a virgin then.

It's time to quit this silly dithering, she told herself, squaring her shoulders. She'd made her choice, and in all honesty, she wouldn't change it even if she could. Sam was too fine a man to allow him to become entangled in Sherry Phillips's web.

She reached for the door, then hesitated, tempted for an instant to put on one of the terry-cloth robes the hotel provided, but dismissed the idea as cowardly. Drawing a deep, fortifying breath, Elise opened the door and stepped into the bedroom.

Her feet were bare, but she must have made a slight sound, for Sam turned from the window. Something hot and urgent flared in his eyes when he saw her, and the mask of indifference slipped from his face as it tightened with desire. Slowly, taking in every inch of her, his gaze ran from the top of her fiery hair to the small bare toes peeking from beneath the hem of the satin nightgown. Elise's courage faltered under that intent look, and only a few feet into the room she came to a halt.

Without taking his eyes from her, Sam crossed the room with slow, measured steps. Somehow, Elise found the controlled, sinuous grace of his movements both threatening and almost unbearably exciting. As he drew near she waited with her heart booming, her insides aquiver.

He had removed his suit coat and tie and unbuttoned his shirt, but the casual image merely heightened the impact of his maleness. Sam halted in front of Elise, and her nostrils flared as his scent drifted to her, dark and heady.

His searing gaze lifted from the womanly roundness of her hips to linger on her breasts and the pebble-hard nubs pushing against the satin gown. Then he stared at the spot where the shiny cloth fluttered rhythmically, betraying the wild beating of her heart.

"You're beautiful." His voice was a rough whisper. When his eyes lifted to her face, they burned like silver fire. He stroked the side of her neck with his fingertips, and Elise thought her knees would give way beneath her as the gossamer touch trailed fire over her skin. She thought he would take her in his arms then, but he merely looked at her for a long tense moment, then stepped around her with a murmured, "I'll just be a minute."

Except for the trembling that shook her, Elise didn't move until the sound of the shower penetrated. Realizing that if she didn't want Sam to think she'd taken root she'd better stir herself, she took a step toward the bed, then pulled up short. While she had been in the bathroom, Sam had removed the spread and turned the covers down, but somehow she couldn't bring herself to simply climb into bed and wait for him.

Elise swung around, her gaze darting about for an alternative. Spotting her purse, she dashed to the dresser and withdrew her hairbrush.

When Sam emerged from the bathroom she was sitting at the dressing table, using the age-old method of slow, repetitive brushing to calm her frazzled nerves.

Whatever small success she'd had was nullified when she turned her head and saw Sam walking toward her, wearing nothing but a towel tied low about his hips.

Elise stared. She couldn't help herself. Sam was beautiful.

She had seen him before in just his briefs, but at the time she'd been too sick and upset to appreciate the sinewy strength in that big, rangy body. And in any case, she'd tried to put that embarrassing episode out of her mind.

Now she could not have looked away had her life depended on it. Sam's legs were long and well-shaped, corded with muscles and dusted with hair. Broad shoulders and a powerful chest tapered to a narrow waist and lean hips. Above the towel, his navel was a shadowy cavity amid the whorl of black hair that arrowed downward from the thatch on his chest. In that glossy mat, Elise saw the glint of silver, and her breasts swelled and tingled as she recalled the feel of that warm disk against her flesh.

Sam came to a stop behind her, and in the mirror their eyes met and held. His big hands closed over her shoulders and caressed the taut muscles there. Then one slid up the side of her neck and his spread fingers sifted through the bright curls. "I've always loved your hair," he whispered, watching it cling and twine about his hand. "It almost seems alive."

All across her bare back and shoulders Elise could feel his heat, and a tremor started deep inside her. "I . . . I've always wished it weren't so red," she said inanely.

"No, it's beautiful. Like a dancing flame." The words flowed from him, soft and evocative, as the pads of his fingers glided over her scalp, sending a delicious tingle racing down her neck and over her shoulders and arms. Elise shivered.

Sam's expression did not alter, but in the mirror she saw the flare of heat the tiny reaction brought to his eyes. Still holding her gaze, he leaned over her shoulder, gently pried the hairbrush from her hand and placed it on the dressing table. Grasping both her hands, he urged her to her feet and brought her to stand before him. As his silver gaze devoured her Elise felt her body run hot, then cold, then hot again.

His eyes found hers again, and the look in them increased the trembling deep inside of her.

"I've dreamed of seeing you like this," he whispered, stunning her. "You're even more beautiful than I imagined."

She stared at him through the haze of passion, struggling to make sense of his words. Was that just desire talking or was he serious? Had she been blind? Had Sam really been dreaming of her, wanting her all this time?

"Sam, I— Oh!" Her breath caught on a gasp as he cupped her breast in his palm.

"Your heart is pounding," he murmured. "Don't be afraid, Elise. I'd never hurt you."

"I . . . I'm not afraid." The words were an automatic response, but to her surprise, she realized they were true. She was excited beyond belief. Her head was spinning, her heart was pounding and she could scarcely draw breath. Very soon, if Sam didn't take her in his arms, she was afraid she would disgrace herself by collapsing in a heap at his feet . . . but she wasn't afraid of Sam. For an instant she wondered if she ever really had been.

Then the moment passed as Sam grasped her hips and brought her trembling body against his.

At the first touch Elise's dwindling strength deserted her. She melted within his embrace, her eyes fluttering shut with a tiny moan as his arms encircled her and his mouth met hers in a long, hot kiss, rife with hunger and need.

Sensations flooded her, delicious, dizzying sensations that filled her being and made coherent thought impossible: the crisp feel of his chest hair against her fingers as they threaded through it, the warmth of his skin beneath, the slight dampness seeping through the satin gown from the towel at his waist, the heat of their bodies that seemed to fuse them together. His scent surrounded her, heady and male and tinged with soap. Beneath her palm she could feel his heart pounding as fiercely as her own, and lower, pressed tormentingly close to that throbbing, hollow ache at the apex of her thighs, she felt his aroused manhood.

His lips devoured hers as his stroking tongue moved evocatively in the dark recesses of her mouth. At the same time his hands explored her back and hips, sliding sensuously over the slick satin to cup her buttocks and pull her hard against him.

Elise moved restlessly, as desire spiraled through her. She tried to wind her arms around Sam's neck, but he broke off the kiss and grasped her wrists, pulling them down to her sides. Her little moan of protest died a moment later when he eased the thin straps off her shoulders and down her arms. The ivory nightgown slithered down her body, satin against silk, and formed a shimmering pool about her ankles.

"Now it's your turn," Sam whispered, bringing her hands to his waist.

Though her hands shook over the task, Elise didn't hesitate, and the damp towel quickly joined her gown on the floor.

Sam brought her back into his heated embrace, and she gasped as her sensitive nipples sank into the crisp hair on his chest, but the gasp became a moan as their flesh met and melded. "Oh, Sam. Sam," she sobbed, pressing urgent kisses on his neck as he held her close and rocked against her.

"Let's go to bed, Elise," he murmured against her hair. "I want to make love to you. Now."

The low rumble pushed her over the edge, and she clung to him as he eased them both down onto the mattress. Lord, had she ever thought his voice was lifeless? The deep and dark tones vibrated with a sizzling passion that drove her wild.

"Your body was made for loving," he murmured, cupping her breast. The next instant his mouth closed over the engorged nipple, and she cried out, her body arching as he drew on her with a slow, sweet suction.

Awash with a need she was beyond questioning, Elise moved her head from side to side on the pillow. Restlessly, her hands slid over his shoulders, his neck, the back of his head, her fingertips kneading the hard, warm flesh, urging him closer.

Moving lower, Sam kissed the underside of her breasts, her belly, the points of her hipbones, and she felt the medallion he wore about his neck sliding over her skin. When the tip of his tongue stabbed into the hollow of her navel a violent shudder went through Elise.

As if the shudder were the nudge that finally snapped his control, Sam took her mouth again. With hot, openmouthed kisses and urgent, teasing hands, he brought Elise to frenzied readiness. When his searching fingers threaded through the triangle of deep copper curls and found the moist heart of her desire, Elise cried out in fierce pleasure, her hips bucking against his hand as her legs parted.

Responding to the invitation, Sam moved into position between her thighs, and looked down at her, his eyes glittering—hot chips of ice in the lamplight. Then he made them one, entering her with a slow, silken stroke, the incredible beauty of it wringing a moan from both of them. As though to savor the moment of possession, he grew utterly still, braced above her, his eyes closed in an agony of pleasure, his face flushed and rigid.

But the fire that burned within them would not be denied. With slow, exquisitely sensual movements, he drew her with him into a heady realm where only passion and its beckoning promise existed.

Trembling, Elise clasped his hard body to her, consumed by the raging flames of desire, as they moved as one. The flames grew higher and the terrible sweet tension built until the core of fire within Elise burst into a million pieces, and as the long shudder of release shook her she cried out, "Oh, Sam!"

"Yes!" Sam growled out the word between clenched teeth, his voice harsh and deep with satisfaction.

Drifting in a sea of contentment, Elise clung to him, scarcely aware of the world around them, her body aglow. For what could have been hours, or merely minutes, she floated somewhere between sleep and wakefulness, absently stroking Sam's damp back, a small smile curving her mouth as she listened to his labored breathing close to her ear.

"Are you okay?" Lifting his weight from her, Sam rolled to his back and drew her with him, tucking her close against his side. As she nestled her head on his shoulder, Elise smiled at the revealing action. Cuddling was not something a cold man relished, but apparently Sam didn't know that.

"Yes, I'm fine."

Sam reached out and clicked off the lamp. Several seconds ticked by in silence, and then his arm tightened around her. "We'll make it work, Elise," he said into the darkness. "I promise you."

"I know, Sam," she answered quietly. "I know."

Elise had never been more sure of anything in her life. Long after Sam's breathing grew deep and even, she lay awake thinking.

She could no longer escape the truth. Right to the end, she'd been so sure that all she felt for Sam was compassion. Which was stupid, of course. She did feel compassion for Sam, but that was natural, considering all he had suffered. But she should have known there was more to it than that, simply because if the same things had happened to her neighbor, or a fellow worker, or almost any other man she could think of, her feelings would not have been so strong, or so intensely personal.

Heavens. She'd even told herself that she was marrying him to save him from his ex-fiancée, when really she had simply used Sherry Phillips's sudden appearance as an excuse to do what she wanted, but had lacked the courage, or honesty, to admit.

When had the unwilling attraction turned to love? she wondered, stroking Sam's chest. Or had she loved him all along and just been too stubborn to recognize it? Had the uneasiness she'd felt when around Sam been a subconscious awareness of her growing love? It was possible. Even probable. She was used to planning her own life, and her plans had not included falling in love with a difficult, wounded man like Sam. In truth, given a choice, she still would not have picked him.

But sometimes, she accepted with a sigh, the heart didn't give you any choice. For, like it or not, love Sam, she did—completely and irrevocably.

And someday, some way, Sam Lawford, I'm going to make you love me back, she vowed silently.

Chapter Ten

Elise had no idea what had awakened her. There had been no noise that she could recall, yet she'd been pulled from a deep slumber by a sudden awareness that something was not as it should be. She lay still and opened her eyes partway, searching the darkness.

Then she saw him. Sam was standing by the balcony doors staring out into the night, magnificently naked and bathed in moonlight.

Elise's heart warmed and swelled with pride and love. Lord, he was so beautiful.

She started to speak, but something about him, something in his stance, his utter stillness, stopped the words.

What sort of devils are clawing at him? she wondered sadly, as her gaze ran over his taut back. She longed to go to him, to put her arms around him and share whatever was tormenting him so, but she knew it was too soon. Their lovemaking had been wonderful, but physical closeness and

emotional closeness were two different things. It was going
to take time to build the latter.

So she lay still in the darkness, watching, her heart silently reaching out to him.

Sam stared out at the glittering world of Las Vegas at
night, his face like stone. Uneasiness rode him, his thoughts
roweling spurs that wouldn't leave him alone. What the hell
was he supposed to do now? The silent question brought a
surge of panic that threatened to suffocate him.

He had thought that having her would be enough. He'd
been wrong.

A long-buried hunger had him reaching for a cigarette,
but his hand patted only bare chest instead of a shirt pocket,
and he shook his head, his mouth twisting. It was a sign of
how rattled he was. Hell, he'd kicked that habit years ago.
Or rather, the Cong had kicked it for him. He hadn't had so
much as a taste of tobacco in those four years. It was the
only thing he could thank his captors for.

Sam raked a hand through his hair and pulled it down the
back of his neck to massage the taut muscles there. He had
been so sure—so *damned* sure—that once she was his wife
the urgent, never-ending hunger would disappear.

That was a laugh. The night was barely half gone and he'd
woken her twice. Each time he possessed her it had been as
shatteringly beautiful as the first. And each time had only
made him want her more.

It's early yet, he told himself. Hell, man it's your wedding night. That's why you can't seem to get enough of her.
Besides, you've got months of wanting to make up for. Give
it a month—six weeks at most—and familiarity will have
taken the edge off your appetite.

Sam released his breath in a disgusted sigh. Hell, who was
he trying to kid? It wasn't the physical hunger that was
bothering him. The depth and strength of his desire for Elise
was a bit unsettling, but since she came to him so sweetly,

he'd be a fool to complain. No, he was deliberately focusing on it to take his mind off the real threat to his peace of mind.

Sam's hands curled into tight fists at his sides. Elise was a torment in his soul, stirring feelings and emotions he didn't want to experience again.

He turned away from the balcony door and walked back to the bed, pausing beside it to look down at his bride. His expression softened. *God, she's beautiful. Like a sleeping angel,* he thought, taking in her soft mouth and the long lashes that lay so beguilingly against her cheeks. In the faint moonlight her tousled curls looked almost black against the pillow. He reached out and smoothed a lock from her forehead, then trailed the backs of his knuckles over her cheek.

Carefully, so as not to wake her, he went around to the other side of the bed and eased himself in. He lay still for a minute, staring through the darkness at the ceiling. Then, turning on his side, he aligned his body with his wife's and put his arm around her waist. Very gently, he pulled her against him.

He rubbed his cheek against her hair, then nuzzled his nose into it, inhaling deeply. The sweet, clean scent of those shining tresses, the bewitching woman smell that owed its existence to some wondrous chemistry that was hers alone, were fast becoming an addiction for him.

The urge to put his hands on her, to explore again her warmth, the delicately made body and sleek, silken flesh, was irresistible. With a tenderness that bordered on reverence, Sam caressed her. His fingertips trailed over her earlobe, her neck, stroked her arm from shoulder to wrist. Her collarbone, her breasts, her midriff, the hollow of her navel, the backs of her knees, were all given worshipful attention. Finally his big hand came to rest on her abdomen, his palm moving in a tiny rotation against the slight swell as he held her close.

After a while, Elise felt his chest move against her back as he released a long sigh, and she smiled.

Oh, Sam, Sam, she thought tenderly. *Don't you realize that you give yourself away with every touch?*

Happiness permeated her being with a delicious effervescence, like bubbles in fine champagne, bringing a tingle that made sleep impossible at first. Then, finally, luxuriating in the warmth of Sam's embrace, her heart soaring with hope, she drifted off.

Sunlight was pouring in through the balcony doors hours later when Elise came slowly awake, stretching like a contented cat under the gentle caresses that roamed her body with familiar intimacy. A slow smile broke through even before her heavy eyelids lifted.

Turning toward the magnetic warmth at her back, she found Sam propped up on one elbow, leaning over her, a look of somber fascination on his face. Mingled with it was a shadow of such terrible longing that Elise nearly cried out when she spotted it.

Instinctively, she started to reach out and gather him to her, as she would have a forlorn child, but fortunately she restrained herself in time, knowing he would take the action as pity, and hate it. Instead she smiled and cupped his jaw.

"Good morning," she murmured, her voice low and husky.

Sam blinked, and the shadow disappeared. "Good morning."

His tone was guarded, his expression unreadable, but Elise refused to be discouraged. He had let his guard down, and she had seen the hunger in his soul, felt it in his touch. Even now, though he affected casual indifference, his body betrayed him. And he seemed unaware that his hand was still gliding back and forth over the long curve of her hip and thigh.

"Are you always such a sleepyhead?" he asked.

"No, actually, I'm one of those disgustingly cheerful people who usually wakes up early, but since I didn't get much sleep last night..." As her voice trailed away, Elise batted her eyes flirtatiously, but Sam frowned.

"Are you all right? How do you feel?"

Elise had to bite back a giggle. She was tempted to tell him that he should know, but she wasn't sure if Sam would appreciate her sense of humor. Besides, she didn't want him to know that she'd been awake when he'd caressed her so tenderly.

She understood the source of his anxiety. Sam was a big man, and though she was fairly tall, her body was fine-boned and slender, and probably appeared delicate to him. For the most part he had been exquisitely gentle, handling her with great care, but once or twice he had lost control and taken her with an explosive power that had left her weak.

Elise didn't waste her breath explaining that she relished his passion. She doubted that he'd believe her, since Sam, like everyone else, seemed determined to treat her as though she were a piece of fragile, translucent china. There were times, she decided, when action was called for.

Whisker stubble made a slight scraping noise against her palm as her hand slid along his jaw and around to the back of his neck. "I'm fine," she assured him, her voice a sultry murmur as she pulled his head down.

Sam resisted at first, watching her warily, but she gave him a heavy-lidded, smoldering look, and as his mouth drew near she raised her head and met it with tormenting little kisses, nibbling, rubbing her parted lips back and forth against his.

"I feel..." The tip of her tongue outlined his seeking mouth. "wonderful, and..." She nipped him. Their breath mingled. "rested, and very..." Her tongue teased the corners of his mouth, and Sam made an inarticulate sound. "very..." She drew his lower lip into her mouth and sucked gently. "...hungry."

Sam's control broke. With a growl he rolled on top of her, pinning her to the mattress, and captured her tormenting lips in a deep, devouring kiss of barely leashed violence.

Elise gloried in the heat and power of it. Control and restraint were forgotten in the erotic clash of their bodies. She couldn't get enough of him, couldn't touch him enough to satisfy the grinding need building inside her. Neither, it seemed, could Sam.

She moved restlessly beneath him, her hands clutching his back, kneading the strong, flat muscles. They slid downward and gripped his buttocks, her fingers digging into the firm flesh, and Sam shivered.

Breaking off the kiss, he buried his face in the side of her neck. He lay still, his breathing harsh and ragged.

"I can't wait. I have to have you. Now," he gasped in her ear, nipping at her lobe.

"Yes." Elise held him tight. "Yes!"

He took her at once. Her body was still warm and rosy from sleep, sweetly welcoming, and she sighed with pleasure and wrapped her legs around him as he made them one.

After the night they had just spent together, Elise was a bit shocked at the depth and urgency of their lovemaking now. Passion spiraled out of control quickly, and they grasped at it like two greedy children, breathless, seeking. Insatiable.

Fulfillment came quickly. Within minutes they lay still in each other's arms, their labored breathing the only sound in the sunlit room.

Sam raised his head, bracing up on his forearms, and looked at her, his gaze intent and searching, faintly puzzled. "You surprise me. I had no idea there was so much passion beneath that sweet exterior."

"Oh?" Elise managed a cool look, which, lying as she was, naked beneath him, took every ounce of control she could muster. "I suppose, given the image you seem to have of me, you expected ladylike compliance and a sigh of relief when the deed was done?''

To her delight, a hint of a smile tugged at Sam's mouth. He gave a little snort. ''I wouldn't say that. But then, I didn't expect an earthy temptress, either.''

Lowering her gaze, Elise ran her fingers through his chest hair, twisting a dark curl around and around her forefinger. ''Are you complaining?''

This time Sam did laugh, though it was a rusty sound, as though his vocal cords had grown stiff from disuse. ''Hardly,'' he said in a dry voice, looking at her with wry humor glinting in his eyes. ''I may not be the brightest guy in the world, but I can assure you, you didn't marry an idiot.'' He stroked the curls at her temples and ran his fingertips over the velvety rims of her ears. ''I'm surprised and pleased. Compatibility in that area is a plus. It speaks well for our future together.''

The cautious optimism she was beginning to feel faded, seeping away like the air out of a deflating balloon. Was that all last night and this morning meant to him? High marks for a good performance? She fought to keep her disappointment from showing, giving him a small wooden smile and agreeing with a soft, ''Yes, it does.''

It's too soon, she scolded herself. *Don't expect too much. Don't push.*

She felt bereft when Sam rolled away from her. She wanted to cuddle, to at least hold on for a while longer to the physical closeness, perhaps talk together softly in the lingering afterglow of lovemaking, as many married couples do, but she swallowed her disappointment and said nothing.

Sam sat up on the side of the bed and swung his feet to the floor, and Elise reached for the sheet to cover herself, feeling abruptly exposed. She allowed herself a longing glance at his bare back, and gasped, her desolation instantly forgotten as she stared in frozen shock.

"Sam! Oh, my God, Sam! Your poor back!"

She sprang up and scrambled across the bed on her knees, her eyes wide with concern. When she reached him, she gingerly touched her fingertips to the thin white lines that crisscrossed the back of his body from shoulders to buttocks. "What *happened* to you?"

But even as the appalled question left her lips, her mind identified those telltale marks, and her face grew pale as her expression changed to horror.

Elise had never seen any like them before, but she knew without being told that those obscene white lines marring her husband's bronze skin were scars from a whip.

At her touch, Sam stiffened. He looked back over his shoulder, his face carefully blank. His silvery gray eyes were so remote they looked dead. Elise, still coming to grips with the terrible discovery, hardly noticed.

Her shaking fingers traced a long thin line with a butterfly touch. She raised her head, her glistening, horrified eyes swimming with pain and anguish as they met his. "Oh, Sam," she crooned in a quavering whisper.

"Forget it, Elise. It happened a long time ago," he replied flatly, and rose from the bed. He picked up the terry-cloth robe from the bedside chair and slipped it on. Tying the belt, he turned and saw the expression on Elise's face. "If the sight offends you, I'm sorry. I'll do my best to keep my back covered when we're together."

"*Sam!* How could you even think such a thing? You know it's not that!"

Giving her a disinterested glance, he dismissed her denial with a shrug and started for the bathroom.

"Sam, please! Don't shut me out," she pleaded. Desperation made her voice a high, thin wail. "Talk to me, please. Sam, for heaven's sake! I'm your wife! Why did you marry me if you won't let me share your life?"

He swung around at that. Deliberately, his gaze swept over the disheveled bed before meeting hers. "For sexual satisfaction and companionship. I'm sure I've been very clear about that from the beginning."

The words were like blows to her heart, but she refused to back down. "Sam, tell me what happened to you in that POW camp. Please."

His head came up just a fraction. "So you know about that, do you?" At her nod, his mouth folded into a grim line. "Well, that's all you need to know."

"Sam, please! You have to tell me. Can't you see, if you don't my imagination will probably paint an even worse picture."

"Oh, I'm not in the least worried about that happening." He gave a humorless snort, his mouth twisting. "You're such an innocent. You couldn't possibly conceive of the hideous things one human being can inflict on another. Or the filth and degradation. Even if I told you, I don't think that sweet pure mind of yours could grasp it." He shook his head. "No, Elise. You may feel that it's your wifely duty to hear all the grisly details, but believe me—you don't want to know."

"Oh, Sam." Her voice wobbled, and she gazed at him with infinite sadness, her brown eyes glistening with tears.

"And I don't want your sympathy."

He turned, walked into the bathroom and shut the door, leaving her sitting in the middle of the bed, clutching the sheet to her breasts, upset, frustrated, hurt . . . and hurting for him.

She stared at the closed door for several seconds, then shut her eyes, her shoulders slumping. He couldn't have made it clearer. He didn't want her pity, nor, apparently, did he want her love.

No, that wasn't true. It was what he wanted her to believe. He might even believe it himself. But though he had retreated again behind that mask of indifference, Elise knew that was merely a defense, not the real Sam. The real Sam was the man who had held her close all night long, the man who had caressed her as though she were the most precious thing in the world to him, the man who gave so freely of himself and his time.

The problem wasn't that Sam didn't want love or was incapable of deep emotion. He was simply afraid to love. Hadn't she known that since the night he proposed? Of course she had, she admitted with a dispirited sigh. But when faced with his cool indifference, that was difficult to remember. It was something she was going to have to keep reminding herself of.

After all he'd been through, she supposed it was understandable. In a way.

Elise thought about those horrible white lines that scarred Sam's back, and shuddered. Why hadn't she seen them before, that first time she had shared a bed with him, after Erin and Max's wedding? Probably, she admitted guiltily, because that morning she'd striven very hard *not* to look at Sam at all.

In part, that had been due to embarrassment, but Elise suspected that the main reason had been because she'd long ago developed the habit of avoiding Sam whenever possible. Until she had started working for him, she'd tried never to speak to him or to look directly at him unless she had to, as though by not doing so she could make herself invisible to him. She'd told herself she did it because he made her nervous, because she didn't like him, but now Elise suspected that all along, on some subconscious level, she'd been fighting the unwanted attraction she felt for him.

Elise sighed at her own foolishness. Had she really believed she could escape her fate?

The question now was, could she deal with Sam's coldness? He obviously wanted her in his life, otherwise he wouldn't have married her, but he seemed so determined to keep her at arm's length. How long could she bear to be no more to him than bed partner and dinner companion?

Elise sighed. In her heart of hearts she was sure that Sam loved her. She had glimpsed that terrible longing he denied so fiercely. She'd also seen his kindness and affection, his thoughtfulness. Those things couldn't be faked.

Elise moaned and dropped her head into her hands. Oh, why did she, of all people, have to fall in love with a hurt, embittered man? She had never been a scrapper. With her protective family she'd never had to be. And besides, it wasn't her nature. Patience and passive determination were the weapons she had always used to get what she wanted.

She would need those traits now, but every feminine instinct she possessed warned her that, alone, they simply wouldn't be enough. Not this time. If she were ever going to reach Sam, she would have to tear down those defenses of his, and that would take direct action.

The sound of the shower running stopped. Elise raised her head and stared at the bathroom door, then threw aside the sheet and rose from the bed. She retrieved the satin gown, and as the shimmering garment settled over her curves it occurred to her that only six months before she would not have dared what she was about to do. The thought brought a self-satisfied smile to her face and bolstered her courage. Maybe the family's ewe lamb was at long last learning to fend for herself.

Without giving herself time to reconsider, Elise crossed to the bathroom door, opened it and stepped inside.

Sam looked up at her entrance. Though he masked it quickly, she caught the look of surprise on his face.

He stood at the sink shaving with one of those little plastic razors they'd bought in the hotel pharmacy. He was stark naked, his body still glistening with droplets of water, his black hair hanging in wet ringlets.

Sam raked another swath through the lather on his cheek, casting her a sidelong glance as she walked toward him. "I'll be through in a couple of minutes."

"That's okay. I don't mind sharing," Elise replied cheerfully. She stopped behind him, and Sam stiffened when she slid her arms around his middle and pressed against him. Water soaked through the satin gown, melding the garment to his skin as well as hers. Very delicately, she lifted several droplets from his back with the tip of her tongue, then pressed her lips against one of the thin white scars.

"What are you doing?"

"I'm kissing your back."

"Why?"

She kissed several more of the marks and lightly grazed the point of his shoulder blade with her teeth. At Sam's reflexive jerk she tightened her hold and grinned. With a sigh, she laid her cheek against his back and rubbed against him like an affectionate kitten. "Sam? Aren't you the least bit curious?" she asked mysteriously, ignoring his question.

"About what?"

Elise rose up on tiptoes, propped her chin on his bare shoulder and smiled at his wary reflection in the mirror. "About why I married you. I mean—you told me why you wanted to marry me, but when I accepted you never asked what my reasons were."

A sharp look came into his eyes, but he quickly concealed it behind lowered lids, fixing his gaze on the razor he was rinsing beneath the faucet. When he raised his head and raked away another strip of lather and whiskers the look was gone, but Elise felt the tension in his body. "I hadn't given it any thought, but I suppose I assumed you found my terms agreeable."

"No. Actually I didn't." Her smile faded and her expression became serious. "I married you for one very simple reason, Sam," she said quietly, holding his gaze in the mirror. "Because I love you."

She felt the shock jolt through him. Sam made a restive movement, but she didn't release him or look away from that sharp, pale stare.

Her insides were aquiver and her heart was thumping like crazy. She was slightly appalled at her own boldness, but she wasn't going to settle for a polite, civilized marriage of pretense. She loved him, and if that made him uncomfortable, so much the better. She was fighting for her life, here. For their future.

"I didn't ask for your love," Sam said woodenly. "I don't want it."

She didn't even flinch, though every word pierced her heart like a hot knife. "I know," she said, silently congratulating herself on her light tone. "To tell you the truth, I'm not too pleased myself, but there doesn't seem to be a whole lot I can do about it. I love you, and that's that. So I'm afraid you're just going to have to accept it."

His body was as rigid as a post, and he was looking at her as though she'd suddenly grown two heads, but Elise had come too far to give up now. Her heels dropped back to the floor, and once again she snuggled her face against his back.

"So, you see, it's pointless to tell me not to feel compassion or sympathy when I look at what those horrible people did to you. When you love someone, their pain is your pain. When they're happy, you're happy, when they're sad, you're sad, and when they've been abused, you hurt and cry and rage...because you care.

"I love you, Sam. If that makes you uncomfortable, I'm sorry. But I thought you ought to know how I feel."

She gave him an affectionate squeeze and kissed his back one last time before stepping blithely away. Sam remained motionless, as though he had turned to stone.

Aware that he was watching her in the mirror, Elise slipped the thin straps off her shoulders, announcing as the gown slithered to the floor, "I'm going to shower now. If you order room service I'd like eggs, bacon, toast...oh, just get me the works." She laughed and stepped into the glass-enclosed stall that was almost as big as the entire bathroom in her apartment. "I'm starving this morning."

Humming off-key, Elise adjusted the spray and reached for the tiny bottle of shampoo the hotel provided, surreptitiously watching Sam through the water-beaded glass.

He remained absolutely still for a moment longer, his gaze riveted to her. Then, with quick, jerky movements, he scraped away the remaining lather and whiskers, rinsed and patted his face dry. He snatched up a thick towel, gave his hair and body a cursory once-over, spritzed deodorant under each arm and left the bathroom without so much as another glance at the enticing hazy figure behind the foggy glass.

When the door closed behind him Elise stopped humming. Pressing her lips together, she closed her eyes and turned her face up to the warm spray, letting it sluice away the mounds of lather along with the stupid tears that squeezed from beneath her closed lids.

"Oh, God, please, please let this be the right thing to do!"

Sam dressed mechanically in the navy slacks and pale blue silk sport shirt he'd purchased the previous day. He went to the dresser, rummaged through the pile of items he'd emptied from his pockets the night before, extracted a comb and raked it through his damp hair, sweeping the thick shock of ebony away from his face. He stared straight at his reflection.

"I married you for one very simple reason, Sam. Because I love you."

Sam drew in a sharp breath and closed his eyes, his jaw clenching tight. His eyes popped open again quickly, and he snatched up his watch, fastened it about his wrist and stuffed comb, wallet, handkerchief and loose change into his pockets. He looked around for something else to do, but there was nothing, and with a muttered curse, he raked a hand through his freshly combed hair in uncharacteristic agitation.

He considered calling room service but decided against it. A crowded dining room seemed preferable at the moment to a cozy breakfast in the room.

Restless, he shoved his hands into his pockets, walked to the balcony doors and stared out at the brilliant sunlit scene. What he saw was soft brown eyes gazing earnestly at him over his shoulder.

"I love you, Sam. If that makes you uncomfortable, I'm sorry. But I thought you ought to know how I feel."

"Damn!" Sam's hand closed around a fistful of change. He squeezed until the coins bit painfully into his palm. Grinding his teeth, he struggled to subdue the surge of emotions that filled his chest almost to bursting. Fear, anger and, yes—God help him—pure sweet elation.

Hell, he didn't need this! He didn't want it! Didn't she realize what a risk love was? And how people became defenseless when they let themselves care that much? He didn't want to hurt her. Not Elise. Not ever.

And love did hurt. How many times had his captors played on his feelings to inflict pain? Taunting him? Smiling those toothy, vicious smiles as they twisted the knife a little deeper into his heart?

"Hey, Sam. Who your woman sleep with now, huh? This pretty Sher-ree. She forget you, I bet. Maybe marry. Have two, three babies. Or maybe sleep with lotta guys. Pretty woman like that! She no wait for pig like you."

Of course, he had known they'd read the letter, the one and only that he'd received from Sherry after landing in Vietnam. He had carried it and her picture with him all the time, like a lovesick fool.

The memory produced a cynical, twisted smile. The damned thing should have been a Dear John letter, since she was already sleeping with Ken Phillips at the time. But Sherry had always been one to keep her options open, so the letter was filled with passionate promises and avowals of love.

In the beginning, he'd ignored their taunts, refusing to believe them, and when he could take their goading no longer he had angrily shaken the bars of his cage and shouted at the guards to shut their filthy mouths, much to their amusement. But as the years went by, he began to wonder...and doubt. By the time he returned home, he wasn't even surprised to find that Sherry had married, just that it had happened only six weeks after he'd shipped out.

Even more painful had been the constant gibes about his parents, how they had given him up for dead. How he'd never see them again.

After a while, he'd learned to simply blank it all out, to shut off the feeling and survive.

He hadn't been quite as successful where Elise was concerned, he admitted uneasily. That had bothered him some, but still, he'd thought he could handle the situation. Like an arrogant fool, he'd assumed he could marry her, enjoy her warmth and her gentle sweetness, her delectable body, without emotions getting in the way. They would be friends and grow old together in contentment, with none of the heart-wrenching despair and grief that love brings.

It had never occurred to him that she might fall in love with him.

Sam closed his eyes against the yearning ache in his heart. Elise would love completely, with all the depth and steadfastness of her sweet nature. How in hell was a man supposed to resist that?

He turned at the sound of the bathroom door opening, and his gut clenched at the sight of Elise, all clean and rosy, wrapped from chin to toes in a fluffy white robe. Her bright hair was darkened to a rich, deep red, rioting about her scrubbed face in a halo of wet curls.

She gave him a soft smile as she walked to the dresser. "Did you call room service?" she asked, searching through the drawers for the panties and bra she'd purchased the day before.

Sam's head spun and his body hardened as he inhaled the intoxicating smell of sweet, clean woman. With each small movement, it radiated from her warm, glowing body and wafted through the air in tantalizing waves, a heady mixture of soap, shampoo and talc, mixed with that delightful scent that was hers alone. The cloud of moist air that rolled from the bathroom was redolent with the same bewitching fragrance. It was all Sam could do not to cross the few feet separating them and snatch her into his arms.

"No," he replied stiffly. "I'd rather eat in the restaurant."

"Oh. Well..." She glanced at him, her slight smile a trifle disappointed, but she shrugged agreeably. "In that case, I'll hurry."

She slipped out of the robe and tossed it onto the bed.

Sam's heart rate soared. He ground his teeth. *Look away, you fool. Don't stand here gaping like a randy teenager*, he told himself angrily. But he didn't. He couldn't.

Instead his gaze roamed over her, avidly tracing the elegant curves, the long, long legs, the lush breasts, the tight, delightfully rounded derriere, that alluring nest of silky curls at the top of her thighs, darker and tighter than those on her head. She was beautiful, every inch of her, and her complexion, he noted, was smooth rich cream. All over.

Elise bent from the waist to step into a pair of bikini panties, and the heated throb in Sam's loins worsened as her breasts shifted under the pull of gravity.

Damn! He stared at those pert nipples, pointing so impudently at the floor, and recalled their velvety texture against his lips.

Straightening, she pulled the ridiculous wisp of lavender silk and lace up over her legs and it settled into place, clinging low on her hips and hiding little more than those nether curls and the rounded swells of her bottom.

Slipping her arms through the straps of the matching bra, she bent forward and let the lace cups take the weight of her breasts. She straightened again, arching her back, and reached around with both hands to hook the bra between her shoulder blades. Each movement was graceful, innately feminine, and totally, excruciatingly provocative.

Sam stood motionless, unable to tear his gaze away, torn between the need to reestablish some distance between them and the need to throw her down on that disheveled bed and ravish her until neither of them could move.

She sent him another sweet look. "Don't worry. I won't be but a few more minutes."

"That's okay. Take your time." *Hurry. Oh, God, please hurry. If there's an ounce of mercy in that innocent heart you'll put your clothes on so we can get out of here.*

Her hair was drying rapidly, shining like polished copper in the shaft of sunlight from the window. Sam thought about how it felt against his skin, so silky soft and touchable, its heavenly scent.

As though she had divined his thoughts, Elise raised both arms, speared her fingers through her hair and fluffed it. The action displayed the tender undersides of her arms and lifted her breasts until they swelled voluptuously above the lacy bra. The pose was at once both wanton and innocent.

Sam's mouth went dry.

With a tremendous effort, he dragged his gaze away and stared out the window. He focused on a jet, streaking across the morning sky, leaving a vapor trail like a white slash mark on a blue chalkboard. But from the corner of his eye he could still see her, sitting at the dressing table now, wearing nothing more than those two enticing scraps of cloth. He was aware of her every move, every subtle shift of her body.

And he was sweating blood. She was beautiful, and desirable . . . and she was his.

And she loves you.

The thought tugged at something deep inside him, something he didn't want to acknowledge. His heart pounded, his manhood throbbed, but he knew with a gut-deep certainty that if he took her now he was lost.

Clenching his jaw so tight his teeth hurt, he fought the desire, he fought the need, and most of all, he fought that nameless yearning deep in his soul.

Elise leaned forward, flicked the mascara wand over her lashes and peeked at Sam. He was staring out the window now, but she'd seen his dazed expression when she'd shed the robe, and the desperation in his eyes when she'd put on her underthings. Her insides were still quivering, and in truth, she was a little shocked at her own behavior. She hadn't been sure that she could do it.

Perhaps it was unfair to torment him, she thought guiltily. But, darn it! It was his own fault. She knew her confession had made a small dent in his armor, but then she'd stepped from the bathroom, met that hateful blank stare and realized that he had retreated from her again. She'd wanted to scream.

Well, she wasn't going to allow it. So far, the sizzling physical attraction between them was the only weapon she had with which to batter down that wall of indifference, and by heaven, she intended to use it to the hilt. She was going to tempt him every chance she got because intuition told her that was her best chance. Perhaps her only chance.

In bed, she'd discovered the night before, Sam's cool control disappeared. There were no polite distances between them there. Just power and need and trembling eagerness, and those hot, thrilling words whispered in the darkness. When caught in the throes of passion, Sam was as much a supplicant as she.

If she had to enthrall him sexually to keep his attention, so be it, but at the same time she intended to remind him of her love, every day, in every way possible. She wouldn't burden him with her feelings, but neither would she let him ignore them. A wise woman could show her love in a thousand and one ways without ever saying the words.

Finished with her makeup, Elise rose, smiling innocently at Sam when he looked her way. "I'll be ready as soon as I finish dressing."

He merely nodded, but she felt his searing gaze follow her every move. Though Elise still felt self-conscious, she managed to stretch languorously and stroll back to the dresser with a naughty little sway in her walk. Her hands trembled as she hooked the lacy garter belt around her waist and drew on the silky stockings.

She stood and shimmied daintily into a white satin half-slip. Sam sucked in his breath, and as though in a trance he started toward her. He had taken only three jerky steps when the telephone rang. Surprised, Elise and Sam looked at one another. She was closest, and when it rang a second time she picked up the receiver.

"Hello."

Several seconds of silence followed, and then, "Elise? Elise, is that . . . is that *you*?"

Chapter Eleven

Elise rolled her eyes and made a wry face in answer to Sam's questioning look.

"Yes, Margo, it's me," she replied with a beleaguered sigh.

"What the devil are you doing in Sam's hotel room at this hour of the morn—?" Margo broke off with a groan and a muttered "Oh, hell. Look, forget I asked that. Okay? It's obvious what you're doing."

"Margo—"

"What I want to know is when did you two get together?"

"Margo—"

"I mean, only a week ago, we were all beating the bushes trying to find Mr. Right for you. And now you're having a fling with Sam."

"Margo, if you'll just lis—"

"Not that I'm criticizing, mind you. Sam's yummy. Hell, if he'd offered me an illicit weekend in Las Vegas, I would've accepted like a shot. That is . . . if I hadn't already met Paul.''

"Margo—"

"But honey, are you sure this is right for you? I know you want wedding bells and love and kids and the whole thing. Sam isn't exactly—"

"Margo, for heaven's sake! Will you stop clucking like a mother hen for a minute and listen! Sam and I were married yesterday."

Silence.

"Margo? Are you still there?"

"Married?" came her friend's shocked whisper. And then, louder, "Oh, my Lord, did you say *married*? I don't believe this! You and Sam? Really?"

"Yes, really," Elise confirmed, wry amusement lacing her voice. Her twitching lips conveyed her friend's reaction to Sam, and he rounded the bed and took the receiver from her hand.

"Margo, this is Sam. What—" Before he could say more Elise heard the murmur of Margo's excited voice coming through the receiver. "Yes, that's right. Yesterday."

Sam's tone did not encourage friendly chatter, but Margo was so wound up Elise doubted that her friend even noticed. From the look on Sam's face and the long silence, she was going on and on, nonstop. Stifling a grin, Elise went to the closet and removed her new lilac dress from the hanger.

"Thank you, Margo. We will." Another pause, longer this time, and Sam frowned. "Yes, I know she is. I—" Sam drew a deep breath and looked impatiently toward the ceiling. "Look, Margo," he broke in finally. "I appreciate your good wishes, but I assume you had a reason for calling me here at this hour. If you don't mind, I'd like to hear it."

As Elise stepped into the simple wool sheath and zipped it partway, Sam grew silent. She glanced at him and saw that his impatience had changed to grim concern. Belatedly, she realized that Margo would not have called unless it was important. From Sam's expression, she knew that something was very wrong.

"When?" He snapped out the one-word question. "I see."

Standing before the dresser, Elise inserted a gold loop in one ear, her uneasiness growing as she watched Sam in the mirror. He turned and ran his eyes over her. For a fleeting instant she saw conflicting emotions in that pale gaze, then his expression locked, and he looked away.

"All right, I'll catch the next flight and meet you at the office as soon as I can." Margo must have argued with him because he shook his head impatiently and said, "No, no, you did the right thing. I know you can handle it, but that's not the point. Look, Margo, I'll see you in a few hours. And in the meantime, check on Harry for me, will you?"

He replaced the receiver, then stood there for a moment with his hand still on it before turning to meet her questioning gaze.

"I'm sorry, Elise, but I have to go back. There's been some trouble at the warehouse."

"Oh." The single word quavered with a wealth of disappointment, and she silently cursed fate and bad timing, and all the other nebulous powers she could think of for conspiring against her. She had so wanted these two days of privacy with Sam.

"There's been a break-in. Harry Deats, the night watchman, was hurt."

"I see." Elise turned back to the dresser and inserted a gold loop in the other ear, but when she tried to slide the back onto the post her fingers fumbled over the task. "Well, in that case, I guess we'd better go," she said, striving for a matter-of-fact tone. "Would you mind zipping my dress? It seems to be stuck."

"Sure." He moved up behind her. For a moment, before he reached for the tiny metal tab, they stared at each other in the mirror. It was a small chore, the kind husbands had

been performing for their wives for aeons, but for them it
was a first, the beginning of a lifetime of such simple inti-
macies, and the knowledge heightened emotions, imbuing
the moment with a poignancy that was at once painfully
moving and wildly exciting. The sensual awareness that had
been brewing between them before Margo's call came surg-
ing back, as vibrant and hot as before.

The silence thrummed between them, taut, expectant,
heavy with thoughts and feelings not expressed.

Elise wet her lips nervously, and Sam ducked his head to
inspect the snagged fabric.

His warm breath feathered across her bare back in a moist
caress. She gripped the edge of the dresser as a tiny shiver
rippled through her and a wave of gooseflesh spread across
her shoulders, neck and scalp.

"This doesn't look too bad."

"Oh, good." Her constricted lungs barely held enough air
to produce the words. They came out in a soft exclamation
that was little more than a sigh.

Sam slipped his hand inside her dress beneath the stuck
fabric, and the backs of his fingers pressed against her spine.
With agonizing slowness, he eased the zipper down. His
knuckles followed, leaving a trail of fire. Cool air struck the
flushed skin of her back as the dress parted. Caught in a
sensuous spell she didn't dare break, Elise stood motionless
as he drew the zipper slide all the way to her waist. With a
little tug, the fabric slipped free.

Again, their eyes met in the mirror. Hers were wide with
longing. Misty. Vulnerable.

His smoldered.

Elise knew that if she leaned back just the slightest bit, let
her bottom brush the front of his trousers, she would find
him hard and ready. Control over whether they stayed or
went was in her hands. It would take only the slightest
movement on her part and Sam would tumble her onto that

bed, without thought to business, or emergencies, or fighting the love that she knew was in his heart.

Elise sighed. It would be so easy, but she wouldn't. It would be neither wise nor fair. Sam obviously felt he should return to Santa Fe. She could distract him from that purpose—for a while—but he would probably end up resenting her for it.

Reluctantly, wisely perhaps, but with a heavy heart, she lowered her eyes. Sam hesitated only a second before pulling the zipper up. "There you go. All set."

"Thank you." She looked up with a wan smile, but Sam had already crossed to the nightstand and was reaching for the telephone.

Within minutes he had them booked on a flight. Three hours later they landed in Albuquerque and retrieved Sam's car. They arrived in Santa Fe in an amazingly short amount of time, thanks to her husband's driving.

The first time she had ridden with Sam he had been angry, and the day before she had assumed he was just in a hurry to get to the airport, but Elise was beginning to realize that Sam always drove like a bat out of hell. It was a bit unnerving, and surprising, since he always seemed so controlled.

Elise had assumed that she would go with him to the office, but as they entered the outskirts of town Sam announced his intention to drop her off at her apartment.

"While I take care of things at work, you can pack what you'll need for the next day or so. Sometime next week you can sort through the rest and decide what you want to keep."

"Oh, but—" Before she could voice her objections his next comment wiped them out of her mind.

"You know, don't you, that you can't work at Global now?"

Startled, Elise looked at him. "Why not?"

"We have a strict policy against employing relatives or husbands and wives, and if Max and I didn't adhere to it ourselves we'd never make it stick." He glanced at her. "You don't have to work at all unless you want to, you know. Would you object to being a full-time home-maker?"

Elise blinked, surprised once again. She could have sworn she detected a note of hope in his voice. Thoughtfully, she studied his profile for a clue to what he was thinking, but came up blank. "No, I wouldn't mind at all."

Actually, it was what she preferred. She had always been the domestic type, and the thought of having her own home again, a husband to fuss over, thrilled her.

After Tommy's death she'd had to sell the huge old Victorian house they'd owned in Crockett. She'd used the money from both the sale and his life insurance to pay off the horrendous mountain of medical bills that had resulted from his illness. These past three years she had worked out of necessity, not because she was career-minded or bored.

With a shock, it occurred to Elise that she had no idea where Sam lived. She didn't even know whether he had a house, an apartment or a condo.

That she'd shown so little interest in him in the past filled her with guilt, but she was too embarrassed to come right out and ask.

"How, uh...how big is your place?" she probed. When he slanted her a knowing look, she added quickly, "Just so I'll have some idea how much I can bring of my own."

"Big enough. It's mostly empty, so there's plenty of room for your things. I've never gotten around to doing much with the inside. But you'll see for yourself in a few hours." He pulled into the driveway behind Elise's apartment, stopping outside her back door.

At the sight of her empty parking slot Elise sat bolt upright. "My car! It's still in the office parking lot!"

"Don't worry. I'll have someone drive it out to my place."

"Oh. All right," she said in a small, unsure voice.

They'd been married less than twenty-four hours and Elise hated to part from him, but she knew he was waiting for her to get out of the car. She fiddled with the clasp on her purse and looked at him wistfully out of the corner of her eye. Sam would probably think she was being a silly, sentimental fool if he knew. Stifling a little sigh, she reached for the door handle. "Well...I, uh...I guess I'll see you later."

She opened the door but before she could move Sam leaned over, cupped his hand around the back of her neck and hauled her to him for a quick but intensely thorough kiss. Elise's heart gave a little leap, then settled down to a heavy thud as she melted under the hot urgency of his hungry lips and thrusting tongue.

He raised his head and drew back just a few inches to stare into her bemused face. For an unguarded few seconds Elise glimpsed something in his expression that told her he was as surprised as she was, that he hadn't intended to kiss her at all and was disturbed by his lack of control. Hope and joy swelled within her even as she watched his face take on that familiar blank hardness. Sam wanted to be immune to the feelings between them, but he wasn't.

"I'll be back to pick you up as soon as I can," he said in a voice rough with resentment and undeniable need.

All Elise could do was nod.

When she let herself into her tiny apartment she wandered through the rooms in a daze. Being there felt strange. *She* felt strange. Everything was neat and in order, exactly as she had left it. Every piece of furniture, every knick-knack, every picture was a cherished, familiar item she'd lived with for years, and yet, somehow, it was no longer home. She laughed aloud at that, a startled little sound that erupted from her without warning. She had no idea where "home" was—only that it was with Sam.

It was strange, she thought pensively, trailing her fingers over the back of her grandmother's platform rocker, how abruptly life could change course. When she'd left for work the previous morning, marrying Sam had been the farthest thing from her mind, and yet here she was...Mrs. Sam Lawford.

Elise stopped in the middle of the living room. "Elise Lawford," she said aloud, testing the name.

She smiled, liking the sound of it.

Sam's home was not at all what Elise expected.

"You live on a ranch?" she exclaimed in obvious surprise when Sam turned off the highway and guided the sleek Cadillac through a nondescript metal gate and onto a narrow dirt road. Set in the endless miles of barbed wire that followed the highway to the south of Santa Fe, the gate was unmarked and almost indistinguishable from the rest of the fence. Elise hadn't even seen it until Sam had touched a button beneath the dash and it had swung open.

The little snort of laughter Sam gave was heavy with irony. "You're probably the only person at Global who didn't know that."

Catching her bottom lip between her teeth, Elise glanced guiltily at Sam's hard profile. There was nothing she could say to that.

Falling silent, she looked around. As far as she could tell, they were about fifteen miles out of Santa Fe. Here the mountains were smaller, mostly rolling, arid foothills, and in between were great, sweeping valleys that seemed to go on into infinity. Patches of melting snow lay in sheltered creases and folds of the land. Tenacious and tough, the sparse vegetation spotted the land, but Elise couldn't see another sign of life anywhere—no cattle or horses or people—just the undulating earth stretching out for miles, empty and awesome, and ruggedly beautiful. Elise knew, too, that it could be unforgiving.

Today the sun spread its weak winter warmth like a benediction, but in the summer it beat down mercilessly on the rugged terrain. Altitude and lack of pollution lent the air a sparkling clarity that made distances deceptive. In the past year, Elise had learned that in this vast country what looked to be no more than a few hundred yards was often ten miles or more.

The emptiness, the sense of aloneness, had taken some getting used to, even coming, as Elise had, from a small, sleepy East Texas town. But now she found the emptiness was one of the things she liked best about that part of the country.

She looked over her shoulder but, except for the plume of dust that trailed behind the car, the view in back was much the same as ahead; there was still no sign of any structure.

"How far off the highway is your house?" she asked, unable to contain her curiosity any longer.

"Three miles. It's over the next rise."

Elise sat forward, anxious to see the home Sam had chosen for himself.

When the car topped the rise, her eyes widened. Whatever she'd been expecting, it wasn't the homey ranch house that sat among a stand of cottonwoods.

Even at a distance she could see that it was old—maybe even older than the Victorian house she and Tommy had owned in Crockett, but more western in flavor. As the road angled down the slope into the wide valley, Elise noticed corrals beyond the house. On the other side of a creek were two large barns and several other buildings.

She felt Sam glance her way every few seconds but he didn't speak, and she was too busy craning her neck trying to take in everything to comment.

As the road neared the house, it forked, the left branch forming a curving path among the cottonwoods before looping back upon itself, while the right made a wide circle around to the barn in the back. Sam took the left branch and brought the Cadillac to a halt in the drive at the front of the house.

Elise was so intrigued she didn't even realize they had stopped until Sam came around and opened the door on her side. "Well, this is it," he said, extending his hand to assist her.

Missing the uncertain note in his voice, Elise murmured a polite "Thank you" and climbed out, her fascinated gaze still sweeping over his home. The bare, interlacing branches of the cottonwoods cast a mottled shade over the drive and made small screeching noises as they rubbed and bumped together in the wind. Elise shivered and pulled her cape tighter around her but did not hurry her inspection.

Like many of the houses in the area, Sam's was made of adobe, with walls that looked to be at least two feet thick, but the Spanish influence ended there. The one-story structure appeared to be a long rectangle, with a steeply pitched roof and a wide covered porch running all the way around it. The posts and porch railing were some sort of twisted, gnarled wood whose surface had been worn smooth by years of exposure to weather and the touch of human hands.

Elise's gaze swept down the long length of the porch, and she noticed that every room seemed to have at least one door that opened onto it. The glass in the wide windows was obviously an addition of modern times, but each was still flanked with sturdy wooden shutters.

As she climbed the wide, shallow steps she saw that the porch was dotted with small handmade tables and wooden rocking chairs, the backs and seats of which were made of cowhide. To the right of the door there was also an old-fashioned porch swing, which creaked as it swayed in the breeze.

"Shall we go inside?"

Elise replied with a distracted, "Mmm."

She barely noticed when Sam took her arm and led her through the front door. Her mind was filled with thoughts of warm summer evenings on the porch, of starlit skies and fireflies and lemonade, of the gentle night sounds of cicadas, clattering cottonwood leaves, and the lulling creak of a swing.

Inside, the house was cozy and warm, and Elise was surprised to hear the soft hum of central heat. Sam took her cape and hung it on the copper hook of an ancient hall tree with a hinged seat and curved arms and a wavy, beveled mirror set in its high back. She glanced at it admiringly, then wandered from the entry into the living room.

Sam followed, the disquiet he'd been experiencing for the past hour growing. It was funny; during the past months, in all his plotting and planning to make her his, he'd never once questioned the wisdom of bringing a fragile flower like Elise to the ranch to live—not, that is, until he'd left the office to pick her up.

Of course, by then he'd been feeling guilty as sin. There had been no real reason for him to cut short their honeymoon, such as it was. Everything that could be done, had been done, by Margo and the rest of the staff. He'd known that, but he'd used the break-in at the warehouse as an excuse to escape from a situation he'd been unable to deal with. If he'd stayed in that hotel room with Elise even five minutes longer he doubted he would have had the strength—or the will—to resist the maelstrom of desire and emotion that had been pulling at him.

By the time they'd reached Santa Fe he'd been almost desperate to put some distance between himself and Elise and regain his equilibrium. So he'd dumped her at her apartment.

For all the good that had done, Sam thought, thoroughly disgusted. By the time he'd gotten to the office he'd been missing Elise so, he'd almost turned around and gone back for her. As a result, he'd rushed through the briefing with Margo and the staff, spent a scant five minutes on the phone with the police detective in charge of the case, paid a lightning visit to Harry in the hospital and hurried right back.

He'd been sure that Elise had known all along what he was doing. Guilty conscience at work again, he supposed. He'd half expected her to be so furious she would refuse to move to the ranch with him. That thought had, in turn, started him wondering how, or if, Elise would take to ranch life.

He'd braced himself for her anger, but when he'd arrived back at her apartment she'd greeted him with a blinding smile that had turned his insides to melted butter.

Still, all the way home, especially after he realized that she hadn't known he lived on a ranch, he'd worried about what her reaction would be.

He watched her inspect the living room, his gut twisting in a knot. He'd never noticed before how bare it looked. Except for the television set, the sofa and his comfortable brown leather chair, it was empty.

The rest of the house wasn't any better. He had moved here with the few furnishings from his one-bedroom bachelor apartment in town. He hadn't bothered to fix it up himself because he knew nothing about that sort of thing, and he hadn't hired a decorator because he simply hadn't thought about it. Besides, he hated that look of impersonal perfection they always created.

Damn. She's bound to hate it. The place is old, for Pete's sake. And rustic. Plain, to boot. Whatever made me think that a woman like Elise could be happy here?

He watched her come to a stop in the middle of the large room and gaze slowly around at the wide-planked wooden floors, the rough-hewn beams and massive stone hearth, and his mouth folded into a grim line.

"I'm sorry if you're disappointed. I guess you were expecting something a lot fancier and more luxurious. I'm afraid in the two years since I bought this place I've spent most of my time improving the herd and the ranch facilities.''

Elise turned and saw him standing just inside the room, watching her, his face set.

"Disappointed?" She shook her head, her eyes widening. "Oh, Sam, how could I be disappointed?" she said in a small, awed voice. "It's wonderful!"

Hope flared, but still he looked at her askance, not daring to believe her, a small frown forming between his eyebrows. "You like it?"

"*Like* it? I *love* it!"

A delighted smile lit up her face and, with a laugh, she launched herself at him.

Her enthusiasm disarmed him, and his own face split in a relieved grin. He opened his arms wide to receive her and lifted her clear of the floor as she clamped her arms around his neck.

"Whoa," he commanded with a low chuckle. "Don't strangle me to death, woman. Lord, if this is how you behave when you're happy I shudder to think what you would've done had you hated the place."

Elise laughed again, and the husky sound lit a fire low in Sam's gut. He couldn't remember ever hearing her laugh quite like that before, all happy and eager and full of excitement.

"Oh, Sam, darling, I adore this place! Almost as much as I adore you." She kissed him soundly and squeezed his neck even tighter before releasing him and dancing away. Spreading her arms wide she twirled around twice, enthusing. "Just look at these lovely old floors, and that molding. And you just don't find rooms this size anymore."

"I'm glad you're pleased," Sam said, but Elise was so excited she didn't seem to notice that once again his voice had taken on a cool edge.

"I'm more than pleased. I've always loved old houses with lots of character. And I have loads of antiques that will look terrific here. Oh, my love, this place is going to be just beautiful.''

The endearment, like the first one, shook Sam to his core. Every muscle, tendon and nerve in his body tightened. Confusion, joy and panic blended together, creating a terrible pressure in his chest. He felt as though he were being pulled in two directions at once.

"Good," he said stiffly. Taking her elbow, he led her back into the entry and retrieved her bag. "I'll show you to the master bedroom. Then I have some things to tend to down at the barn. While I'm gone you can unpack and look around at the rest of the house."

"Oh, but I was hoping—" Something in his tone finally penetrated her bubble of happiness, and Elise broke off to look up at him, her heart sinking at the wooden expression on his face.

"Very well," she agreed. Her voice was soft and quivering with hurt, despite her forced smile. "You go ahead. I'm sure I can manage."

The master bedroom was at the opposite side of the house from the living room, at the back, a large square room with off-white plaster walls and dark beams spanning the ceiling. It contained only a massive walnut chest of drawers, a small bedside table and a king-size brass bed.

Sam wasted no time. He placed her bag on the bed, and after showing her the attached bathroom he hurriedly changed into jeans, a flannel western shirt and boots. Then he instructed her to make whatever room she needed in the closet and chest of drawers, crammed a sweat-stained Stetson on his head and left, using the door that opened directly onto the porch.

Elise watched him vault over the rail and stride away. With dragging steps, she moved to stand by the glass-paned door, her forlorn gaze following him until he disappeared into the barn. What had gone wrong? For a few minutes everything had been easy and relaxed. Sam had even laughed. Then he'd frozen up again.

She saw Sam emerge from the barn with a saddle slung over his shoulder and a bridle in his other hand. When he entered the corral an enormous black stallion came trotting across the lot to him, his magnificent head bobbing in greeting. Within minutes, Sam was swinging into the saddle, astride the stallion's back. The animal shook his head and did an impatient sidestepping prance as Sam guided him out of the corral. Leaning from the saddle, he latched the gate, then straightened and dug his heels into the black horse's sides.

Elise swallowed the hard, hurting knot in her throat as man and horse cleared a fence and took off toward the mountains in the distance as though the hounds of hell were nipping at their heels.

Chapter Twelve

It took almost three miles of hard riding before Sam accepted that he could not outrun his thoughts.

"Whoa, boy. Whoa, Blazer." The black stallion slowed to a trot, then a sedate walk. Finally Sam brought him to a halt atop a knoll. Leaning forward, he rested his forearm across the saddle horn and gazed down at the house in the stand of cottonwoods. Leather creaked and the bridle jingled as Blazer lowered his head to munch on a clump of winter-dried grass.

Elise was there, in his home. His wife.

There was no denying it; the knowledge afforded him bone-deep satisfaction, a pleasure so sharp it was almost pain.

But along with it was that terrible fear—fear of losing control, of being weak, vulnerable. Dammit! He didn't want to be at the mercy of his emotions.

Sam sighed and pinched the bridge of his nose between his thumb and forefinger. But Elise loved him.

He broke out into a cold sweat at the thought. Even so, he had to admit there was a part of him that relished the idea. It was no small thing, being loved by a woman like Elise. Her devotion would warm the years ahead, provide a haven, an escape from all he wanted to forget.

The trouble was, he was no longer certain that he could live with her and remain unscathed. Already he cared for her more than was wise.

He felt as though he were stretched out on a rack, being pulled apart. What made it worse, the whole mess was his own damned fault. Sam closed his eyes and rubbed them with his thumb and forefinger. Sweet God in heaven, how could he have been so arrogant as to think he could have a woman like Elise, take all she had to give, and remain detached? He'd wanted her, he wanted her still, now more than ever. But damn! He didn't want this wrenching need.

Like a dog chasing his tail, Sam's thoughts went around and around, leading nowhere.

He stayed on the knoll for another half hour, but the endless soul-searching produced only one solid conclusion: from now on, no matter how uneasy it made him, he wouldn't run for the hills when Elise showed her love. He wouldn't hurt her that way again, as he knew he had today.

Sam heaved a sigh and straightened in the saddle. It wasn't a solution to his dilemma, but the decision eased the knot of tension in his chest. Resolutely, he turned the horse toward the stand of cottonwoods and urged him into a smooth, ground-eating lope.

By the time Sam reached the corral, the light had the ghostly golden haze of winter sunset and long shadows were stretching across the ground like bluish fingers. The temperature was dropping rapidly. His breath and Blazer's blew out in foggy puffs.

Sam glanced toward the house as he led the stallion into the barn. He was used to coming home to a dark house, to emptiness. The warm glow that spilled from the windows drew him like a powerful magnet. He felt its pull as he un-saddled the stallion. As he rubbed and brushed the glossy black coat and filled the grain box he had to fight the urge to rush through the chores.

He entered the house through the kitchen and found Elise there, standing at the stove. She had changed into a mid-night-blue velvet caftan, and he noted the way the lush ma-terial draped her breasts and flowed gently against her body as she moved. She darted him a glance and an uncertain smile, and just as quickly looked away again, not quite meeting his eyes.

"Something smells wonderful," he said, sniffing the air and covertly watching her with more than a little uneasi-ness, wondering what his reception would be. Running off and leaving her as he'd done had been inexcusable, and he felt like a heel. She had every right to be angry and upset.

"It's nothing fancy, I'm afraid," she said with an apol-ogetic shrug. "Just chicken-fried steak and gravy, mashed potatoes and green beans. Oh, and there're biscuits in the oven."

Relief seeped through Sam. She seemed a little wary, a little anxious, but not angry. It was a helluva lot more than he deserved.

He shucked out of his fleece-lined jacket and hung it and his Stetson on the rack by the door. "Chicken-fried steak, huh? Don't they call that the national dish of Texas?" he asked as he washed his hands in the small bathroom off the kitchen.

"No, that's chili," she replied absently, then looked up as the teasing note in Sam's voice registered. "Oh, Sam, I'm sorry! Look, if you don't like it I can cook something else. It was just the easiest, and—"

"Hey. I was just kidding. Chicken-fried steak is great. I love it. Really." Hell, he was grateful she was cooking his dinner at all. Most women would have been throwing the pots *at* him for the stunt he'd pulled.

"You're sure?"

"Positive."

It took a minute to convince her but soon they were seated at the kitchen table. The hearty meal was as delicious as it smelled, and Sam discovered that he was starving. After the first tentative taste he dug into his food with gusto. Watching his reaction, Elise smiled and relaxed.

As they ate, she asked about the buildings she'd glimpsed on the other side of the creek, and Sam explained that one was the bunkhouse and the rest were houses for the married hands and their families, the largest of which was occupied by John Vogel, the ranch manager.

"So you see, you won't be totally isolated here. If you want, I'll take you around tomorrow and introduce you to everyone," he offered.

"I'd like that," she agreed softly, then placed her hand on his forearm. "But, Sam, please don't worry about me feeling lonely or isolated. I promise you, I'm going to love it here."

He looked at her hard for a moment, then nodded. After that, their talk switched to other things—the burglary at the warehouse, having her belongings moved, when and how to notify their friends and Elise's family of their marriage.

Through it all, Sam was sharply aware of the subtle difference she had already made in his home. The kitchen was filled with the delicious aromas of her excellent cooking. From somewhere she had unearthed colorful quilted place mats, and a fat candle sat in the middle of the table, its flame flickering cozily.

Having her here felt good. He enjoyed talking quietly with her, listening to her soft voice, just basking in that exquisite feminine aura she radiated.

When they reached the coffee stage Sam looked up and found her studying him, her head cocked to the side. He raised one eyebrow.

"What's wrong?"

"Nothing. It's just that...well...to tell you the truth, I'm having difficulty adjusting my image of you. Not even in my wildest dreams would I have pictured you on a ranch. Somehow, I always thought you'd have a penthouse. Or a place like Max's."

Sam gave her a wry look. "Hardly. Oh, Max's house is okay, and the view is great, but unless you're an eagle there's only one way down off that mountain. And I don't like being trapped."

She frowned. "Is that why you bought a ranch? For the wide-open spaces?"

"Partly." Sam looked out the window, and her gaze followed. The sun was going down in a blaze of brilliance behind the mountains to the west. Mauve, orange and crimson ribboned the dusky blue sky and silver rimmed a bank of dark, low-hanging clouds. Beyond the corral and barns, the valley swept away into endless shadows, touched here and there with a kiss of rose from the setting sun. "It gives you a sense of freedom. I don't feel caged here."

Elise's eyes widened, but Sam went on. "But I also bought this place because I enjoy ranching, being outdoors. I don't actually run it myself, of course—I don't have the time—but I do enjoy working with the men when I can."

"Well, at least now I know what put those calluses on your hands." Again she gave that low, husky chuckle, and again Sam felt a fire ignite low in his gut. "But I just can't quite get used to seeing you in jeans and cowboy boots. You always look so...I don't know...sophisticated, I suppose. I've never seen you wear anything but tailored three-piece suits or elegant casual clothes."

Sam looked at her steadily for a moment. "I'll admit I tend to overcompensate, but when you spend four years wearing only filthy rags you develop a penchant for nice clothes."

Elise sucked in a sharp breath and stared at him, horrified. Her small hands clenched into fists on either side of her coffee cup. "Oh, Sam," she said in an appalled whisper. "They kept you in a cage, didn't they? Like an animal?"

Her wobbly voice broke on the last word. She stared at him, her chin quivering helplessly as her brown eyes filled with tears.

Sam cursed himself. He was as surprised as she was by what he'd revealed. He'd never told anyone about the things that had happened to him, but the words had just popped out before he could stop them. Now, looking at the anguish and grief in Elise's face, he understood what she'd meant about loving. Because he had been hurt, she was hurting.

Once he might have lashed out in angry repudiation of such a display of sympathy, but Elise's pain was real—as real as his own—and it touched him as nothing had in a long, long while.

He cupped his palm over one of her clenched fists and squeezed it, his big hand engulfing hers. "Elise, it's okay. Really. I survived it, and it's over now," he said in a low, comforting voice.

She just looked at him, unable to speak. Her throat worked with emotion, and she pressed her quivering lips together. A tear overflowed and hung from her lower lashes for an instant, then plopped onto her cheek and trickled down. Another followed. And another.

"Elise, don't. Please," Sam begged, but to no avail. Her tears flowed faster, until they dripped from her chin like gentle rain, and the sobs she tried so hard to suppress shook her chest.

They tore at her throat, harsh little guttural sounds, and with each one Sam felt as though his heart were being rent in two. Unable to bear her suffering a moment longer, he grasped both her hands and pulled her out of the chair and onto his lap.

"Hush, honey. Hush," he murmured, wrapping her in his arms and hugging her close. "Don't cry."

The need to comfort and soothe her rose with an urgency that drove every other consideration from his mind. He rocked her gently and stroked her bright hair, pressing her head against his chest. His strong fingers kneaded her bare back above the low rounded neckline of the caftan.

"Oh, Sam," she gasped. Her voice was raw with pain, the words muffled against him. "H-how could they have done . . . done that to y-you?" A fresh spasm of tears shook her, the hot wetness melding his shirt to his skin. She clung to him desperately, her fingers clutching handfuls of the flannel cloth.

"Oh, God, honey, don't. Don't cry like that. You'll make yourself sick. Damn! I'm sorry I said anything. I hate to see you so upset."

Elise sniffed and struggled to get hold of herself. "No. No, I'm. . .glad you did. I understand th-things better now."

Sam could feel her trembling, and he cradled her as though she were a hurt child. He rubbed her back, his big, rough hands gliding with a hypnotic rhythm over the plush velvet, moving up and down her spine. "Some things you're better off not knowing," he muttered, his voice rough with self-reproach.

"No, I want to know everything about you," she insisted softly over a hiccup. "I want us to share everything, the b-bad as well as the good." Unconsciously, she sought his warmth, her fingers releasing the buttons on his shirt and slipping inside. With a sigh, she burrowed her face against him. "Besides," she insisted in a quavery voice, "you shouldn't keep things like that locked inside you. Sharing problems and hurts always makes them easier to bear."

Sam made a wry face and rubbed his cheek against her temple, catching the silky strands of hair in his beard stubble. He was touched by her sweetness, the generosity of her love, but though he suspected that she was right, he couldn't do as she wanted. God, did she really think he could dump all that garbage on her fragile shoulders?

He wanted to protect her from harsh realities, keep her safe from all the ugliness in the world.

She was growing calmer, he noted with relief, her breathing becoming gentler, gradually slowing. Still he rocked her, liking the way she cuddled against him. She was so slender, so delicately built, barely a feather in his arms, as light as a child, but with the warm, alluring curves of a woman.

Elise gave a long, shuddering sigh and slid her arms around him, running her hands up over the strong muscles of his back. Sam's body tightened under the innocent caress and delight rippled through him. He buried his face in her hair, inhaling its sweet freshness. He rubbed his mouth against it, felt the silky strands slide against his lips, tasted them on his tongue.

The elasticized neckline of her caftan had slipped off one shoulder and gaped open in front. A bewitching scent rose from the velvety curves of her breasts, not a perfume, but that special essence that was hers alone, womanly, warm and intoxicating. It made his head spin, his blood pound hotly.

Desire rose, heavy and urgent, tightening his body. Sam nuzzled his face against her neck, trailed his lips down the slender column, over the creamy slope of her shoulder, nibbling, his teeth gently nipping as he edged lower toward the source of that enticing female fragrance. "I want to share many things with you, Elise," he murmured as he discovered the revealing pulse at the base of her throat. Slowly, erotically, the tip of his tongue traced a wet line downward. "Especially this."

With a little moan, Elise leaned away to give him better access. Her eyes were closed, her head tilted to the side. Tears still glistened wetly on her cheeks, but her features were taut with a look of ecstasy.

Sam rubbed his mouth back and forth over the upper curves of her breasts. The warm, moist caress of his breath against her sensitive flesh drew a little sound of pleasure from her, and she shivered violently.

His hands slid down to her bottom, cupping and kneading the firm roundness. He had already discovered she wasn't wearing a bra, and now he began to wonder if she wore anything at all beneath the lush folds of velvet.

The enticing thought sent his hand sliding along her thigh to her knee. Busy fingers worked the soft material upward, then slipped beneath the hem and retraced the path. Delight, and something more, shot through Sam when he encountered only a long, unbroken line of warm flesh, as soft and smooth as the cloth that covered it.

His hand closed possessively around her hip, his thumb tracing the protruding bone, the slight hollow beneath it. His fingers skimmed her belly. The soft flesh quivered at his touch.

"Oh, Sam," she cried as his forefinger dipped into her navel. Her voice was shaky, the merest wisp of sound.

"Do you like that?"

"Yes...yes." Her lips parted as her head lolled back. Her hands were buried in the thick mat of hair on his chest, and unconsciously she flexed her fingers, her nails digging into the hard muscles.

He withdrew his hand from beneath the caftan, and a little moan of distress escaped her, but it turned to a gasp as he hooked his fingers beneath the elastic at the neck of the garment and pulled it down to her elbows, baring her breasts and pinning her arms to her sides.

"Oh!" The cry of pleasure was wrung from her as he bent his head and closed his hot mouth over a sensitive nipple.

"And that? Do you like that?" he demanded fiercely against the engorged bud, filling his hands with the warm weight of her breasts.

"Yes ... yes ... yes."

He squeezed, lifted, stroked, then pressed the pearly globes together. "And this?" Bending his head, he buried his face in the lush flesh, and Elise shuddered, her answer coming out in a high moan as his tongue dipped evocatively into the warm cleavage.

He was driving her crazy. Elise wanted to put her arms around him, to bury her fingers in his hair and press him closer still, but the velvet binding held fast, and the delightful torment was too wonderful to halt. All she could do was sigh and gasp as it went on and on.

Finally, Sam kissed his way back to her mouth, claiming it with the deep, sensual thrusts of his tongue. With a growl, he shoved the caftan down farther, and as she pulled her arms free it collapsed in a soft roll about her hips.

Burning, nearly mindless with desire, Elise yanked his shirt free of his jeans and spread the edges wide. She twisted on his lap and sought to press against him, to bury her aching breasts in the crisp curls on his chest. The innate shyness that was so much a part of her vanished. She gave no thought to where they were, to the foolishness, the incongruity of making love on a hard chair when there was a bed available. All she knew was need. Urgent. Desperate.

She came to her senses briefly when Sam made a rough sound and abruptly lifted and turned her until she was astride his lap. "Sam. Darling, we're in the kitchen," she protested weakly as he jerked the caftan up until it was bunched around her middle and her naked bottom was nestled against his thighs.

"I don't give a...damn...where...we are," he growled, snatching at his jeans. "I . . . want . . . you . . . now!"

He nearly tore the buttons off in his haste to get them open and shove the jeans out of the way. "Kiss me," he commanded in a rough whisper, and Elise obeyed, leaning forward, her lips meeting his with a sigh as his big hands cupped her hips and lifted her onto him.

Completion. It felt so right, so wonderful. He filled her—her body, her heart, her soul.

She rocked against him, moaning his name, on fire. Outside the night closed in and the room grew dark but for the flickering glow of the candle flame. The only sounds were desperate, incoherent words of passion and need, the harsh rasp of labored breathing. Elise's slender body moved in the frantic, undulating rhythm, setting a pace that drove him to the edge of madness. Sam gritted his teeth, his body taut as a bowstring as he held back, wanting, needing to give her that final pleasure, to feel her body grip his with those sweet, pulsing contractions.

His hands on her hips guided her, aided her, keeping the driving rhythm even when she grew tired. Her pants became desperate little sobs and he caught them with his mouth, urging her on with his thrusting tongue and the hard pressure of his hands. The tension built and spiraled until the world exploded in a starburst of unbearable ecstasy, and she cried out her joy, collapsing against Sam's chest as pleasure overtook him.

Elise lay tiredly against Sam as their breathing became less labored and their pounding hearts gradually slowed. She felt boneless and replete and unbearably happy. She'd been so afraid when he'd left her alone and ridden off, afraid he didn't want her anymore, that he'd changed his mind about the marriage. But the urgency and hunger with which he'd taken her had given her new hope.

Sighing contentedly, she closed her eyes and snuggled her face into the side of his neck, brushing tiny kisses against his skin.

She felt him shudder and his arms tighten around her, and she smiled.

"Sam!" she gasped in surprise when he stood up with her in his arms and strode from the kitchen. "Sam! The dishes!"

"To hell with them," he growled. "We're going to bed."

"Oh, Sam," she said with aching tenderness, laying her cheek against his shoulder.

Despite getting very little sleep, Elise woke early the next morning, as usual. The digital clock beside the bed showed 6:45.

She glanced at Sam and saw that he was sleeping soundly, sprawled on his back, one arm flung over his head, the other draped across his abdomen. Dark beard stubble shadowed his jaw and cheeks and his mouth was open, his thin lips softened by sleep. His mussed hair was dark as a raven's wing against the white pillowcase. He looked tough and virile and all male, and yet surprisingly vulnerable. Elise's expression softened with love as she gazed down at him.

He had kicked off the covers in his sleep, and when she leaned over and kissed his shoulder his skin was cold, so she drew the blanket up over him. Sam made an appreciative sound and snuggled deeper into the warmth. Smiling, Elise eased from the bed and tiptoed into the bathroom.

A lot of things made sense to her now, she mused as she stood under the steamy shower spray—Sam's remoteness, his need to protect himself, his control. Lord, how helpless he must have felt all those years, caged like an animal, at the mercy of those people. She shuddered just to think about it. It was no wonder he'd been drawn to this place, with its wide-open spaces, out of sight of the highway and prying eyes. No doubt this sturdy house with its abundance of windows had influenced his decision to buy it. He probably even drove fast because it gave him a sense of freedom and power. And who could blame him?

Finding him still sleeping after she had showered, she pulled on her warm robe and quietly left the room.

In the kitchen she filled the coffee maker and turned it on, and then debated about whether to start breakfast. Happiness always increased her appetite, and that morning she felt on top of the world.

The night had been magic, even more so than their wedding night had been. It was due, Elise was sure, to the subtle change she'd detected in Sam. She stared dreamily out the window above the sink, a small smile on her lips.

No endearments or words of love had left his lips, but his every touch, the look in his beautiful pale eyes, had made her heart soar.

Her stomach rumbled and she laughed. Humming an atrociously off-key version of a popular song, she began to assemble the ingredients for pancakes.

The smell of fresh coffee drew Sam from the bed, but as he neared the kitchen a puzzled frown creased his brow. What the devil was that noise? It sounded like a funeral dirge being played on a defective bagpipe. At the kitchen door he stopped and stared at his wife in amazement.

"What are you doing?" he asked, smothering a yawn as he propped his shoulder against the jamb.

Elise whirled, a glowing smile lighting her face at the sight of him. She had a butcher knife in one hand and a roll of sausage in the other. "Good morning." Her voice was soft and husky and held a touch of shyness. "I'm cooking breakfast."

"No, I mean why are you making that god-awful racket?"

"Racket!" She huffed and tilted her chin. "I'll have you know I was humming."

"Really? Well, I hate to tell you this, Elise, but I've heard better sounds from a rusty hinge. I thought for a minute that you were in pain."

"Too bad. You're just going to have to get used to it," she informed him haughtily. "Because I always hum when I'm happy."

Sam's mouth twitched as he bit back a relieved grin at her feigned annoyance. For a second there he'd been afraid he'd gone too far. He hadn't wanted to hurt her feelings, but the temptation to tease her had been irresistible. He had always thought of her as being perfect, and wouldn't have been surprised if she sang like a nightingale, but the tiny flaw was strangely endearing.

"Oh, Lord." Heaving a beleaguered sigh, he pushed away from the door, poured himself a mug of coffee and sat down at the table, stretching his long legs out in front of him. "Well, I suppose I could buy some earplugs."

"Very funny. Hasn't anyone ever told you it isn't smart to insult the cook?" She narrowed her eyes and gave him a slow, wicked smile. "Especially one holding a knife?"

That startled a laugh out of Sam. He'd always thought of Elise as being serious and serene, a proper lady right down to her fingertips. He found he was delighted to discover she had a droll wit and a lively sense of humor.

Laughter was something that had been missing from his life for a long time. It felt good to joke with her, laugh with her, he realized in astonishment. Perhaps a little too good.

Elise bustled around the kitchen, so buoyant with happiness she felt as though she were walking on air. Sam's teasing was more precious to her than diamonds.

As she flipped pancakes and turned sizzling sausage, chattering all the while, she couldn't resist glancing at him. His hair was still wet from his shower, and he was dressed more casually than she'd ever seen him, in old jeans and a faded sweatshirt that was clean but speckled with several different colors of dried paint. He wore heavy white socks but no shoes. The look was so different from his usual pristine elegance that she wondered if he had chosen his attire because of the comments she had made the night before. Whatever his reason, she liked it. Sam looked wonderful and sexy no matter what he wore, but seeing him in his comfortable, slightly slovenly clothes made her feel ridiculously happy. There was something so homey and domestic about it.

"There you are." She set a plate of pancakes and sausage on the table in front of him and refilled his coffee mug. Standing with one hand on the back of his chair, she caught the scents of soap and damp hair and minty toothpaste. And male. She looked at the comb lines in his hair, the fine peach fuzz on the rim of his ear, the crinkles at the corner of his eye, and felt a tug at her heart. Unable to resist, she stooped and placed a soft kiss on his cheek. "Good morning, darling."

"Good morning."

His voice was clipped. Sam didn't move or even look at her. When she took her seat she saw that his face was expressionless. Her heart gave a little flutter of panic, but she refused to give in to it.

"After you've taken me around to meet the hands and their families maybe we can start on those riding lessons you suggested," she said brightly.

"If you'd like." He took a bite of pancake and washed it down with coffee. When he looked at her his eyes were clear and direct, but impersonal. "But I'm afraid both are going to have to wait until later in the day. I need to spend the morning working with John Vogel."

Elise could almost see him retreating from her, pulling his defenses back into place, and she wanted to weep.

Fighting to keep her voice even, she nodded and said, "All right. Just let me know when you're ready."

She cut through the stack of pancakes with the side of her fork and put the bite into her mouth. It tasted like sawdust, and even though the pancakes were soaked in syrup she had to chew until they dissolved in her mouth before she could swallow past the lump in her throat. After the night they had just shared, Sam's coolness was harder than ever to take. At that moment, her spirits were so low she despaired of ever reaching him.

But gradually during the days that followed, Elise began to realize that no matter how hard Sam tried, no matter how much he wanted to be, he was not indifferent to her. Several times, she caught him looking at her with such hunger and longing that her heart almost melted. Though he didn't seem to be aware of it, he touched her constantly—running his hand down her arm, brushing a stray curl from her cheek, giving her shoulder a squeeze whenever he passed by, placing a hand at her elbow or the small of her back when they walked together. It was more than tactile pleasure; it was a compulsive need for physical contact that he was powerless to resist. And all the emotions he wouldn't express—couldn't express—were revealed in those gentle touches.

Elise could see in his eyes, in his brooding expression, the inner struggle he was having. Sam was torn, pulled one way by instincts shaped through bitter experience, and another by a heart that yearned for happiness no matter the risk.

Resolute in her determination, Elise waged a quiet battle of her own. She showered Sam with affection, both obvious and subtle. Hugs and kisses were bestowed for the flimsiest of reasons. In the beginning he responded with stiff awkwardness but she persevered, and he soon relaxed, even came to accept them as his due.

No matter what his mood, Elise was unfailingly pleasant. When Sam returned from work, she met him with a loving smile and a drink. She rubbed his back when he was tired, massaged his neck when he had a headache. She cooked his favorite dishes and filled his house with flowers and warmth and love. She gave the old ranch house the personal touches it had been missing—pictures, ornaments, small items of whimsy. And she furnished it with the lovely antiques she'd been collecting for years, slowly transforming it into a beautiful, warm, cozy home—a home that beckoned to him with open arms, as did the woman who resided there.

Chapter Thirteen

The reactions to their marriage were varied. Elise's parents smugly claimed they were not in the least surprised.

"Your mother knew the minute she saw the two of you together, and I've learned to trust her intuition about these things," Joe Blaine said when Elise called with the news. "She told me when we were in Santa Fe that you'd be married within six months."

Other than bemoaning the fact that they missed the wedding, both her parents were pleased and offered their congratulations and best wishes. They had apparently been impressed with both Max and Sam during their Christmas visit.

No amount of arguing or protestations would convince her friends that she had not been seeing Sam before the wedding, but once they got beyond being annoyed with her for being, as Colleen put it, "unforgivably sneaky" they all expressed surprise, good-natured envy and outright delight over the marriage. And each one of them teased her unmercifully about how she'd sworn that Sam wasn't her type.

Elise was sure that Max and Erin would be ecstatic over the news. But when she finally reached them overseas, they were both reserved and lukewarm with their congratulations. Elise was disappointed and more than a little hurt, but Sam shrugged off their reaction as unimportant.

The only person she dreaded telling, though she wasn't quite sure why, since things had never gotten serious between them, was Keith Hawthorne. And, as she expected, it wasn't easy.

She sought him out as soon as she arrived at the Youth Center the following weekend. For an instant she saw sorrow in his eyes, but then he took her hands and asked, "Do you love him?"

"Yes. Very much," she whispered shakily, feeling sad that she hadn't been able to love Keith. He was a wonderful man, and he would have returned her love openly, joyously. Intuitively she knew that if she hadn't already met Sam, they might have made a match of it. But the timing had been wrong. Though she hadn't known it, she had already given her heart.

"And Sam? Does he love you?"

"Why, ye—" Assurances rushed to her tongue, but under that steady gaze she found she couldn't voice them. "That is, I...I think so."

"I see." Keith looked at her with deep concern. "Elise...are you very sure about this marriage?" When she would have spoken, he rushed on. "Please don't misunderstand me. I like Sam. A lot. He's a good man, and he's certainly been generous where the kids are concerned. But he's...well...hard, I'm afraid. He guards his heart closely, Elise. I'm not sure he's capable of opening it to any woman." Lowering his voice, Keith asked gently, "Can you live with that?"

Elise drew in a quivering breath. "I don't really have a choice," she answered in a small, wobbly voice. "I love him."

Keith's gentle expression held compassion and pity, and a lingering trace of regret. "Then that's all that matters. Sam's a very lucky man, and if he has any sense at all, I'm sure he'll realize it." He squeezed her hands and smiled, his kind eyes soft and warm. "I wish you all the best. Both of you."

"Thank you," Elise managed, perilously close to tears.

Keith looked around. "Where is Sam, by the way? Didn't he come with you? I'd like to give him my congratulations."

"He's, uh . . . he went straight to the gym." Sam was not pleased with her that morning. He had walked off without a word the moment they arrived.

"Such dedication. But I have to admit, I'm relieved. When both you and Sam phoned that you couldn't be here last weekend, I was afraid I'd lost my two best volunteers."

Elise gave a nervous laugh. "There's no chance of that. Sam and I both love working here. Which reminds me, if I don't hurry I'm going to be late."

With a wave, she hurried out the door, but as she started down the hall her smile faded.

Actually, it had been her refusal to quit working at the center that had caused the strain between her and Sam that morning. She couldn't say they'd argued; Sam simply didn't argue. If she disagreed with him, or opposed him, he either shrugged it off or clammed up and grew colder. Although she usually detested strife, Elise was now beginning to wonder if anything or anyone was important enough to him to rouse his anger.

Still, she knew from his stony silence that he was displeased. She also knew that, in part at least, he objected to her working in that neighborhood, which he believed to be unsafe. She knew he'd expected her to quit her volunteer work at the center now that they were married, and her refusal to do so appeared to surprise him. He obviously thought he'd married a docile little lamb who would acquiesce to her husband's slightest wish.

Sam, she thought with a determined little smile as she pushed open the nursery door, had a lot to learn about his bride.

Elise's greatest strength was her gentle tenacity, and it took every ounce of it she possessed to get through the next couple of months.

In the beginning her life with Sam seemed to settle into a comfortable routine. She spent a lot of time working on the house, making curtains, shopping for the additional furnishings it needed. As spring approached she cleared the long-neglected flower beds around the porch and prepared them for planting. Sam scolded her for doing such heavy work and told her to have one of the hands do the spading, but she paid him no heed. She enjoyed working in the soil and being outdoors. She even enjoyed the physical labor.

Sam came straight home from work every night, and he seemed pleased to have her there. Though Elise cautioned herself against being too optimistic, it seemed to her that his cool reserve was fading, little by little.

She had harbored the fear that once they were married, once she was in his home and his bed, he might ignore her, but Sam seemed to enjoy her company and deliberately sought her out. There were quiet evenings before the fire, watching television or just reading. Even when he worked on the ranch records in his study he liked to have her there, and she would curl up with a book or work on her needlepoint. On lazy Sunday mornings they read the newspaper before going to church, and in the afternoons he gave her riding lessons. The contentment they felt with each other became an almost tangible thing that was growing day by day.

And physically they were extremely compatible. More than compatible; their sex life was fantastic. Sam was a healthy, virile man, and hardly a night went by that he didn't make love to her. She was amazed but delighted at how un-inhibited he was sexually, considering the cool control he exhibited at other times. When his passions flared he took her wherever they happened to be, once even in the hay-loft, and though at first she'd been terrified that one of the hands might return and discover them, he soon had her so hot and panting with need that nothing else mattered but the exquisite pleasure they shared.

Elise had high hopes that eventually the stability of their daily life and the constancy of her love would allow Sam to abandon his defenses completely.

But then, suddenly, things changed. Sam began working late night after night, and the frequency and duration of his out-of-town trips increased. Many times he came in after she was in bed, and she would lie there waiting for him to take her in his arms, but he never did. The one time she had made the first move he had told her he was too tired—gently, it was true, but the rebuff had hurt too much for her to ap-proach him again. The few evenings he was home, he was withdrawn and moody.

Elise told herself that he was just overworked, that it would pass, but she was frightened.

With Sam gone so much she had time on her hands, and to keep herself from worrying she decided to volunteer more at the Youth Center. Keith was delighted, and immediately put her to work teaching a needlepoint class on Tuesday af-ternoons and a course on computer literacy on Thursday evenings.

She intended to tell Sam of her new schedule before-hand, but she saw so little of him the opportunity did not arise.

Her first Tuesday class went very well. The girls, and the one brave boy who attended, were eager to learn and coop-erative, and Elise drove home euphoric and alight with suc-cess. When she arrived, Sam's car was in the drive, and she hurried inside, determined to tell him, no matter how busy he was or what mood he was in.

"Sam. I'm home. I have something to—" At the door to their bedroom she stopped short, her heart sinking at the sight of the open suitcase on the bed.

Sam turned from the dresser with a stack of shirts in his hands. As he added them to the contents of the suitcase, he flicked her a preoccupied glance and announced, "Some-thing's come up. I have to fly to Atlanta. I left you a note in the kitchen with the name of the hotel where I can be reached."

"I see." Her voice was low and despondent. Shoulders slumping, she entered the room and sank down on the side of the bed. "Do you know when you'll be back?"

"That depends on how things go. But don't expect me before Friday."

"Don't worry. I'm learning not to expect much from you," she said, and for the first time since their marriage she let her hurt and disappointment show.

Sam dropped a stack of underwear into the suitcase and looked at her unhappy face. Something akin to guilt flick-ered across his harsh features. "Elise," he began hesi-tantly. "I know I've neglected you lately, but if you'll be patient just a little longer I'll have this mess all cleared up. I promise."

"Do you?" she questioned in a doubtful little voice, her face sulky and accusing.

Sam was accustomed to sweet serenity from Elise, an endless supply of patience that was spiced only occasionally with a bit of temper. He stared at her pouting mouth, and for the first time since she'd known him, he seemed at a loss. "Elise...I..." He paused and groped for the right words. When they didn't come he muttered an impatient, "Oh, hell" and shoved the suitcase aside.

Taken by surprise, Elise gasped when Sam pushed her back on the bed and came down beside her, his body half covering hers. He took her mouth in a hot, hungry kiss, and the tension and pent-up passion of the past few weeks exploded between them.

Elise spared not a thought to resistance; she was too grateful to have him back in her arms. She clutched him to her and kissed him back with all the passion and warmth of her loving nature, her bruised heart finding solace in the rough urgency of the embrace.

"Damn, I need you," Sam swore, breaking off the kiss. He rolled off her and stood, and Elise gasped again as he pushed her dress up to her waist and stripped away her underthings. His face was rigid with desire, and she felt her body throb with the heat and excitement that he aroused in her so easily.

"Sam, your plane," she reminded him weakly, her eyes smoldering beneath half-closed lids.

"If I miss it I'll take the next one." He unzipped his pants and stepped out of them. Nudging her legs apart, he knelt between her thighs. "This can't wait."

Smiling, she made a soft purring sound and twined her arms around his neck as he lowered his weight onto her. "Oh, Sam, Sam, I love you so." She sighed, but the soft sound turned to a moan and tears of joy filled her eyes as he made them one.

"Elise!" Her name was a harsh, guttural cry on his lips as he began the deep, strong thrusts that carried them quickly into a wondrous oblivion where only pleasure existed.

A short while later they clung to each other, their labored breathing slowly returning to normal as they floated back to earth. Her face wreathed in contentment, Elise rubbed her palms over Sam's damp back beneath the rumpled shirt.

"Sam?"

"Mmm?"

"Why are you going to Atlanta?"

Sam went still. Then he rolled away from her and stood up. "It's business," he said shortly, pulling on his pants. He traded the wrinkled shirt for a fresh one and looped a burgundy silk tie beneath the collar.

"What kind of business?" she prodded.

"Uh... just some employee trouble at the outlet there." Sam adjusted the knot in his tie and thrust his arms into his suit coat, then snapped the suitcase shut and picked it up.

Curled on her side, Elise watched him from the bed. A look of supreme male satisfaction stamped his features as he bent over her and ran his rough palm over the long curve of her hip and thigh. "Don't get up," he murmured. Then he kissed her, his tongue sliding back and forth over hers with erotic friction. When he raised his head, he touched her cheek. "I have to run or I really will miss my plane. I'll see you at the end of the week."

Elise remained motionless, listening to his footsteps recede down the hallway, the click of the front door closing behind him. Outside the sun was going down, and as the room grew dim she pulled the bedspread over her and huddled beneath it, a painful heaviness settling over her heart.

Global Imports didn't have an outlet in Atlanta.

Two days later Sam opened the door and stepped inside the house, feeling an enormous sense of relief. He'd done it.

It was over. One more meeting, and the whole nasty mess would be dealt with.

Then things could return to normal, he could settle back into the satisfying life he'd found with Elise.

That thought had filled him with anticipation ever since yesterday, when the trip to Atlanta had proved successful. God, how he had missed her.

If nothing else, at least the past few weeks had driven home exactly how much Elise had come to mean to him. Worry, lack of time and energy and frequent physical distance had played havoc with their love life and left him frustrated and aching, but it was more than just sex that he needed. He was constantly surprised and delighted by the fire that ran just below Elise's calm surface, by the contrast between the serene, genteel lady the world saw, and the writhing, moaning woman who melted beneath him. But slowly the realization had come to him that he missed more than the startling passion of her lovemaking. He missed talking to her, just being with her, the comfortable, undemanding silences that sometimes fell between them. Hell, he'd even missed her atrocious humming. He felt at ease with Elise, whole once again, like a misplaced soul who has finally come home.

Sam gave a wry little chuckle and shook his head. Not too long ago the admission would have scared the hell out of him and produced a storm of denial. He still wasn't comfortable with it, but at that moment he didn't care. The need to hold Elise, just to relax and be with her, had become so compelling he had driven all the way from the Albuquerque airport like a madman, practically burning up the highway.

"Elise?" He set his suitcase down and walked into the living room. Shafts of light beamed through the west windows from the setting sun, bathing the room in a rosy glow. As Sam stood waiting, listening for her, he looked around, and became sharply aware of the changes she had brought to his house.

The place was beautiful and comfortable and there wasn't so much as an ashtray out of place. Elise, he'd discovered, had a penchant for neatness—a place for everything and everything in its place. She straightened and arranged without even being aware she was doing it. It occurred to him that you could put her in a junkyard, and within a week it would be immaculate.

It certainly hadn't taken her long at all to put her stamp on the house. New curtains framed the wide windows and glass-paned doors, lush plants were scattered around the room and her needlepoint pillows, each an exquisite work of art, dotted the couch and numerous comfortable chairs. Colorful braided rugs adorned the planked floors, which gleamed with the patina of age and a fresh coat of wax.

Before their marriage, the ranch house had merely been a place to sleep and shower and, occasionally, eat, but now, looking around, he experienced a profound sense of home-coming.

Sam grinned and shook his head, marveling at what a difference one small, soft woman could make.

A delicious aroma wafted on the air and, sniffing appreciatively, his anticipation growing, he followed it to the kitchen. "Elise, I'm home."

All he found was an empty, spotless room and a simmering Crockpot filled with stew sitting on the counter. Impatiently, he went through the house, room by room, his frown growing darker as he realized she wasn't there.

Where was she? He was home a day earlier than he'd told her he would be, but, dammit, he'd expected her to be there. She could be shopping, he supposed. Or with her sister. Erin and Max had returned from the Far East trip a couple of weeks before, thank God, or he wouldn't have felt com-

fortable about spending so much time away from the office.

He went to the phone and dialed his partner's home but
no one answered. Most likely Elise and Erin were off somewhere together. Sam checked his watch. They'd probably be
back soon. Elise knew he didn't like her to be out alone after dark.

He unpacked and changed his clothes, then went through
the mail she had left in a neat stack on his desk in the study.
There was nothing important, so he settled down in the living room with the evening paper. A while later he tried to
watch television but his mind kept wandering, so he turned
it off. He paced. Darkness had fallen, and every few minutes he looked out the window and checked the road for a
sign of her car's headlights.

When she hadn't returned by eight he called the Delany
home again, and this time Erin answered.

"No, I haven't seen her at all today," she told him when
he asked if Elise was there. "She called this morning and we
made a date to have lunch on Monday, but she didn't tell me
what her plans were for today."

Sam thanked her shortly and hung up.

He helped himself to a bowl of stew and ate it alone at the
kitchen table. As he stared at the centerpiece of dried flowers
Elise had made, anger grew apace with worry. What could
she be doing? What if something had happened to her?

His heart gave a sickening lurch. No. No, he wouldn't let
himself think like that. He *couldn't* think like that. He'd go
mad if he did.

But, dammit, *where was she?*

It was almost eleven when he heard her key in the front
door. A knee-buckling relief seized Sam, followed instantly
by black rage. He bolted off the couch and stormed into the
entry a half second before she stepped inside.

"Where have you been?"

"Sam!" She stopped in her tracks, her face lighting up like a neon sign at the sight of him.

"Oh, Sam!" she cried, and flung herself at his chest.

Her response mollified him somewhat but anger still held sway, and Sam grabbed her shoulders, holding her away from him. "Elise, I asked you a question. It's late and I want to know where you've been."

She blinked at the coldness of his tone, the joy fading from her face. "At the center."

"The Youth Center?" A puzzled frown drew Sam's black brows together.

"Well, actually, for the past couple of hours I've been going through the hassle of having my car towed to a garage and renting another one." Her mouth twisted in a disgusted grimace. "The darned thing broke down on the outskirts of town, and I had the devil of a time finding a telephone."

"What were you doing at the center today? Especially at that hour?"

"I'm teaching a computer literacy class on Thursday evenings and one on needlepointing on Tuesday afternoons. I was going to tell you the day you left," she said, and her eyes began to sparkle. "But you kept me so busy I didn't have a chance."

Sam ignored her teasing reference to the urgent, unbearably exciting way he had taken her two days before. "I suppose this was Keith Hawthorne's bright idea. Well, you can tell him I said he can forget it."

For an instant Elise was stunned. She stepped back, her delicate shoulders erect, and looked him square in the eye. "No," she said clearly. Her voice was soft but firm.

"No?" Sam's face went slack with disbelief. "What do you mean, no?"

"I mean no, I will not tell Keith to forget it. I volunteered to teach the classes because I wanted to, and I won't disappoint the kids who've signed up for them. Besides, I have to have something to fill my time. You're never here anymore, and I refuse to sit around and twiddle my thumbs waiting and wondering when you're going to come home."

The small jab was right on target. Elise felt a bitter satisfaction at the guilty flash in Sam's eyes.

It passed quickly, and his face was stoic once again. "I told you that was almost over. And one thing has nothing to do with the other. Now I want you to forget about those classes."

"No."

Elise turned on her heel and started down the hall to their bedroom. Behind her Sam bit out, "Dammit, Elise! I'm your husband!"

This time she knew she had not imagined it; beneath the cold tones there was a hard edge of temper. Uneasiness and elation intermingled. Her heart beat faster.

She stopped and faced him, her delicate face pale but determined. "That's right, you're my husband, but not my lord and master. I married you, Sam, because I love you and I wanted to share my life with you, but that doesn't mean that I have to give up my freedom or the right to make my own decisions," she said calmly. "Now if you'll excuse me, I'm going to take a shower and go to bed. I'm very tired."

"Elise, don't you realize that your car could just as easily have broken down in that slum area around the center," he demanded of her back as she walked away.

"If it had I could have reached a telephone a lot sooner and been home an hour ago," she tossed over her shoulder.

Elise knew she was deliberately picking a fight, and she was amazed at her own temerity. But she was tired of beating her head against a stone wall of indifference. She had tried reaching Sam through loving patience and it had gotten her exactly nowhere. Maybe—just maybe—she could reach him through anger.

She hated fighting and unpleasantness, but at least she had finally managed to arouse *some* sort of emotional response in him.

"Elise, we are not through talking," he insisted.

Without slowing her pace, she glanced back over her shoulder. He stood where she had left him, his pale eyes boring into her. His face was hard as stone.

She walked into the bedroom and closed the door behind her with an insulting little click. In the middle of the floor she halted. Her hands clenched at her sides. Closing her eyes, she pressed her lips together tightly. *Come after me,* she willed silently. *Come after me, Sam. Please!*

Her insides quivering, she waited.

A minute went by. Then another. But there was only silence.

Elise's shoulders slumped. Fighting the urge to weep, she walked into the bathroom.

Hours later when Sam came to bed she was still awake. She lay motionless, feigning sleep, but she need not have bothered. As soon as he slipped beneath the covers he turned on his side, and within minutes his breathing was slow and deep.

The next morning when she awoke he was gone. Despondent, Elise moped around the house, wondering what to do. At midmorning she was sitting at the kitchen table drinking her fifth cup of coffee, still in her robe, when he telephoned.

"I've bought you a new car," he announced without preamble as soon as she said hello. "The dealer is getting it ready now so that you can pick it up today. I've called the bank and they have a cashier's check for the purchase price ready for you."

"But, Sam—"

"I don't want to argue about this, Elise. If you insist on working all hours at the center I at least want you to have a reliable car. That junk heap you've been driving should have been scrapped long ago. Especially after Erin rammed it into the mountainside last summer.''

Her spine stiffened. ''That couldn't be helped,'' she said frostily in defense of her twin. ''And I couldn't afford a new car.''

''Well you can now. Look, Elise, consider this a favor to me. I don't want to worry about you driving around in a car that might break down at any moment.''

Heaven forbid that you should worry, she thought waspishly. *That would be too human.* Elise sighed and swallowed the retort that hovered on the tip of her tongue. She wanted to goad Sam into anger, but in person, not over the telephone. ''Very well,'' she agreed without enthusiasm. ''Where do I pick it up.''

Two hours later at the automobile dealer's, Elise took one look at the car Sam had chosen and balked. It was the biggest, heaviest, most sedate sedan made.

''There you go, lady. Isn't she a beauty?'' the salesman said, beaming. ''You just go right ahead and inspect it, and when you're through we'll go into my office and sign the papers.''

Elise looked at him, her face brightening. ''You mean the sale isn't final until I sign those papers?''

''We-ell...technically, no. But—''

''How much is that one over there?'' she interrupted, pointing to a fire-engine-red sports car.

''That? It's a couple of grand more than the sedan.''

''Good. I'll take it instead.''

''But...but your husband wanted you to—''

''I know what my husband wanted.'' The smile she gave him was soft and sweetly feminine, and as implacable as steel. ''But I'm afraid it's the sports car or no sale.''

That evening when Sam came home and saw the little red fireball of a car parked in front of the house, he felt an ominous tightening in his gut. Nothing had gone right the whole day, and he had a suspicion that wasn't about to change.

"What is that thing doing in the driveway?" he demanded when he stalked into the living room.

Elise looked up from the magazine she was reading. "That's my new car," she replied placidly.

"That is not the car I ordered."

"I know. But I liked this one better."

Sam's jaws clenched and a muscle twitched in his cheek. Damn. *First that scene with Elise last night. Then today Sherry didn't show up for work, and he couldn't even reach her at her home. And now this! Hellfire! Didn't anything go right anymore?*

Fury and frustration rose inside him to a level he had not experienced in years. The urge was strong to release it, to rant and rave and demand to know why she was behaving this way. He wanted to haul her into his arms and kiss that adorable impudent mouth until all she could utter were the sweet words of love he'd missed so these past weeks. Most of all, he wanted to take her to bed and hold her close, to pour out his soul and tell her how much she meant to him.

But old fears and the rigid self-control of years weren't easily overcome. Sam drew in several deep breaths and clamped down on the unwanted emotions. "Elise," he began with strained patience. "That car won't do."

"Why not? It's new, and it's reliable. That's what you said you wanted me to drive."

"I want you to drive a *safe* car, not some expensive toy."

"I made up the difference in price with money from my savings."

He came close to showing anger at that. "It's not the money, and you know it."

"Then what is your objection?"

"That thing is too fast and too powerful. You'll get yourself killed." He turned his head and looked at the car through one of the windows. "Besides, it's not the car for you."

"How would you know? You didn't ask me what kind of car I wanted. You just decided for yourself that helpless little Elise should have a big stodgy sedan because they're heavier, therefore safer. I'm surprised you didn't buy me a tank."

"Come on, Elise, be reasonable. There's more to it than that. I wouldn't be surprised to see Erin tooling around in an outlandish machine like that, but it's hardly your style."

Elise was suddenly, outrageously incensed. "Oh, *really*. Well, I'm tired of everyone deciding what *is* and what *isn't* right for me. For your information, I've always wanted a red sports car."

It was true. She hadn't bought the car solely to annoy Sam, though, of course, she'd known that it would. For years she'd had a secret passion to own a fast, zippy little sports car. The only reason she hadn't bought one before was that she'd never quite had the nerve, or the money. But lately she'd found herself doing a lot she wouldn't have dared to do before.

"Are you saying you intend to keep that car? No matter how I feel about it?"

She lifted her chin defiantly. "That's exactly what I'm saying."

Elise waited, braced for an explosion, but Sam simply stared at her in frigid, tight-lipped silence.

"Very well," he said finally. "Since you insist."

He shrugged out of his coat, tossed it over the back of the sofa and loosened his tie. Sitting down in the brown leather chair he liked so much, he picked up the newspaper and gave it a little snap as he opened it up and spread the pages wide in front of his face.

Elise was so disappointed and exasperated she was torn between the need to cry and an uncharacteristic, consuming desire to give him a good swift kick. Controlling both urges, she picked up her magazine again and pretended to read.

They ate dinner in silence, and afterward Sam went into his study to do some ranch work. For the first time, he didn't ask Elise to join him. Neither did he make love to her when he finally came to bed around midnight.

The next morning Sam acted as though nothing at all had happened, which depressed Elise even more, and she was relieved when they reached the center and parted company.

The Mothers' Morning Out program was a huge success, and within minutes of Elise's arrival the nursery was filled. For the next six hours she was kept so busy changing diapers, rocking crying babies and running after inquisitive toddlers that she didn't have time to worry about her floundering relationship with Sam.

When the last infant had been reclaimed by her mother, Elise was so exhausted all she could think about was immersing her weary body in a tub of hot water. Once the nursery had been put in order she said a hurried goodbye to the other women and went in search of Sam.

There was no sign of him or his players when she entered the gym. Assuming they had already gone to the showers, Elise glanced at her watch and debated whether to wait there for Sam or go stand by the dressing-room door out in the hall. Tiredness won out, and she trudged across the court toward the bleachers.

She had almost reached them when a hand clamped over her mouth from behind. At the same time a muscular arm encircled her midriff, pinning her arms against her sides, and jerked her back against a hard body.

The instinctive scream that tore from her throat was muffled by a dirty palm, but more followed anyway. Elise struggled frantically, twisting her body and kicking out as hard as she could, but she was no match for her captor's strength.

"Stop fighting and you won't get hurt," he snarled in her ear as he wrestled her around the end of the bleachers. Above the filthy hand Elise's eyes widened, and her skin crawled with real fear as she recognized the rough voice of the boy called Wolf. "You and I are just going to go back here and have a little fun, lady, that's all. Who knows, you might even enjoy it," he taunted with a nasty chuckle.

Terror made Elise's heart boom when she realized he intended to drag her beneath the bleachers. Her screams were smothered against his palm and she fought even harder, twisting and straining with every ounce of strength she possessed.

Her efforts only seemed to enrage Wolf. He muttered a stream of obscenities in her ear and jerked and shoved viciously, edging her ever closer to the dark shadows. His fingers dug into her cheeks cruelly. Ignoring the pain, Elise pried her jaws apart and snapped them together again, biting down on his fleshy palm as hard as she could.

"You bitch!" Wolf shrieked.

The instant he jerked his hand away Elise let out a scream.

"Why you stupid—" He spun her around and backhanded her across the face, cutting off the shrill sound and sending her sprawling onto her back. Before she could move he was on her, his body pinning her to the hard wooden floor.

His hand covered her mouth again before she could manage another scream. "You're gonna be sorry you did that, lady." His fetid breath nearly gagged her as he issued the threat close to her face in a low, furious voice.

Elise squirmed and bucked beneath him, small whimpering sounds coming from her throat as he clawed at her clothes.

"You filthy little bastard!"

Suddenly he was lifted from her and she was free. Disoriented, Elise struggled up on her knees in time to see Sam hurl the boy to the floor like a sack of garbage. At the same moment Keith came barreling in through the gym doors, with Dr. Rosenthal and several of the volunteers right on his heels.

With the quickness and agility of youth, Wolf rolled away and sprang to his feet in a crouch position.

"Look out, Sam! He's got a knife!"

The warning wrung a cry from Elise, but Sam didn't even blink. Assuming the same threatening stance, he moved in on the youth, his hard face murderous.

Keith and Bernie started to circle around Wolf but Sam waved them away. "Keep out of this," he commanded, never taking his eyes from the boy. "He's mine."

"Sam, don't!" Elise cried, but he ignored her.

Wolf waved the knife in front of him. "C'mon, big man," he sneered. "You think you're tough? Well, I'm gonna gut you like a fish."

Sam moved closer.

Keith circled around the pair and helped Elise to her feet, keeping a supporting arm around her. She was barely aware of him. Trembling, she put a hand over her mouth, her terrified gaze glued to her husband.

Sam lunged and Wolf swung the knife. Elise's shrill scream bounced off the walls of the cavernous gym and echoed through the rafters. Wolf cried out in pain when Sam bent his arm back at an unnatural angle. The weapon clattered against the wooden floor. Before anyone could move, he had the youth pinned to the wall, one big, powerful hand around his throat.

"You dared to touch my wife, you little piece of filth," Sam snarled between his teeth as his hand squeezed tighter. His face, just a hairbreadth from Wolf's, was livid with fury.

Wolf's eyes bulged. He made a desperate choking sound and clawed at Sam's powerful wrist with his uninjured hand as his dark complexion began to turn blue.

"Sam! Sam, stop it! You'll kill him."

Keith and Bernie surged forward and grabbed Sam's arms. It took all their combined strength to pull him off the boy. Wolf slid down the wall and slumped to the floor, gasping for breath and holding his neck.

"Let me go!" Sam raged, struggling to free himself. "That little bastard tried to rape my wife!"

"We know, we know. But the police will take care of him now. Just calm down, Sam."

"Oh, Sam!" Elise flung herself at his chest, and when the men released him his arms closed around her. He pulled her close and held her so tightly she could barely breathe, but she didn't care. He was safe.

"Are you all right? Did he hurt you?" Sam asked anxiously.

"No. No, I'm fine. Really." She clung to him for a moment, then, unable to stand it, she pulled back to look at him. "And you? Are you okay?" As she spoke she ran her hands frantically over his beloved face, his chest, then gasped sharply when she encountered the blood on his sleeve.

"Sam! You're hurt!"

"It's just a scratch, Elise. Nothing to get upset about," Sam assured her, but she wasn't listening.

Making distressed little sounds, she tried to tear his sleeve so she could see the wound but her hands were shaking so she couldn't manage it. "Help me, somebody!" she wailed.

Her voice verged on hysteria, and Keith moved forward and put his arm around her waist. "Come on, Elise," he urged gently. "I think we'd better get you both to the infirmary."

"First, you get that scum out of here," Sam ordered, jerking his head toward Wolf. "And second, you take your hands off my wife, Hawthorne."

Elise stepped back, her mouth dropping open. "Sam!"

Chapter Fourteen

Ow! Not so tight," Sam complained. "You know, for an angel of mercy, you leave a bit to be desired."

The teasing note in his voice had no effect on Elise. She continued to wrap the gauze strip around his upper arm with brisk efficiency. "I've told you several times— I'm no angel. Besides, if you're going to be pigheaded and refuse to see a doctor you'll just have to accept whatever treatment you get."

Sam looked up at her set face and grimaced. "Still mad, huh?"

She shot him a blistering glance. "How perceptive." Bending again to her task, she tried to ignore him, which, given the circumstances, was impossible.

Stripped to the waist, Sam sat on the side of their bed as she rebandaged the cut on his upper right arm. Her nerves were jangled and raw, and his nearness, the sight of that broad bare chest, weren't helping matters. Against the stark white gauze his skin looked like burnished bronze. The silver medallion kept winking at her from the forest of dark curls, and again and again, no matter how hard she tried to resist, her gaze kept sliding over those sleek, sinewy muscles that banded his chest and shoulders and ridged his hard belly. His musky scent, mingled with the sharp bite of antiseptic, made her nostrils flare and her stomach quiver.

Elise's feelings were in a muddle. She wanted to be angry with him. She *was* angry with him, darn it, but mixed with the feeling was a welter of other emotions—gratitude, pride, elation, lingering fear. Most of all, though, she was just so wretchedly relieved that he was alive and not seriously hurt that it was all she could do not to throw herself on him and smother him with hugs and kisses.

Which, of course, he most certainly did not deserve, she reminded herself as she tied the gauze in place, jerking on the knot with a bit more force than necessary.

"I still think you're being foolish. I'm sure you need a few stitches," she said stiffly as she gathered up the first-aid supplies and put them back into the kit. "To say nothing of a tetanus shot."

The nurse at the center had applied a pressure bandage to Sam's wound while they waited for the police to arrive, but her suggestion that he visit the hospital emergency room had fallen on deaf ears. By the time they had given their statements and she had apologized to Keith for Sam's boorish behavior and driven home, the pad had stuck to the cut and it had taken almost another hour to soak it free.

"It'll be fine," he insisted.

She started to move away, but Sam caught her wrist in a hard grasp, his strong fingers wrapping around the delicate bones. "Elise, a man has a right to protect his wife," he said, and this time there wasn't a hint of teasing in his voice or expression.

His steady gaze held her, and after a moment she sighed. "All right. I can understand that, but I still can't believe you were so insufferably rude to Keith."

"I don't like him touching you," he declared flatly, not in the least repentant.

"Sam, he's a minister!"

"He's still a man."

"He was just trying to comfort me. That's part of his job."

"If you need comforting, I'll do it. Keith Hawthorne can get his own woman."

Why, he was jealous! Elise stared at him, feeling as though a tiny explosion had just occurred in her heart.

Carefully, she set the first-aid kit down on the bedside table and moved to stand between Sam's spread thighs. He released her wrist and placed his hands on her hips, drawing her close. Gazing at him tenderly, she touched his cheeks and ran shaking fingers through the hair at his temples. "What is it, Sam?" she asked softly. "Why does Keith's kindness to me bother you?"

"In case you haven't noticed, he's attracted to you."

The edge in his voice was music to her ears, and Elise had to fight back a smile. "So? Keith's an honorable man. He won't act on the attraction, and you know it."

"I still don't like it."

"Why, Sam?"

"You're my wife."

"Oh, Sam," she chided gently. "That's not a reason." Giving him a pitying look, she rubbed her thumbs over the wiry silk of his eyebrows, brushed them across his cheeks, the corners of his mouth, her touch growing steadier, more assured.

"Elise..."

"Tell me, Sam. Why?"

Gazing into her soft brown eyes Sam saw all the love she made no effort to hide, and felt his chest expand and tighten. He knew what she wanted to hear. What she deserved to hear.

He breathed deeply and swallowed against the ache in his throat. Still the words hovered on the tip of his tongue.

It wasn't that he didn't want to say them. No matter how foolish it might be, no matter the risk, he could no longer deny his feelings. They swelled his heart and permeated his very soul.

He started to speak, hesitated, then closed his eyes and hauled her against him, pressing his face into her abdomen. As he locked her fiercely within his embrace she bent over him and cradled his head in her arms.

"Elise. Oh, God...Elise..." Sam's chest hurt so badly he thought surely he would die. He knew he should tell her how he felt. He wanted to tell her, but no matter how hard he tried he simply could not.

The admission brought bitter self-recrimination, but Sam refused to accept defeat. He might not be able to say the words, but he could show her what was in his heart.

He fell back on the bed, pulling her with him.

"Sam, be careful of your arm," Elise cried anxiously. "Sam? Sam, what—? Oh, darling, we mustn't. You'll hurt—"

Sam cut off her protests with a kiss. He seduced her with his mouth, his agile tongue and clever hands easily overcoming her feeble attempts to thwart him. Desperation and hunger and heartfelt need aided his effort, and within minutes he had stripped away her clothes and what remained of his.

"Oh, Sam. Darling," Elise said on a trembling sigh of need and love as he drew her into his heat.

The night that followed was the most thrilling Elise had ever known. Sam filled the darkness with passionate whispers and murmurs of praise. He told her how lovely she was, how much he admired her slender body, her creamy skin. With hands and tongue and mouth and hot, shockingly intimate words, he paid homage to her breasts, her belly, her legs. No part of her was left untouched, unadored. He rained kisses over her shoulders and spine, the backs of her knees, her buttocks, the tender undersides of her arms, the arches of her feet. Like a virtuoso, he played her body, wringing cries of ecstasy, purrs of delight. When he discovered that a nip on her earlobe made her shiver and moan his rusty chuckle rumbled wickedly through the darkness.

Elise melted under the exquisite assault, a mass of longing and love.

It wasn't until she awoke, late the next morning, that she realized Sam had not said the one thing her yearning heart had wanted to hear.

On Monday, Elise picked up her twin for their luncheon date, and the minute Erin got in the car, she said, "All right, do you want to tell me what's troubling you, or do I have to figure it out for myself?"

Elise gave her an annoyed look and groaned.

"Come on, out with it."

"Oh, it's nothing new," Elise said despondently as she gunned the sporty little car, sending it shooting down the drive.

"I see. So silent Sam still hasn't told you that he loves you."

Elise shook her head, then gave a weak chuckle when her twin pronounced Sam a thickheaded jerk.

Erin sighed, her eyes filled with compassion and worry. "This is exactly what I was afraid of. Oh, I know I was all for the marriage at first, but then I realized that you are the kind of woman who needs affection and declarations of love. And watch these curves, will you. I don't think this Tinkertoy would make a very good hang glider."

Elise laughed and reduced her speed. "Actually, Sam has been very affectionate lately," she said. Her face softened as she recalled the way he had made love to her, and the attention he'd showered on her the day before.

Seeing the look, Erin grinned knowingly. "Really? Well that's encouraging. Look, I have an idea. Why don't we stop by the office and drag our husbands out to lunch. Not only will Max be a good example of a loving mate, we'll get *them* to pick up the tab."

Elise had almost called to cancel their luncheon date but now she was glad she hadn't. Just being around her irrepressible twin was enough to lift anyone's spirits. "You've got a deal," she said gaily, as she whipped the flashy little car around a curve with panache.

A few minutes later, she brought the car to a halt in the Global parking lot—just in time to see Sam escort Sherry Phillips from the office and solicitously hand her into his Cadillac. Unable to move, Elise sat with her hands on the steering wheel and watched them drive away.

"Why that dirty, low-down, sneaky rat!" Erin blurted out in a low, furious voice, only to turn instantly contrite when she noticed Elise's stricken expression. "Oh, honey, I'm sorry. Look, I'm sure there's a perfectly reasonable explanation."

"Of course," Elise agreed, but the little chuckle she gave shook with the threat of tears. "I mean, there could be any number of reasons why a man would take his ex-fiancée out to lunch." Her chin wobbled, and she looked away. "Assuming, of course, that that's where they're going."

Elise's precarious emotional state galvanized her twin into action. Before she even knew what was happening, Erin hustled her out of the car and into the building. "Before you start jumping to conclusions we're going to talk to Max," she insisted sotto voce in Elise's ear as she hauled her through the reception room. At the same time, she returned Peggy's greeting with a wave and a false smile.

Max looked up, surprised, when they walked unannounced into his office. "Well, hello, you two. What brings—" He halted abruptly and stood up at the sight of Elise's white face. "What's wrong? What happened?"

Erin turned from settling her sister on the sofa, bristling like an enraged lioness. "I'll tell you what's wrong. We just saw *your* dear friend, Sam, leaving for a cozy tête-à-tête with Sherry Phillips," she spit out accusingly, as though the entire thing were his fault. "I told you no good would come from that woman working here."

Even in the midst of her distress, Elise could not help but smile at her sister's vehemence. Erin had been incensed when she discovered that Sam had hired his ex-fiancée.

Max groaned and ran a hand through his hair, his face taking on a pained expression. "Oh, hell. Of all the lousy timing. Sam didn't want Elise to know anything about this mess."

"Oh, I'll just *bet* he didn't," Erin snapped.

Elise turned paler.

"No, no. You don't understand." Max sat down beside Elise on the couch and took one of her hands. "Elise, listen to me. Sam is not in any way interested in Sherry Phillips. She was furious when you married Sam, and a few weeks after the wedding she started threatening him with a paternity suit."

"What!" both Elise and Erin exclaimed in unison.

"She claimed that her daughter, who was born after she married Ken Phillips, was fathered by Sam before he left for Vietnam. Sam was sure she was lying, and as it turns out she was, but she had a faked birth certificate, coincidentally from a hospital whose records had been destroyed in a fire, which showed the child was born seven months after Sam left.''

"But...I don't understand. What did she hope to gain?" Erin asked. Elise simply stared at Max, absorbing it all without a word.

"At first Sherry seemed to think that Sam would divorce Elise and marry her, but when he made it clear that was out of the question she started demanding a cash settlement. A very hefty cash settlement," Max added disgustedly.

"Anyway, Sam stalled her, hoping he could find proof that she was lying. He had several meetings with her attorney and pretended to work out an agreement, while at the same time he was contacting people who had known Sherry. After they married, she and Ken Phillips moved around a lot, but after several false leads, Sam finally located some people who knew they'd been living in Atlanta at the time of the child's birth.''

"So that explains all those late nights and trips," Elise said in a dazed voice.

"Yes. And last week he hit pay dirt. He located the hospital Sherry used and got a copy of her daughter's real birth certificate. It shows that the child was born fourteen months after Sam shipped out. Sam took Sherry to lunch today to confront her with it, mainly because he didn't want her to create a scene here.''

"I see," Elise said tonelessly. "And Sam didn't see fit to tell me about any of this.''

"He didn't want you upset. He was hoping to get the whole nasty mess settled without it ever touching you.''

Max obviously thought she should feel relieved, but the explanation merely deepened her distress. Despite everything she had said, everything she had done, Sam was still treating her like a Dresden doll instead of a woman. Instead of a wife.

Elise got to her feet like someone who has just received a stunning blow. "Thank you, Max, for telling me. Now, if you don't mind, would one of you please drive me to the airport?"

Erin and Max exchanged a worried glance. "The airport?" her sister questioned warily. "Why?"

"Because I'm leaving Sam."

"Elise!"

"For God's sake, why?"

The other two spoke at once, and Elise looked at them with calm determination.

"Because I'm tired of beating my head against a stone wall. I want to truly be a wife to Sam, to share his life, and that means both the good and bad, but he won't let me. I had thought that I could make this marriage work, that eventually his heart would thaw."

Head held high, she looked at Max, her expression filled with hurt and wounded pride. "Has Erin told you he's never said he loves me? Not once. I've finally come to realize that all I am to Sam is exactly what he said he wanted: a companion and bedmate. No more, no less." She waged a battle with her emotions as her chin quivered uncontrollably, and after a moment she added in a shaky voice, "Well, I'm sorry. That's simply not enough."

"Elise—"

"My mind is made up, Erin," she insisted. "I'm going back to Texas—for a while, anyway. Either you take me to the airport or I'll drive myself."

Her sister hesitated, her look pleading, but after a moment she heaved a resigned sigh. "All right. I still think you're making a terrible mistake, but we'll take you."

Erin drove the sports car to the ranch and Max followed them in his Continental. Numbly, Elise packed a bag and wrote Sam a note explaining exactly why she was leaving.

Within an hour they were on their way to the Albuquerque airport.

When Sam arrived at the ranch house, he was delighted to see the saucy little red car parked in the drive. It hadn't occurred to him until he was almost there that Elise might still be shopping with her sister.

It was the middle of the afternoon, and he was ruefully aware that he should have returned to the office, but he was so relieved all he wanted was to find Elise and share his happiness with her. Anyway, after that distasteful scene with Sherry, he had a compelling need to hold his wife in his arms.

It was finally over, thank God. That bitch was out of his life for good. He felt as though an enormous weight had been lifted from his back. God! He couldn't believe he had ever loved her.

"Elise! Honey, I'm home," he called out, hurrying through the house. When the living room and kitchen proved empty he headed for their bedroom. There he found the note, propped against his pillow.

As he read it, all the blood seemed to drain from his body. Unaware he was doing so, he sank down weakly on the edge of the bed. When he'd finished he slumped forward, propped his elbows on his spread knees and held his head in his hands.

He'd lost her. Dear God, he'd lost her.

It was his own fault. That was the bitterest thing of all. He should have told her he loved her. He should have had the guts to trust her with his heart. No matter how hard it was for him, he should have been open with her, shared everything with her, as she had wanted.

He sat there for what could have been minutes or hours, indulging in an orgy of self-flagellation, bitterly listing his faults and shortcomings, and all the things he had done wrong or handled badly. When the telephone on the bed-side table rang, he merely looked at it and willed whoever it was to leave him alone. He was too heartsick to talk to any-one. But the caller was persistent, and finally he snatched it up just to stop the incessant ringing.

"What is it?" he demanded viciously.

"Sam! Thank God. I was beginning to think you weren't there."

Sam raked a hand through his hair. "Look, Max, what-ever it is will have to wait. I can't talk right now—"

"Dammit, don't you dare hang up on me!" Max roared. "Not if you want your wife back."

Sam's spine straightened. "What do you mean?"

"I mean Erin and I are at the airport with Elise right now. I'm stalling every way I can think of. I even booked her on a later flight than was necessary, but if you want to stop her you'd better haul your tail over here in a hurry, old friend. The plane leaves in an hour."

"I'm on my way."

"They should be calling my flight soon," Elise said, checking her watch. "The plane was right on time."

"Yeah," Max acknowledged sourly. He paced up and down in front of his wife and sister-in-law, nervously jin-gling the change in his pockets, and searching the crowded concourse for the umpteenth time.

"Elise, it's not too late to change your mind," Erin urged. "We can turn in your ticket. I'm sure if you'd just explain to Sam—"

"I have explained. I've tried everything I—" She broke off as a commotion occurred at the far end of the con-course. "What on earth—?" Elise sucked in her breath and stared, her eyes enormous in her stunned face. "Oh . . . my . . . word! It's Sam!"

But the wild-eyed, disheveled man who raced toward her, shouting and shoving people aside, bore little resemblance to the Sam she knew. He had discarded his coat and tie and his shirt was half unbuttoned, the tail hanging out of his trousers on one side. His hair was mussed and his eyes were fixed on her with such a look of desperation that Elise felt her heart turn over.

"Elise! Elise, wait!"

She stood and watched him draw near, scarcely able to breathe. He skidded to a stop a few feet from her. For a moment he just stood there gasping for air, unable to speak, but in his eyes was all the love for which Elise had yearned.

He held out his hands in silent entreaty, and the temptation was strong to throw herself into his arms, but she resisted it.

"E...Elise...don't go. Please...don't...don't go," Sam pleaded as he struggled to control his labored breathing. "S-stay with me."

"Why, Sam?" she said in a low, intense voice. "Why should I stay?"

"Be...because I...I want you."

"Why?"

"Because...because..."

"Why?"

"You're my wife, Elise. We belong together."

"Not good enough, Sam," Elise said stoutly, though her voice was unsteady. "Why?"

Sam looked to Max for help, but his friend merely shrugged. When his gaze sought Erin, she tilted her chin and said, "Yes, Sam. Why should she stay? I'd like to know that, too."

"Elise, please..." Sam glanced around at the faces of the strangers about them who were avidly taking in the confrontation, but Elise was unyielding.

"Why, Sam? You're going to have to tell me."

He looked at her beseechingly, his face working with emotion. Slowly, his eyes filled with tears, and the sight wrung Elise's heart.

She wanted to go to him, to put her arms around him and tell him that everything would be all right, but though it took every ounce of strength she possessed, she held her ground.

She was fighting for their marriage. If they were to have a future together, she had to smash, once and for all, the wall that Sam had built around his heart.

Her flight was announced, but no one around them moved.

"Because..." Sam's voice caught, and he swallowed hard. A tear spilled over and trickled down his lean cheek as he held his hand out to her and said huskily, "Because I love you. Oh, God, Elise, I love you so."

Before he could get all the words out her feet were moving. She flew across the space that separated them and launched herself against his chest.

Sam's arms closed about her in a rib-crushing embrace that lifted her off the floor, and their lips met in a long, desperate, soul-stirring kiss. They clung to each other, oblivious to the murmurs of approval from the people around them.

"Oh, sweetheart, I'm sorry. I'm sorry," Sam vowed in between kisses.

"Shh. I know, my love. I know." Elise ran her hands over his face, his ears, threaded her fingers through his hair, unable to touch him enough.

"I didn't tell you about Sherry because I didn't know what your reaction would be. I was afraid you'd believe her lies and leave me."

"Oh, Sam," Elise crooned. "I wouldn't have left you. I'll never leave you again. Never. I want us to be together for always." She stopped and looked at him uncertainly, her eyes pleading. "I'd...I'd like for us to have a family."

Sam swallowed hard. She could see that he still had demons to fight, but he'd taken the first step. Framing his face between her palms, she said gently, "Oh, Sam. It'll be okay. Just go with your heart, my love."

"I...I want children, too, darling. Honestly. It still scares me, I'll admit, but the thought of you having my child..." He shook his head and looked at her adoringly. Tears flooded Elise's eyes.

"Don't worry about it, my love. We'll work it out. Together."

Sam rained kisses over her eyelids, her cheeks, her nose, her chin. Squeezing his eyes shut, he held her tight and pressed his cheek against her temple. "Oh, God, Elise, I love you. I love you. I love you." Over and over he told her, as though having finally declared it, he could not seem to stop.

The final boarding call was announced, and as the remaining passengers headed reluctantly for the tunnel, Max cleared his throat and tapped Sam on the shoulder.

"Listen, pal, I'm happy for you and all that, but this is getting a little embarrassing," he teased. "Whaddaya say you take your wife home and continue this in private?"

Sam raised his head, and Elise's breath caught as a slow, heart-stopping grin spread across her husband's face. "You know, Delany, that's the best idea you've had in years."

He looked down at Elise lovingly. "Well, wife? Are you ready to go home?"

Emotion clogged her throat, and all she could do was nod.

Unable to resist, Sam dropped another kiss on her mouth, then tucked her against his side. As they walked back down the concourse with their arms around each other, Elise leaned her head on her husband's shoulder.

Behind them, her sister, similarly embraced, sniffed and sighed tremulously. "Oh, Max. Isn't it wonderful?"

*   *   *   *   *

TALES OF THE RISING MOON
A Desire trilogy by Joyce Thies

MOON OF THE RAVEN—June

Conlan Fox was part American Indian and as tough
as the Montana land he rode, but it took fragile yet
strong-willed Kerry Armstrong to make his dreams
come true.

REACH FOR THE MOON—August

It would take a heart of stone for Steven Armstrong
to evict the woman and children living on his land.
But when Steven met Samantha, eviction was the
last thing on his mind!

GYPSY MOON—October

Robert Armstrong met Serena when he returned to
his ancestral estate in Connecticut. Their fiery
temperaments clashed from the start, but despite
himself, Rob was falling under the Gypsy's spell.

Don't miss any of Joyce Thies's enchanting
TALES OF THE RISING MOON,
coming to you from Silhouette Desire.

SD 432

Silhouette Romance

LONG, TALL TEXANS

A Trilogy by Diana Palmer

Bestselling Diana Palmer has rustled up three rugged heroes in a trilogy sure to lasso your heart! The titles of the books are your introduction to these unforgettable men:

CALHOUN

In June, meet Calhoun Ballenger. He wants to protect Abby Clark from the world, but can he protect her from himself?

JUSTIN

Calhoun's brother, Justin—the strong, silent type—has a second chance with the woman of his dreams, Shelby Jacobs, in August.

TYLER

October's long, tall Texan is Shelby's virile brother, Tyler, who teaches shy Nell Regan to trust her instincts—especially when they lead her into his arms!

Don't miss CALHOUN, JUSTIN and TYLER—three gripping new stories coming soon from Silhouette Romance!

SRLTT

Silhouette Intimate Moments

At Dodd Memorial Hospital, Love is the Best Medicine

When temperatures are rising and pulses are racing, Dodd Memorial Hospital is the place to be. Every doctor, nurse and patient is a heart specialist, and their favorite prescription is a little romance. This month, finish Lucy Hamilton's Dodd Memorial Hospital Trilogy with HEARTBEATS, IM #245.

Nurse Vanessa Rice thought police sergeant Clay Williams was the most annoying man she knew. Then he showed up at Dodd Memorial with a gunshot wound, and the least she could do was be friends with him—if he'd let her. But Clay was interested in something more, and Vanessa didn't want that kind of commitment. She had a career that was important to her, and there was no room in her life for any man. But Clay was determined to show her that they could have a future together—and that there are times when the patient knows best.

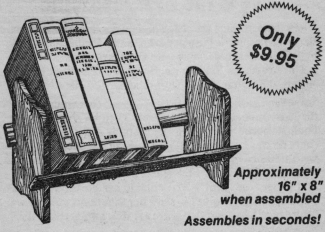